The Avenger

E. PHILLIPS OPPENHEIM

1st WORLD
LIBRARY
Literary Society

The Avenger

E. Phillips Oppenheim

© 1st World Library – Literary Society, 2004
PO Box 2211
Fairfield, IA 52556
www.1stworldlibrary.org
First Edition

LCCN: 2004195288

Softcover ISBN: 1-4218-0115-9
Hardcover ISBN: 1-4218-0015-2
eBook ISBN: 1-4218-0215-5

Purchase *"The Avenger"*
as a traditional bound book at:
www.1stWorldLibrary.org/purchase.asp?ISBN=1-4218-0115-9

1st World Library Literary Society is a nonprofit
organization dedicated to promoting literacy by:

- Creating a free internet library accessible from any
  computer worldwide.
- Hosting writing competitions and offering book
  publishing scholarships.

**Readers interested in supporting literacy
through sponsorship, donations or
membership please contact:
literacy@1stworldlibrary.org
Check us out at: www.1stworldlibrary.ORG
and start downloading free ebooks today.**

The Avenger
contributed by Tim, Ed & Rodney
in support of
1st World Library Literary Society

CONTENTS

CHAPTER I

A MYSTERIOUS VISITOR

The man and the woman stood facing one another, although in the uncertain firelight which alone illuminated the room neither could see much save the outline of the other's form. The woman stood at the further end of the apartment by the side of the desk - his desk. The slim trembling fingers of one hand rested lightly upon it, the other was hanging by her side, nervously crumpling up the glove which she had only taken off a few minutes before. The man stood with his back to the door through which he had just entered. He was in evening dress; he carried an overcoat over his arm, and his hat was slightly on the back of his head. A cigarette was still burning between his lips, the key by means of which he had entered was swinging from his little finger. So far no words had passed between them. Both were apparently stupefied for the moment by the other's unexpected presence.

It was the man who recovered his self-possession first. He threw his overcoat into a chair, and touched the brass knobs behind the door. Instantly the room was flooded with the soft radiance of the electric lights. They could see one another now distinctly. The woman leaned a little forward, and there was amazement as well as fear flashing in her soft, dark eyes. Her voice, when she spoke, sounded to herself unnatural. To him it came as a surprise, for the world of men and women was his study, and he recognized at once its quality.

"Who are you?" she exclaimed. "What do you want?"

He shrugged his shoulders.

"It seems to me," he answered, "that I might more fittingly assume the role of questioner. However, I have no objection to introduce myself. My name is Herbert Wrayson. May I ask," he continued with quiet sarcasm, "to what I am indebted for this unexpected visit?"

She was silent for a moment, and as he watched her his surprise grew. Equivocal though her position was, he knew very well that this was no ordinary thief whom he had surprised in his rooms, engaged to all appearance in rifling his desk. The fact that she was a beautiful woman was one which he scarcely took into account. There were other things more surprising which he could not ignore. Her evening dress of black net was faultlessly made, and he knew enough of such things to be well aware that it came from the hands of no ordinary dressmaker. A string of pearls, her only ornament, hung from her neck, and her black hat with its drooping feathers was the fellow of one which he had admired a few evenings ago at the Ritz in Paris. It flashed upon him that this was a woman of distinction, one who belonged naturally, if not in effect, to the world of which even he could not claim to be a habitant. What was she doing in his rooms? - of what interest to her were he and his few possessions?

"Herbert Wrayson," she repeated, leaning a little

E. Phillips Oppenheim

towards him. "If your name is Herbert Wrayson, what are you doing in these rooms?"

"They happen to be mine," he answered calmly.

"Yours!"

She picked up a small latch-key from the desk.

"This is number 11, isn't it?" she asked quickly.

"No! Number 11 is the flat immediately overhead," he told her.

She appeared unconvinced.

"But I opened the door with this key," she declared.

"Mr. Barnes and I have similar locks," he said. "The fact remains that this is number 9, and number 11 is one story overhead."

She drew a long breath, presumably of relief, and moved a step forward.

"I am very sorry!" she declared. "I have made a mistake. You must please accept my apologies."

He stood motionless in front of the door. He was pale, clean-shaven, and slim, and in his correct evening clothes he seemed a somewhat ordinary type of the well-bred young Englishman. But his eyes were grey, and his mouth straight and firm.

She came to a standstill. Her eyes seemed to be questioning him. She scarcely understood his attitude.

"Kindly allow me to pass!" she said coldly.

"Presently!" he answered.

Her veil was still raised, and the flash of her eyes would surely have made a weaker man quail. But Wrayson never flinched.

"What do you mean by that?" she demanded. "I have explained my presence in your room. It was an accident which I regret. Let me pass at once."

"You have explained your presence here," he answered, "after a fashion! But you have not explained what your object may be in making use of that key to enter Mr. Barnes' flat. Are you proposing to subject his belongings to the same inspection as mine?" he asked, pointing to his disordered desk.

"My business with Mr. Barnes is no concern of yours!" she exclaimed haughtily.

"Under ordinary circumstances, no!" he admitted. "But these are not ordinary circumstances. Forgive me if I speak plainly. I found you engaged in searching my desk. The presumption is that you wish to do the same thing to Mr. Barnes'."

"And if I do, sir!" she demanded, "what concern is it of yours? How do you know that I have not permission to visit his rooms - that he did not himself give me this key?"

She held it out before him. He glanced at it and back into her face.

"The supposition," he said, "does not commend itself to me."

"Why not?"

He looked at the clock.

"You see," he declared, "that it is within a few minutes of midnight. To be frank with you, you do not seem to me the sort of person likely to visit a bachelor such as Mr. Barnes, in a bachelor flat, at this hour, without some serious object."

She kept silence for several moments. Her bosom was rising and falling quickly, and a brilliant spot of colour was burning in her cheeks. Her head was thrown a little back, she was regarding him with an intentness which he found almost disconcerting. He had an uncomfortable sense that he was in the presence of a human being who, if it had lain in her power, would have killed him where he stood. Further, he was realizing that the woman whom at first glance he had pronounced beautiful, was absolutely the first of her sex whom he had ever seen who satisfied completely the demands of a somewhat critical and highly cultivated taste. The silence between them seemed extended over a time crowded and rich with sensations. He found time to marvel at the delicate whiteness of her bosom, gleaming like polished ivory under the network of her black gown, to appreciate with a quick throb of delight the slim roundness of her perfect figure, the wonderful poise of her head, the soft richness of her braided hair. Every detail of feature and of toilet seemed to satisfy to the last degree each critical faculty of which he was possessed. He felt a little shiver of apprehension when he recalled the cold brutality of the words which had just left his lips! Yet how could he deal with her differently?

"Is this man - Morris Barnes - your friend?" she asked, breaking a silence which had done more than anything else to unnerve him.

"No!" he answered. "I scarcely know the man. I have never seen him except in the lift, or on the stairs."

"Then you have no excuse for keeping me here," she declared. "I may be his friend, or I may be his enemy. At least I possess the key of his flat, presumably with his permission. My presence here I have explained. I can assure you that it is entirely accidental! You have no right to detain me for a moment."

The clock on the mantelpiece struck midnight. A sudden passion surged in his veins, a passion which, although at the time he could not have classified it, was assuredly a passion of jealousy! He remembered the man Barnes, whom he hated.

"You shall not go to his rooms - at this hour!" he exclaimed. "You don't know the man! If you were seen -"

She laughed mockingly.

"Let me pass!" she insisted.

He hesitated. She saw very clearly that she was conquering. A moment before she had respected this man. After all, though, he was like the others.

"I will go with you and wait outside," he said doggedly. "Barnes, at this hour - is not always sober!"

Her lips curled.

"Be wise," she said, "and let me go. I do not need your protection or - "

She broke off suddenly. The interruption was certainly startling enough. From a table only a few feet off came the shrill tinkle of a telephone bell. Wrayson mechanically stepped backwards and took the receiver into his hand.

"Who is it?" he asked.

The voice which answered him was faint but clear. It seemed to Wrayson to come from a long way off.

"Is that Mr. Wrayson's flat in Cavendish Mansions?" it asked.

"Yes!" Wrayson answered. "Who are you?"

"I am a friend of Mr. Morris Barnes," the voice answered. "May I apologize for calling you up, but the matter is urgent. Can you tell me if Mr. Barnes is in?"

"I am not sure, but I believe he is never in before one or two o'clock," Wrayson answered.

"Will you write down a message and leave it in his letter-box?" the voice asked anxiously. "It is very important or I would not trouble you."

"Very well," Wrayson answered. "What is it?"

"Tell him instantly he returns to leave his flat and go to the Hotel Francis. A friend is waiting there for him, the friend whom he has been expecting!"

"A lady?" Wrayson remarked a little sarcastically.

"No!" the voice answered. "A friend. Will you do this?
Will you promise to do it?"

"Very well," Wrayson said. "Who are you, and where
are you ringing up from?"

"Remember you have promised!" was the only reply.

"All right! Tell me your name," Wrayson demanded.

No answer. Wrayson turned the handle of the
instrument viciously.

"Exchange," he asked, "who was that talking to me just
now?"

"Don't know," was the prompt answer. "We can't
remember all the calls we get. Ring off, please!"

Wrayson laid down the receiver and turned round with
a sudden sense of apprehension. There was a feeling of
emptiness in the room. He had not heard a sound, but
he knew very well what had happened. The door was
slightly open and the room was empty. She had taken
advantage of his momentary absorption to slip away.

He stepped outside and stood by the lift, listening. The
landing was deserted, and there was no sound of any
one moving anywhere. The lift itself was on the
ground floor. It had not ascended recently or he must
have heard it. He returned to his room and softly
closed the door. Again the sense of emptiness

E. Phillips Oppenheim

oppressed him. A faint perfume around the place where she had stood came to him like a whiff of some delicious memory. He set his teeth, lit a cigarette, and sitting down at his desk wrote a few lines to his neighbour, embodying the message which had been given him. With the note in his hand he ascended to the next floor.

There was apparently no light in flat number 11, but he rang the bell and listened. There was no answer, no sound of any one moving within. For nearly ten minutes he waited - listening. He was strongly tempted to open the door with his own key and see for himself if she was there. Then he remembered that Barnes was a man whom he barely knew, and cordially disliked, and that if he should return unexpectedly, the situation would be a little difficult to explain. Reluctantly he descended to his own flat, and mixing himself a whisky and soda, lit a pipe and sat down, determined to wait until he heard Barnes return. In less than a quarter of an hour he was asleep!

CHAPTER II

THE HORROR OF THE HANSOM

Wrayson sat up with a sudden and violent start. His pipe had fallen on to the floor, leaving a long trail of grey ash upon his waistcoat and trousers. The electric lights were still burning, but of the fire nothing remained but a pile of ashes. As soon as he could be said to be conscious of anything, he was conscious of two things. One was that he was shivering with cold, the other that he was afraid.

Wrayson was by no means a coward. He had come once or twice in his life into close touch with dangerous happenings, and conducted himself with average pluck. He never attempted to conceal from himself, however, that these few minutes were minutes of breathless, unreasoning fear. His heart was thumping against his side, and the muscles at the back of his neck were almost numb as he slowly looked round the room. His eyes paused at the door. It was slightly open, to his nervous fancy it seemed to be shaking. His teeth chattered, he felt his forehead, and it was wet.

He rose to his feet and listened. There was no sound anywhere, from above or below. He tried to remember what it was that had awakened him so suddenly. He

E. Phillips Oppenheim

could remember nothing except that awful start. Something must have disturbed him! He listened again. Still no sound. He drew a little breath, and, with his eyes glued upon the half-closed door, recollected that he himself had left it open that he might hear Barnes go upstairs. With a little laugh, still not altogether natural, he moved to the spirit decanter and drank off half a wineglassful of neat whisky!

"Nerves," he said softly to himself. "This won't do! What an idiot I was to go to sleep there!"

He glanced at the clock. It was five minutes to three. Then he moved towards the door, and stood for several moments with the handle in his hand. Gradually his confidence was returning. He listened attentively. There was not a sound to be heard in the entire building. He turned back into the room with a little sigh of relief.

"Time I turned in," he muttered. "Wonder if that's rain."

He lifted the blind and looked out. A few stars were shining still in a misty sky, but a bank of clouds was rolling up and rain was beginning to fall. The pavements were already wet, and the lamp-posts obscured. He was about to turn away when a familiar, but unexpected, sound from the street immediately below attracted his notice. The window was open at the top, and he had distinctly heard the jingling of a hansom bell.

He threw open the bottom sash and leaned out. A hansom cab was waiting at the entrance to the flats. Wrayson glanced once more instinctively towards the clock. Who on earth of his neighbours could be keeping a cab waiting outside at that hour in the morning? With the exception of Barnes and himself, they were most of them early people. Once more he looked out of the window. The cabman was leaning forward in his seat with his head resting upon his folded arms. He was either tired out or asleep. The attitude of the horse was one of extreme and wearied dejection. Wrayson was on the point of closing the window when he became aware for the first time that the cab had an occupant. He could see the figure of a man leaning back in one corner, he could even distinguish a white-gloved hand resting upon the apron. The figure was not unlike the figure of Barnes, and Barnes, as he happened to remember, always wore white gloves in the evening. Barnes it probably was, waiting - for what? Wrayson closed the window a little impatiently, and turned back into the room.

"Barnes and his friends can go to the devil," he muttered. "I am off to bed."

He took a couple of steps across the room, and then stopped short. The fear was upon him again. He felt his heart almost stop beating, a cold shiver shook his whole frame. He was standing facing his half-open door, and outside on the stone steps he heard the soft, even footfall of slippered feet, and the gentle rustling of a woman's gown.

He was not conscious of any movement, but when she reached the landing he was standing there on the threshold, with the soft halo of light from behind shining on to his white, fiercely questioning face. She came towards him without speech, and her veil was lowered so that he could only imperfectly see her face, but she walked as one newly recovered from illness, with trembling footsteps, and with one hand always upon the banisters. When she reached the corner she stopped, and seemed about to collapse. She spoke to him, and her voice had lost all its quality. It sounded harsh and unreal.

"Why are you - spying on me?" she asked.

"I am not spying," he answered. "I have been asleep - and woke up suddenly."

"Give me - some brandy!" she begged.

She stood upon the threshold and drank from the wineglass which he had filled. When she gave it back to him, he noticed that her fingers were steady.

"Will you come downstairs and let me out?" she asked. "I have looked down and it is all dark on the ground floor. I am not sure that I know my way."

He hesitated, but only for a moment. Side by side they walked down four flights of steps in unbroken silence. He asked no question, she attempted no explanation. Only when he opened the door and she saw the waiting hansom she very nearly collapsed. For a moment she clung to him.

"He is there - in the cab," she moaned. "Where can I hide?"

"Whoever it is," Wrayson answered, with his eyes fixed upon the hansom, "he is either drunk or asleep."

"Or dead!" she whispered in his ear. "Go and see!"

Then, before Wrayson could recover from the shock of her words, she was gone, flitting down the unlit side of the street with swift silent footsteps. His eyes followed her mechanically. Then, when she had turned the corner, he crossed the pavement towards the cab. Even now he could see little of the figure in the corner, for his silk hat was drawn down over his eyes.

"Is that you, Barnes?" he asked.

There came not the slightest response. Then for the first time the hideous meaning of those farewell words of hers broke in upon his brain. Had she meant it? Had she known or guessed? He leaned forward and touched the white-gloved hand. He raised it and let go. It fell like a dead, inert thing. He stepped back and confronted the cabman, who was rubbing his eyes.

"There's something wrong with your fare, cabby," he said.

The cabby raised the trap door, looked down, and descended heavily on to the pavement.

"Well, I'm blowed!" he said. "Here, wake up, guv'nor!"

There was no response. The cabby threw open the apron of the cab and gently shook the recumbent figure.

"I can't wait 'ere all night for my fare!" he exclaimed. "Wake up, God luv us!" he broke off.

He stepped hastily back on to the pavement, and began tugging at one of his lamps.

"Push his hat back, sir," he said. "Let's 'ave a look at 'im."

Wrayson stood upon the step of the cab and lifted the silk hat from the head of the recumbent figure. Then he sprang back quickly with a little exclamation of horror. The lamp was shining full now upon the man's face, livid and white, upon his staring but sightless eyes, upon something around his neck, a fragment of silken cord, drawn so tightly that the flesh seemed to hang over and almost conceal it.

"Throttled, by God!" the cabman exclaimed. "I'm off to the police station."

He clambered up to his seat, and without another word struck his horse with the whip. The cab drove off and disappeared. Wrayson turned slowly round, and, closing the door of the flats, mounted with leaden feet to the fourth story.

He entered his own rooms, and walked without hesitation to the window, which was still open. The fresh air was almost a necessity, for he felt himself being slowly stifled. His knees were shaking, a cold icy horror was numbing his heart and senses. A feeling of nightmare was upon him, as though he had risen unexpectedly from a bed of delirium. There in front of him, a little to the left, was the broad empty street amongst whose shadows she had disappeared. On one side was the Park, and there was obscurity indefinable, mysterious; on the other a long row of tall mansions, a rain-soaked pavement, and a curving line of gas lamps. Beyond, the river, marked with a glittering arc of yellow dots; further away the glow of the sleeping city. Shelter enough there for any one - even for her. A soft, damp breeze was blowing in his face; from amongst the dripping trees of the Park the birds were beginning to make their morning music. Already the blackness of night was passing away, the clouds were lightening, the stars were growing fainter. Wrayson leaned a little forward. His eyes were fixed upon the exact spot where she had crossed the road and disappeared. All the horror of the coming day and the days to come loomed out from the background of his thoughts.

E. Phillips Oppenheim

CHAPTER III

DISCUSSING THE CRIME

The murder of Morris Barnes, considered merely as an event, came as a Godsend to the halfpenny press, which has an unwritten but immutable contract with the public to provide it with so much sensation during the week, in season or out of season. Nothing else was talked about anywhere. Under the influence of the general example, Wrayson found himself within a few days discussing its details with perfect coolness, and with an interest which never flagged. He seemed continually to forget his own personal and actual connection with the affair.

It was discussed, amongst other places, at the Sheridan Club, of which Wrayson was a member, and where he spent most of his spare time. At one particular luncheon party the day after the inquest, nothing else was spoken of. For the first time, in Wrayson's hearing, a new and somewhat ominous light was thrown upon the affair.

There were four men at the luncheon party, which was really not a luncheon party at all, but a promiscuous coming together of four of the men who usually sat at what was called the Colonel's table. First of all there was the Colonel himself, - Colonel Edgar Fitzmaurice,

C.B., D.S.O., - easily the most popular member of the club, a distinguished retired officer, white-haired, kindly and genial, a man of whom no one had ever heard another say an unkind word, whose hand was always in his none too well-filled pockets, and whose sympathies were always ready to be enlisted in any forlorn cause, deserving or otherwise. At his right hand sat Wrayson; on his left Sydney Mason, a rising young sculptor, and also a popular member of this somewhat Bohemian circle. Opposite was Stephen Heneage, a man of a different and more secretive type. He called himself a barrister, but he never practised; a journalist at times, but he seldom put his name to anything he wrote. His interests, if he had any, he kept to himself. In a club where a man's standing was reckoned by what he was and what he produced, he owed such consideration as he received to a certain air of reserved strength, the more noteworthy amongst a little coterie of men, who amongst themselves were accustomed to speak their minds freely, and at all times. If he was never brilliant, he had never been heard to say a foolish thing or make a pointless remark. He moved on his way through life, and held his place there more by reason of certain negative qualities which, amongst a community of optimists, were universally ascribed to him, than through any more personal or likable gifts. He had a dark, strong face, but a slim, weakly body. He was never unduly silent, but he was a better listener than talker. If he had no close friends, he certainly had no enemies. Whether he was rich or poor no man knew, but next to the Colonel himself, no one was more ready to subscribe to any of those charities which the Sheridanites were continually inaugurating on behalf of their less fortunate members. The man who succeeds in keeping the "ego" out of sight as a rule neither irritates nor greatly attracts. Stephen Heneage was one of those who stood in this position.

They were talking about the murder, or rather the Colonel was talking and they were listening.

"There is one point," he remarked, filling his glass and beaming good-humouredly upon his companions, "which seems to have been entirely overlooked. I am referring to the sex of the supposed assassin!"

Wrayson looked up inquiringly. It was a point which interested him.

"Nearly all of you have assumed," the Colonel continued, "that it must have taken a strong man to draw the cord tight enough to have killed that poor fellow without any noticeable struggle. As a matter of fact, a child with that particular knot could have done it. It requires no strength, only delicacy of touch, rapidity and nerve."

"A woman, then - " Wrayson began.

"Bless you, yes! a woman could have done it easily," the Colonel declared, "only unfortunately there don't seem to have been any women about. Why, I've seen it done in Korea with a turn of the wrist. It's all knack."

Wrayson shuddered slightly. The Colonel's words had troubled him more than he would have cared to let any one know.

"Woman or man or child," Mason remarked, "the person who did it seems to have vanished in some remarkable manner from the face of the earth."

"He certainly seems," the Colonel admitted, "to have covered up his traces with admirable skill. I have read every word of the evidence at the inquest, and I can understand that the police are completely confused."

Heneage and Mason exchanged glances of quiet amusement whilst the Colonel helped himself to cheese.

"Dear old boy," the latter murmured, "he's off on his hobby. Let him go on! He enjoys it more than anything in the world."

Heneage nodded assent, and the Colonel returned to the subject with avidity a few moments later.

"This man Morris Barnes," he affirmed, "seems to have been a somewhat despicable, at any rate, a by no means desirable individual. He was of Jewish origin, and he had not long returned from South Africa, where Heaven knows what his occupation was. The money of which he was undoubtedly possessed he seems to have spent, or at any rate some part of it, in aping the life of a dissipated man about town. He was known to the fair promenaders of the Empire and Alhambra, he was an *habitué* of the places where these - er - ladies partake of supper after the exertions of the evening. Of home life or respectable friends he seems to have had none."

"This," Mason declared, leaning back and lighting a cigarette, "is better than the newspapers. Go on, Colonel! Your biography may not be sympathetic, but it is lifelike!"

The Colonel's eyes were full of a distinct and vivid light. He scarcely heard the interruption. He was on

E. Phillips Oppenheim

fire with his subject.

"You see," he continued, "that the man's days were spent amongst a class where the passions run loose, where restraint is an unknown virtue, where self and sensuality are the upraised gods. One can easily imagine that from amongst such a slough might spring at any time the weed of tragedy. In other words, this man Morris Barnes moved amongst a class of people to whom murder, if it could be safely accomplished, would be little more than an incident."

The Colonel lit a cigar and leaned back in his chair. He was enjoying himself immensely.

"The curious part of the affair is, though," he continued deliberately, "that this murder, as I suppose we must call it, bears none of the hall-marks of rude passion. On the contrary, it suggests in more ways than one the touch of the finished artist. The man's whole evening has been traced without the slightest difficulty. He dined at the Café Royal alone, promenaded afterwards at the Alhambra, and drove on about supper-time to the Continental. He left there at 12.30 with a couple of ladies whom he appeared to know fairly well, called at their flat for a drink, and sent one out to his cabby - rather unusual forethought for such a bounder. When he reappeared and directed the man to drive him to Cavendish Mansions, Battersea, the driver tried to excuse himself. Both he and his horse were dead tired, he said. Barnes, however, insisted upon keeping him, and off they went. At Cavendish Mansions, Barnes alighted and offered the man a sovereign. Naturally enough the fellow could not change it, and Barnes went in to get some silver from his rooms, promising to return in a minute or two. The cabby descended and walked to the corner of the street to see if he could beg a match for his pipe from any passer-by. He may have been away for perhaps five minutes, certainly no more, during which time he stood with his back to the Mansions. Seeing no one about, he returned to his cab, ascended to his seat, naturally without looking inside, and fell fast asleep. The next thing he remembers is being awakened by Wrayson here! So much for the cabby."

"What a fine criminal judge was lost to the country, Colonel, when you chose the army for a career," Mason remarked, turning round to order some coffee. "Such coherence - such an eye for detail. Pass the matches, Wrayson. Thanks, old chap!"

The Colonel smiled placidly.

"I am afraid," he said, "that I should never have had the heart to sentence anybody to anything, but I must admit that things of this sort do interest me. I love to weigh them up and theorize. The more melodramatic they are the better."

Heneage helped himself to a cigarette from Mason's case, and leaned back
in his chair.

"I never have the patience," he remarked, "to read about these things in the newspapers, but the Colonel's *résumé* is always thrilling. Do go on. There won't be any pool till four o'clock."

The Colonel smiled good-naturedly.

"It's good of you fellows to listen to my prosing," he

E. Phillips Oppenheim

remarked. "No use denying that it is a sort of hobby of mine. You all know it. Well, we'll say we've finished with the cabby, then. Enter upon the scene, of all people in the world, our friend Wrayson!"

"Hear, hear!" murmured Mason.

Wrayson changed his position slightly. With his head resting upon his hand, he seemed to be engaged in tracing patterns upon the tablecloth.

"Wrayson knows nothing of Barnes beyond the fact that they are neighbours in the same flats. Being the assistant editor of a journal of world-wide fame, however, he has naturally a telephone in his flat. By means of that instrument he receives a message in the middle of the night from an unknown person in an unknown place, which he is begged to convey to Barnes. The message is in itself mysterious. Taken in conjunction with what happened to Barnes, it is deeply interesting. Barnes, it seems, is to go immediately on his arrival, at whatever hour, to the Hotel Francis. Presumably he would know from whom the message came, and the sender does not seem to have doubted that if it was conveyed to Barnes he would obey the summons. Wrayson agrees to and does deliver it. That is to say, he writes it down and leaves it in the letter-box of Barnes door, Barnes not having yet returned. Now we begin to get mysterious. That communication from our friend here has not been discovered. It was not in the letter-box; it was not upon the person of the dead man. We cannot tell whether or not he ever received it. I believe that I am right so far?"

"Absolutely," Wrayson admitted.

"Our friend Wrayson, then," the Colonel continued, beaming upon his neighbour, "instead of going to bed like a sensible man, takes up a book and falls asleep in his easy-chair. He wakes up about three or four o'clock, and his attention is then attracted by the jingling of a hansom bell below. He looks out of window and sees a cab, both the driver and the occupant of which appear to be asleep. The circumstance striking him as somewhat unusual, he descends to the street and finds - well, rather more than he expected. He finds the cabman asleep, and his fare scientifically and effectually throttled by a piece of silken cord."

Wrayson turned to the waiter and ordered a liqueur brandy.

"Have one, you fellows?" he asked. "Good! Four, waiter."

He tossed his own off directly it arrived. His lips were pale, and the hand which raised the glass to his lips shook. Heneage alone, who was watching him through a little cloud of tobacco smoke, noticed this.

"Have you finished with me, Colonel?" Wrayson asked.

"Practically," the Colonel answered, smiling, "unless you can answer one of the three queries suggested by my *résumé*. First, who killed Morris Barnes? Secondly, when was it done? Thirdly, where was it done? I have left out a possible fourth, why was it done? because, in this case, I think that the motive and the man are practically identical. I mean that if you discover one, you discover the other."

E. Phillips Oppenheim

Heneage leaned across the table towards the Colonel.

"You are a magician, Colonel," he declared quietly. "I glanced through this case in the paper, and it did not even interest me. Since I have listened to you I have fallen under the spell of the mysterious. Have you any theories?"

The Colonel's face fell a little.

"Well, I am afraid not," he admitted regretfully. "To be perfectly interesting the affair certainly ought to present something more definite in the shape of a clue. You see, providing we accept the evidence of Wrayson and the cabman, and I suppose," he added, laying his hand affectionately upon Wrayson's shoulder, "we must, the actual murderer is a person absolutely unseen or unheard of by any one. If you are all really interested we will discuss it again in a week's time after the adjourned inquest."

"I, for one, shall look forward to it," Heneage remarked, glancing across towards Wrayson. "What about a pool?"

"I'm on," Wrayson declared, rising a little abruptly.

"And I," Mason assented.

"And I can't," the Colonel said regretfully. "I must go down to Balham and see poor Carlo Mallini I hear he's very queer."

The Colonel loved pool, and he hated a sick-room. The click of the billiard balls reached him as he descended the stairs, but he only sighed and set out manfully for

Charing Cross. On the way he entered a fruiterer's shop and inquired the price of grapes. They were more than he expected, and he counted out the contents of his trousers pockets before purchasing.

"A little short of change," he remarked cheerfully. "Yes! all right, I'll take them."

He marched out, swinging a paper bag between his fingers, travelled third class to Balham, and sat for a couple of hours with the invalid whom he had come to see, a lonely Italian musician, to whom his coming meant more than all the medicine his doctor could prescribe. He talked to him glowingly of the success of his recent concert (more than a score of the tickets sold had been paid for secretly by the Colonel himself and his friends), prophesied great things for the future, and laughed away all the poor fellow's fears as to his condition. There were tears in his eyes as he walked to the station, for he had visited too many sick-beds to have much faith in his own cheerful words, and all the way back to London he was engaged in thinking out the best means of getting the musician sent back to his own country, Arrived at Charing Cross, he looked longingly towards the club, and ruefully at the contents of his pocket. Then with a sigh he turned into a little restaurant and dined for eighteen-pence.

E. Phillips Oppenheim

CHAPTER IV

UNDER A CLOUD

Exactly one week later, six men were smoking their after-dinner cigars at the same round table in the dining-room at the Sheridan Club. As a rule, it was the hour when, with all the reserve of the day thrown aside, badinage and jest reigned supreme, and the humourist came to his own. To-night chairs were drawn a little closer together, voices were subdued, and the conversation was of a more serious order. Not even the pleasant warmth of the room, the fragrance of tobacco, and the comfortable sense of having dined, could altogether dispel a feeling of uneasiness which all more or less shared. It chanced that all six were friends of Herbert Wrayson's.

The Colonel, as usual, was in the chair, but even on his kindly features the cloud hovered.

"Of course," he said, "none of us who know Wrayson well would believe for a moment that he could be connected in any way with this beastly affair. The unfortunate part of it is, that others, who do not know him, might easily be led to think otherwise!"

"It is altogether his own fault, too," Mason remarked. "He gave his evidence shockingly."

"And his movements that night, or rather that morning, were certainly a little peculiar," another man remarked. "His connection with the affair seemed to consist of a series of coincidences. The law does not look favourably upon coincidences!"

"But, after all," the Colonel remarked, "he scarcely knew the fellow! Just nodded to him on the stairs, and that sort of thing. Why, there isn't a shadow of a motive!"

"We can't be sure of that, Colonel," Heneage remarked quietly. "I wonder how much we really know of the inner lives of even our closest friends? I fancy that we should be surprised if we realized our ignorance!"

The Colonel stroked his grey moustache thoughtfully.

"That may be true," he said, "of a good many of us. Wrayson, however, never struck me as being a particularly secretive sort of chap."

"Unfortunately, that counts for very little," Heneage declared. "The things which surprise us most in life come often from the most unlikely people. We none of us mean to be deceitful, but a perfectly honest life is a luxury which few of us dare indulge in."

The Colonel regarded him gravely.

"I hope," he said, "that you don't mean that you consider Wrayson capable -"

"I wasn't thinking of Wrayson at all," Heneage interrupted. "I was generalizing. But I must say this. I think that, given sufficient provocation or motive, there isn't one of us who wouldn't be capable of committing murder. A man's outer life is lived according to the laws of circumstances and society: his inner one no one knows anything about, except himself - and God!"

"Heneage," Mason sighed, "is always cynical after 'kümmel.'"

Heneage shrugged his shoulders and lit a cigarette.

"No!" he said, "I am not cynical. I simply have a weakness for the truth. You will find it rather a hard material to collect if you set out in earnest. But to return to Wrayson. Let me ask you a question. We are all friends of his, more or less intimate friends. You would all of you scout the idea of his having any share in the murder of Morris Barnes. What did you make of his evidence at the inquest this afternoon? What do you think of his whole deportment and condition?"

"I can answer that in one word," the Colonel declared. "I think that it is unfortunate. The poor fellow has been terribly upset, and his nerves have not been able to stand the strain. That is all there is about it!"

"Wrayson has been working up to the limit for years," Mason remarked, "and he's not a particularly strong chap. I should say that he was about due for a nervous breakdown."

A waiter approached the table and addressed the Colonel - he was wanted on the telephone. During his absence, Heneage leaned back in his chair and relapsed into his usual imperturbability. He was known amongst his friends generally as the silent man. It was very seldom that he contributed so much to their discussions as upon this occasion. Perhaps for that reason his words, when he spoke, always carried weight. Mason changed his place and sat beside him. The others had wandered off into a discussion upon a new magazine.

"Between ourselves, Heneage," Mason said quietly, "have you anything at the back of your head about Wrayson?"

Heneage did not immediately reply. He was gazing at the little cloud of blue tobacco smoke which he had just expelled from his lips.

"There is no reason," he declared, "why my opinion should be worth any more than any one else's. I think as highly of Wrayson as any of you."

"Granted," Mason answered. "But you have a theory or an idea of some sort concerning him. What is it?"

"If you really want to know," Heneage said, "I believe that Wrayson has kept something back. It is a very dangerous thing to do, and I believe that he realizes it. I believe that he has some secret knowledge of the affair which he has not disclosed - knowledge which he has kept out of his evidence altogether."

"A - guilty - knowledge?" Mason whispered.

"Not necessarily!" Heneage answered. "He may be shielding some one."

"If you are right," Mason said anxiously, "it is a serious affair."

"Very serious indeed," Heneage assented. "I believe

that he is realizing it."

The Colonel came back looking a little disturbed.

"Sorry, boys, but I must be off," he announced. "Wrayson has just telephoned to ask me to go down and see him. I'm afraid he's queer! I've sent for a hansom."

"Poor chap!" Mason murmured. "Let us know if any of us can do anything."

The Colonel nodded and took his departure. The others drifted up into the billiard-room. Heneage alone remained seated at the end of the table. He was playing idly with his wineglass, but his eyes were fixed steadfastly, if a little absently, upon the Colonel's empty place.

CHAPTER V

ON THE TELEPHONE

It was a little hard even for the Colonel to keep up his affectation of cheerfulness when he found himself alone with the man whom he had come to visit. His experience of life had been large and varied, but he had never yet seen so remarkable a change in any human being in twenty-four hours. There were deep black lines under his eyes, his cheeks were colourless, every now and then his features twitched nervously, as though he were suffering from an attack of St. Vitus' dance. His hand, which had lain weakly in the Colonel's, was as cold as ice, although there was a roaring fire in the room. He had admitted the Colonel himself, and almost dragged him inside the door.

"Did you meet any one outside - upon the stairs?" he asked feverishly.

"No one upon the stairs," the Colonel answered. "There was a man lighting his pipe in the doorway."

Wrayson shivered as he turned away.

"Watching me!" he declared. "There are two of them! They are watching me all the time."

E. Phillips Oppenheim

The Colonel took off his coat. The room seemed to him like a furnace. Then he stretched out his hands and laid them upon Wrayson's shoulders.

"What if they are?" he declared cheerfully. "They won't eat you. Besides, it is very likely the dead man's rooms they are watching."

"They followed me home from the inquest," Wrayson muttered.

The Colonel laughed.

"And if I'd been living here," he remarked, "they'd have followed me home just the same. Now, Herbert, my young friend," he continued, "sit down and tell me all about it like a man. You're in a bit of trouble, of course, underneath all this. Let's hear it, and we'll find the best way out."

The Colonel's figure was dominant; his presence alone seemed to dispel that unreal army of ghosts and fancies which a few moments before had seemed to Wrayson to be making his room like the padded cell of a lunatic asylum. His tone, too, had just enough sympathy to make its cheerfulness reassuring. Wrayson began to feel glimmerings of common sense.

"Yes!" he said, "I've something to tell you. That's why I telephoned."

The Colonel rose again to his feet, and began fumbling in the pocket of his overcoat.

"God bless my soul, I almost forgot!" he exclaimed, "and the fellows would make me bring it. We guessed how you were feeling - much better to have come up and dined with us. Here we are! Get some glasses, there's a good chap."

A gold-foiled bottle appeared, and a packet of hastily cut sandwiches. Wrayson found himself mechanically eating and drinking before he knew where he was. Then in an instant the sandwiches had become delicious, and the wine was rushing through his veins like a new elixir of life. He was himself again, the banging of anvils in his head had ceased; he was shaken perhaps, but a sane man. His eyes filled with tears, and he gripped the Colonel by the hand.

"Colonel, you're - you're - God knows what you are," he murmured. "All the ordinary things sound commonplace. I believe I was going mad."

The Colonel leaned back and laughed as though the idea tickled him.

"Not you!" he declared. "Bless you, I know what nerves are! Out in India, thirty-five years ago, I've had to relieve men on frontier posts who hadn't seen a soul to speak to for six months! Weird places some of them, too - gives me the creeps to think of them sometimes! Now light up that cigar," he added, throwing one across, "and let's hear the trouble."

Wrayson lit his cigar with fingers which scarcely shook. He threw the match away and smoked for a moment in silence.

"It's about this Morris Barnes affair," he said abruptly. "I've kept something back, and I'm a clumsy hand at telling a story that doesn't contain all the truth. The consequence is, of course, that I'm suspected of having had a hand in it myself."

The Colonel's manner had for a moment imperceptibly changed. Lines had come out in his face which were not usually visible, his upper lip had stiffened. One could fancy that he might have led his men into battle looking something like this.

"What is it that you know?" he asked.

"There was another person in the flats that night, who was interested in Morris Barnes, who visited his rooms, who was with me when I first saw him dead."

The Colonel shaded his face with his hand. The heat from the fire was intense.

"Why have you kept back this knowledge?" he asked.

"Because - it was a woman, and I am a fool!" Wrayson answered.

There was a silence. Then the Colonel pushed back his chair and dabbed his forehead with his handkerchief. The room was certainly hot, and the handkerchief was wet.

"Tell me about it," he said quietly. "I expected something of the sort!"

"On that morning," Wrayson began, "I returned home about twelve o'clock, let myself in with my own latch-key, and found a woman standing before my open desk going through my papers."

"A friend?" the Colonel asked.

"A complete stranger!" Wrayson answered. "Her surprise at seeing me was at least equal to my own. I gathered that she had believed herself to be in the flat of Morris Barnes, which is the corresponding one above."

"What did you do?" the Colonel asked.

"What I should have done I am not sure," Wrayson answered, "but while I was talking to her the telephone bell rang, and I received that message which I spoke about at the inquest. It was a mysterious sort of business - I can hear that voice now. I was interested, and while I stood there she slipped away."

"Is that all?" the Colonel asked.

"No!" Wrayson answered with a groan. "I wish to God it was!"

The Colonel moved his position a little. The cigar had burnt out between his fingers, but he made no effort to light it.

"Go on," he said. "Tell me the rest. Tell me what happened afterwards."

"I wrote down the message for Barnes and left it in his letter-box. There seemed then to be no light in his flat. Afterwards I lit a pipe, left my door open, and sat down, with the intention of waiting till Barnes came home and explaining what had happened. I fell asleep in my chair and woke with a start. It was nearly three o'clock. I was going to turn in when I heard the jingling of a hansom bell down below. I looked out of the window and saw the cab standing in the street. Almost at the same time I heard footsteps outside. I went to the door of my flat and came face to face with the girl descending from the floor above."

"At three o'clock in the morning?" the Colonel interrupted.

Wrayson nodded.

"She was white and shaking all over," he continued rapidly. "She asked me for brandy and I gave it to her; she asked me to see her out of the place, and I did so. When I opened the door to let her out and we saw the man leaning back in the cab, she moaned softly to herself. I said something about his being asleep or drunk - 'or dead!' she whispered in my ear, and then she rushed away from me. She turned into the Albert Road and disappeared almost at once. I could not have followed her if I would. I had just begun to realize that something was wrong with the man in the cab!"

"This is all?" the Colonel asked.

"It is all!" Wrayson answered.

"You do not know her name, or why she was here? You have not seen her since?"

Wrayson shook his head.

"I know absolutely nothing," he said, "beyond what I have told you."

The Colonel struck a match and relit his cigar.

"I should like to understand," he said quietly, "why you avoided all mention of her in your evidence."

Wrayson laughed oddly.

"I should like to understand that myself," he declared. "I can only repeat what I said before. She was a woman, and I was a fool."

"In plain English," the Colonel said, "you did it to shield her?"

"Yes!" Wrayson answered.

The Colonel nodded thoughtfully.

"Well," he said, "you were in a difficult position, and you made a deliberate choice. I tell you frankly that I expected to hear worse things. Do you believe that she committed the murder?"

"No!" Wrayson answered. "I do not!"

"You believe that she may be associated with - the person who did?"

"I cannot tell," Wrayson declared.

"In any case," the Colonel continued, "you seem to have been the only person who saw her. Whether you were wise or not to omit all mention of her in your evidence - well, we won't discuss that. The best of us have gone on the wrong side of the hedge for a woman before now - and damned glad to do it. What I can't quite understand, old chap, is why you have worked yourself up into such a shocking state. You don't stand any chance of being hanged, that I can see!"

Wrayson laughed a little shamefacedly.

"To tell you the truth," he said, "I am beginning to feel ashamed of myself. I think it was the sense of being spied upon, and being alone - in this room - which got a bit on my nerves. I feel a different man since you came down."

The Colonel nodded cheerfully.

"That's all right," he declared. "The next thing to -"

The Colonel broke off in the midst of his sentence. A few feet away from him the telephone bell was ringing. Wrayson rose to his feet and took the receiver into his hand.

"Hullo!" he said.

The voice which answered him was faint but clear. Wrayson almost dropped the instrument. He recognized it at once.

"Is that Mr. Herbert Wrayson?" it asked.

"Yes!" Wrayson answered. "Who are you?"

"I am the person who spoke to you a few nights ago," was the answer. "Never mind my name for the present. I wish to arrange a meeting - for some time to-morrow. I have a matter - of business - to discuss with you."

"Anywhere - at any time," Wrayson answered, almost fiercely. "You cannot be as anxious to see me as I am to know who you are."

The voice changed a little in its intonation. A note of mockery had stolen into it.

"You flatter me," it said. "I trust that our meeting will be mutually agreeable. You must excuse my coming to Battersea, as I understand that your flat is subjected to a most inconvenient surveillance. May I call at the office of your paper, at say eleven o'clock tomorrow?"

"Yes!" Wrayson answered. "You know where it is?"

"Certainly! I shall be there. A Mr. Bentham will ask for you. Good night!"

Wrayson's unknown friend had rung off. He replaced the receiver and turned to the Colonel.

"Do you know who that was?" he asked eagerly.

"I can guess," the Colonel answered.

"To-morrow, at eleven o'clock," Wrayson declared, "I shall know who killed Morris Barnes."

CHAPTER VI

ONE THOUSAND POUNDS' REWARD

But when the morrow came, and his visitor was shown into Wrayson's private office, he was not quite so sure about it. Mr. Bentham had not in the least the appearance of a murderer. Clean-shaven, a little slow in speech, quietly dressed, he resembled more than anything a country solicitor in moderate practice.

He bowed in correct professional manner, and laid a brown paper parcel upon the table.

"I believe," he said, "that I have the honour of addressing Mr. Wrayson?"

Wrayson nodded a little curtly.

"And you, I suppose," he remarked, "are the owner of the mysterious voice which summoned Morris Barnes to the Francis Hotel on the night of his murder?"

"It was I who spoke to you," Mr. Bentham admitted.

"Very well," Wrayson said, "I am glad to see you. It was obvious, from your message, that you knew of some danger which was threatening Morris Barnes that night. It is therefore only fair to presume that you are also aware of its source."

"You go a little fast, sir," Mr. Bentham objected.

"My presumption is a fair one," Wrayson declared. "You are perhaps aware of my unfortunate connection with this affair. If so, you will understand that I am particularly anxious to have it cleared up."

"It is not at all certain that I can help you," his visitor said precisely. "It depends entirely upon yourself. Will you permit me to put my case before you?"

"By all means," Wrayson answered. "Go ahead."

Mr. Bentham took the chair towards which Wrayson had somewhat impatiently pointed, and unbuttoned his coat. It was obvious that he was not a person to be hurried.

"In the first place, Mr. Wrayson," he said, "I must ask you distinctly to understand that I am not addressing you on my own account. I am a lawyer, and I am acting on behalf of a client."

"Who is he?" Wrayson asked. "What is his name?"

The ghost of a smile flickered across the lawyer's thin lips.

"I am not at liberty to divulge his identity," he answered. "I am, however, fully empowered to act for him."

Wrayson shrugged his shoulders.

"He may find it necessary to disclose it, and before very long," he remarked. "Well, go on."

Mr. Bentham discreetly ignored the covert threat in Wrayson's words.

"My mission to you, Mr. Wrayson" he declared, "is a somewhat delicate one. It is not, in fact, connected with the actual - tragedy to which you have alluded. My commission is to regain possession of a paper which was stolen either from the person of Morris Barnes or from amongst his effects, on that night."

Wrayson looked up eagerly.

"The motive at last!" he exclaimed. "What was the nature of this paper, sir?"

Mr. Bentham's eyebrows were slowly raised.

"That," he said, "we need not enter into for the moment. The matter of business between you and myself, or rather my client, is this. I am authorized to offer a thousand pounds reward for its recovery."

Wrayson was impressed, although the other's manner left him a little puzzled.

"Why not offer the reward for the discovery of the murderer?" he asked. "It would come, I presume, to the same thing."

"By no means," the lawyer answered dryly. "I am afraid that I have not expressed myself well. My client cares nothing for Morris Barnes, dead or alive. His interest begins and ends with the recovery of that paper."

"But isn't it almost certain," Wrayson persisted, "that the thief and the murderer are the same person? Your client ought to have come forward at the inquest. The thing which has chiefly troubled the police in dealing with this matter is the apparent lack of motive."

"My client is not actuated in any way by philanthropic motives," Mr. Bentham said coldly. "To tell you the truth, he does not care whether the murderer of Morris Barnes is brought to justice or not. He is only anxious to recover possession of the document of which I have spoken."

"If he has a legal claim to it," Wrayson said, "he had better offer his reward openly. He would probably help himself then, and also those who are anxious to have this mystery solved."

"Are you amongst those, Mr. Wrayson?" his visitor asked quietly.

Wrayson started slightly, but he retained his self-composure.

"I am very much amongst them," he answered. "My connection with the affair was an extremely unpleasant one, and it will remain so until the murderer of Morris Barnes is brought to book."

"Or murderess," Mr. Bentham murmured softly.

Wrayson reeled in his chair as though he had been struck a violent and unexpected blow. He understood

E. Phillips Oppenheim

now the guarded menace of his visitor's manner. He felt the man's eyes taking merciless note of his whitening cheeks.

"My client," the lawyer continued, "desires to ask no questions. All that he wants is the document to which he is entitled, and which was stolen on the night when Mr. Morris Barnes met with his unfortunate accident."

Wrayson had pulled himself together with an effort.

"I presume," he said, "from your frequent reiteration, that I may take this as being to some extent a personal offer. If so, let me assure you, sir, that so far as I am concerned I know nothing whatever of any papers or other belongings which were in the possession of my late neighbour. I have never seen or heard of any. I do not even know why you should have come to me at all."

"I came to you," Mr. Bentham said, "because I was very well aware that, for some reason or other, your evidence at the inquest was not quite as comprehensive as it might have been."

"Then, for Heaven's sake, tell me all that you know!" Wrayson exclaimed. "Take my word for it, I know nothing of this document or paper. I have neither seen it nor heard of it. I know nothing whatever of the man or his affairs. I can't help you. I would if I could. On the other hand, you can throw some light upon the motive for the crime. Who is your client? Let me go and see him for myself."

Mr. Bentham rose to his feet, and began slowly to draw on his gloves.

"Mr. Wrayson," he said quietly, "I am disappointed with the result of my visit to you. I admit it frankly. You are either an extremely ingenuous person, or a good deal too clever for me. In either case, if you will not treat with me, I need not waste your time."

Wrayson moved to the door and stood with his back to it.

"I am not at all sure," he said, "that I am justified in letting you go like this. You are in possession of information which would be invaluable to the police in their search for the murderer of Morris Barnes."

Mr. Bentham smiled coldly.

"And are not you," he remarked, "in the same fortunate position - with the unfortunate exception, perhaps, of having already given your testimony? Of the two, if disclosures had to be made, I think that I should prefer my own position."

Wrayson remained where he was.

"I am inclined," he said, "to risk it. At least you would be compelled to disclose your client's name."

Mr. Bentham visibly flinched. He recovered himself almost immediately, but the shadow of fear had rested for a moment, at any rate, upon his impassive features.

"I am entirely at your service," he said coldly. "My client has at least not broken the laws of his country."

Wrayson stood away from the door.

E. Phillips Oppenheim

"You can go," he said shortly, "if you will leave me your address."

Mr. Bentham bowed.

"I regret that I have no card with me," he said, "but I have an office, a single room only, in number 8, Paper Buildings, Adelphi. If you should happen to come across - that document - "

Wrayson held open the door.

"If I should come to see you," he said, "it will be on other business."

*　*　*　*　*

Wrayson lunched at the club that morning, and received a warm greeting from his friends. The subject of the murder was, as though by common consent, avoided. Towards the end of the meal the Colonel received a telegram, which he read and laid down upon the table in front of him.

"By Jove!" he said softly, "I'd forgotten all about it. Boys, you've got to help me out."

"We're on," Mason declared. "What is it? a fight?"

"It's a garden party my girls are giving to-morrow afternoon," the Colonel answered. "I promised to take some of you down. Come, who's going to help me out? Wrayson? Good! Heneage? Excellent! Mason? Good fellows, all of you! Two-twenty from Waterloo, flannels and straw hats."

The little group broke up, and the Colonel was hurried off into the Committee Room. Wrayson and Heneage exchanged dubious glances.

"A garden party in May!" the latter remarked.

"Taking time by the forelock a little, isn't it?"

Wrayson sighed resignedly.

"It's the Colonel!" he declared. "We should have to go if it were December!"

CHAPTER VII

THE COLONEL'S DAUGHTER

After all, the garden party was not so bad. The weather was perfect, and the grounds of Shirley House were large enough to find amusement for all the guests. Wrayson, who had made great friends with the Colonel's younger daughter, enjoyed himself immensely. After a particularly strenuous set of tennis, she led him through the wide-open French windows into a small morning-room.

"We can rest for a few minutes in here," she remarked. "You can consider it a special mark of favour, for this is my own den."

"You are spoiling me," Wrayson declared, laughing. "May I see those photographs?"

"If you like," she answered, "only you mustn't be too critical, for I'm only a beginner, you know. Here's a bookful of them you can look through, while I go and start the next set."

She placed a volume in his hand and swung out of the room, tall, fresh, and graceful. Wrayson watched her admiringly. In her perfect naturalness and unaffected good-humour, she reminded him a good deal of her father, but curiously enough there was some other likeness which appealed to him even more powerfully, and yet which he was unable to identify. It puzzled him so that for a moment or two after her departure he sat watching the door through which she had disappeared, with a slight frown upon his forehead. She was undoubtedly charming, and yet something in connection with her seemed to impress him with an impending sense of trouble. Everything about her person and manners was frank and girlish, and yet she was certainly recalling to his mind things that he had been struggling all the afternoon to forget. Already he began to feel the clouds of nervousness and depression stealing down upon him. He struck the table with his clenched fist. He would have none of it. Outside was the delicious sunshine, through the open window stole in the perfume of the roses which covered the wall, and mignonette from the trim borders, and stocks from the bed fringing the lawn. The murmur of pleasant conversation was incessant and musical. For a time Wrayson had escaped. He swore to himself that he would go back no more into bondage; that he would dwell no more upon the horrors through which he had lived. He would take hold of the pleasant things of life with both hands, and grip them tightly. A man should be master of his thoughts, not the slave of unwilling memories. He would choose for himself whither they should lead him; he would fight with all his nerve and will against the unholy fascination of those few thrilling hours. He looked impatiently towards the door, and longed for the return of his late companion that he might continue his half-laughing flirtation. Then he remembered the album still upon his knee, and opened it quickly. He had dabbled a little in photography; he would find something here to keep his thoughts from the forbidden place. And he did indeed

E. Phillips Oppenheim

find something - something which set his heart thumping, and drew all the colour, which the sun and vigorous exercise had brought, from his cheeks; something at which he stared with wide-open eyes, which he held before him with trembling, nerveless fingers. The picture of a woman! The picture of her!

It had lain loose in the book, with its back towards him. Only chance made him turn it over. As he looked he understood. There was the likeness, such likeness as there may be between a beautiful woman, a little sad, a little scornful, with the faint lines of mockery about her curving lips, the world-weary light in her distant eyes, and the fresh, ingenuous girl with whom he had been bandying pleasantries during the last few hours. He had felt it unknowingly. He realized it now, and the thought of what it might mean made him catch at his breath like a drowning man. Then she came in.

He heard her gay laughter outside, a backward word flung to one of the tennis players, as she stepped in through the window, her cheeks still flushed, and her eyes aglow.

"We really ought to watch this set," she declared. "That is, if you are not too much absorbed in my handiwork. What have you got there?"

He held it out to her with a valiant attempt at unconcern.

"Do you mind telling me who this is?" he asked.

She glanced at it carelessly enough, but at once her whole expression changed. The smile left her lips, her eyes filled with trouble.

"Where did you find it?" she asked, in a low tone.

"In the album," he answered. "It was loose between the pages."

She took it gently from his fingers, and crossing the room locked it in her desk.

"I had no idea that it was here," she said. "It is a picture of my eldest sister, or rather my step-sister."

The change in her manner was so apparent that, under ordinary circumstances, Wrayson would not have dreamed of pursuing the subject. But the conventions of life seemed to him small things just then.

"Your step-sister!" he exclaimed. "I had no idea - shall I meet her this afternoon?"

"No!" she answered, gravely. "What do you say - shall we go out now?"

She took up her racket, but he lingered.

"Please don't think me hopelessly inquisitive, Miss Fitzmaurice," he said, "but I have really a reason for being very interested in the original of that picture. I should like to meet your step-sister."

"You will never do so here, I am afraid," she answered. "My father and she disagreed years ago. He does not allow us to see or hear from her. We may not even mention her name."

"Your father," Wrayson remarked thoughtfully, "is not a stern parent by any means."

"I should think not," she answered, smiling. "Dear old dad! I have never heard him say an unkind word to any one in my life."

"And yet -" Wrayson began, hesitatingly.

"Do you mind if we don't talk any more about it?" she interrupted simply. "I think you can understand that it is not a very pleasant subject. Do you feel like another set, or would you rather do something else?"

"Tennis, by all means, if you are rested," he answered. "We will find our old opponents and challenge them again."

Wrayson made a supreme effort, and his spirits for the rest of the afternoon were almost boisterous. Yet all the time the nightmare was there behind. It crept out whenever he caught sight of his host moving about amongst his guests, beaming and kindly. His daughter! The Colonel's daughter! What was he to do? The problem haunted him continually. All the time he had to be pushing it back.

The guests began to depart at last. By seven o'clock the last carriage was rolling down the avenue. The Colonel, with a huge smile of relief, and a large cigar, came and took Wrayson's arm.

"Good man!" he exclaimed. "You've worked like a Trojan. We'll have one whisky and soda, eh? and then I'll show you your room. Say when!"

"I've enjoyed myself immensely," Wrayson declared. "Miss Edith has been very kind to me."

"I'm glad you've made friends with her," the Colonel said. "She's a harum-scarum lot, I'm afraid, and a sad chatterbox, but she's the right sort of a person for a man with nerves like you! You're looking a bit white still, I see!"

Wrayson would have spoken then, but his tongue seemed to cling to the roof of his mouth. He had been asked to bring his clothes and dine, and in the minutes' solitude while he changed, he made a resolute effort to face this new problem. There was not the slightest doubt in his mind that the girl whom he had surprised in his rooms, ransacking his desk, and whom subsequently he had assisted to escape from the Mansions, was identical with the original of this portrait. She was the Colonel's daughter. With a flash of horror, he remembered that it had been the Colonel himself who had pointed out the possibility of a woman's hands having drawn that silken cord together! Half dressed he sat down in a chair and buried his face in his hands.

The dinner gong disturbed him. He sprang up, tied his tie with trembling fingers, and hastily completed his toilet. Once more, with a great effort, and an almost reckless resort to his host's champagne, he triumphed over the demons of memory which racked his brain. At dinner his gayety was almost feverish. Edith Fitzmaurice, who was his neighbour, found him a delightful companion. Only the Colonel glanced towards him now and then anxiously. He recognized the signs of high-pressure, and the light in Wrayson's eyes puzzled him.

There were no other men dining, and in course of time the two were left alone. The Colonel passed the cigars and touched the port wine decanter, which, however, he only offered in a half-hearted way.

"If you don't care about any more wine," he said, "we might have a smoke in the garden."

Wrayson rose at once.

"I should like it," he said abruptly. "I don't know how it is, but I seem half-stifled to-day."

They passed out into the soft, cool night. A nightingale was singing somewhere in the elm trees which bordered the garden. The air was sweet with the perfume of early summer flowers. Wrayson drew a long, deep breath of content.

"Let us sit down, Colonel," he said; "I have something to tell you."

The Colonel led the way to a rustic seat. A few stars were out, but no moon. In the dusky twilight, the shrubs and trees beyond stood out with black and almost startling distinctness against the clear sky.

"You remember the girl - I told you about, whom I found in my flat, and afterwards?" Wrayson asked hoarsely.

The Colonel nodded.

"Certainly! What about her? To tell you the truth, I am afraid I -"

Wrayson stopped him with a quick, fierce exclamation.

"Don't, Colonel!" he said. "Wait until you have heard what I have to say. I have seen her picture - to-day."

The Colonel removed his cigar from his mouth.

"Her picture!" he exclaimed. "To-day! Where? My dear fellow, this is very interesting! You know my opinion as to that young - "

Again Wrayson stopped him, this time with an oath.

"In your house, Colonel," he said. "Your daughter showed it to me - in an album!"

The Colonel sat like a man turned to stone. The hand which held his cigar shook so that the ash fell upon his waistcoat.

"Go on!" he faltered.

"I asked who it was. I was told that it was your daughter! Miss Edith's step-sister! Forgive me, Colonel! I had to tell you!"

The Colonel seemed to have shrunk in his place. The cigar slipped from his fingers and fell unheeded on to the grass. His mouth trembled and twitched pitifully.

"My - my daughter Louise!" he faltered. "Wrayson, you are not serious!"

"It is God's truth," Wrayson answered. "I would stake my soul upon it that the girl - I told you about - was the original of that picture! When I look at your daughter Edith I can see the likeness."

The Colonel's head was buried in his hands. His exclamation sounded like a sob.

"My God!" he murmured.

Then there was silence. Only the nightingale went on with his song.

CHAPTER VIII

THE BARONESS INTERVENES

The Baroness trifled with some grapes and looked languidly round the room.

"My dear Louise," she declared, "it is the truth what every one tells me of your country. You are a dull people. I weary myself here."

The girl whom she had addressed as Louise shrugged her shoulders.

"So do I, so do all of us," she answered, a little wearily. "What would you have? One must live somewhere."

The Baroness sighed, and from a chatelaine hung with elegant trifles selected a gold cigarette case. An attentive waiter rushed for a match and presented it. The Baroness gave a little sigh of content as she leaned back in her chair. She smoked as one to the manner born.

"One must live somewhere, it is true," she agreed, "but why London? I think that of all great cities it is the most provincial. It lacks what you call the atmosphere.

The people are all so polite, and so deadly, deadly dull. How different in Paris or Berlin, even Brussels!"

"Circumstances are a little against us, aren't they?" Louise remarked. "Our opportunities for making acquaintances are limited."

The Baroness made a little grimace.

"You, my young friend," she said, "are of the English - very English. Quite Saxon, in fact. With you there would never be any making of acquaintances! I feel myself in the bonds of a cast-iron chaperonage whenever I move out with you. Why is it, little one? Have you never any desire to amuse yourself?"

"I don't quite understand you," her companion answered dryly. "If you mean that I have no desire to encourage promiscuous acquaintances, you are certainly right. I prefer to be dull."

The Baroness sighed gently.

"Some of my dearest friends," she murmured, "I have - but there, it is a subject upon which we disagree. We will talk of something else. Shall we go to the theatre to-night?"

"As you will," Louise answered indifferently. "There isn't much that we haven't seen, is there?"

"We will send for a paper and see," the Baroness said. "We cannot sit and look at one another all the evening. With music one can make dinner last out till nine or even half past - an idea, my Louise!" she exclaimed suddenly. "Cannot we go to a music-hall, the

Alhambra, for example? We could take a box and sit back."

"It is not customary," Louise declared coldly. "If you really wish it, though, I don't - I don't -"

Her speech was broken off in a somewhat extraordinary manner. She was leaning a little forward in her chair, all her listlessness and pallor seemed to have been swept away by a sudden rush of emotion. The colour had flooded her cheeks, her tired eyes were suddenly bright; was it with fear or only surprise? The Baroness wasted no time in asking questions. She raised her lorgnettes and turned round, facing the direction in which Louise was looking. Coming directly towards them from the further end of the restaurant was a young man, whose eyes never swerved from their table. He was pale, somewhat slight, but the lines of his mouth were straight and firm, and there was not lacking in him that air of distinction which the Baroness never failed to recognize. She put down her glasses and looked across at Louise with a smile. She was quite prepared to approve.

The young man stopped at their table and addressed himself directly to Louise. The Baroness frowned as she saw how scanty were the signs of encouragement in her young companion's face. She leaned a little forward, ready at the first signs of an introduction to make every effort to atone for Louise's coldness by a most complete amiability. This young man should not be driven away if she could help it!

"I have been hoping, Miss Fitzmaurice," Wrayson said calmly, "that I might meet you somewhere."

She shrank a little back for a moment. There flashed across her face a quiver, as though of pain.

"Why do you think," she asked, "that that is my name?"

"Your father, Colonel Fitzmaurice, is one of my best friends," he answered gravely. "I was at his house yesterday. I only came up this morning. I beg your pardon! You are not well!"

Every vestige of colour had left her cheeks. The Baroness touched her foot under the table, and Louise found her voice with an effort.

"How did you know that Colonel Fitzmaurice was my father?" she asked breathlessly.

"I found a picture in your sister's album," he answered.

The answer seemed somehow to reassure her. She leaned a little towards him. Under cover of the music her voice was inaudible to any one else.

"Mr. Wrayson," she said, "please don't think me unkind. I know that I have a great deal to thank you for, and that there are certain explanations which you have almost a right to demand from me. And yet I ask you to go away, to ask me nothing at all, to believe me when I assure you that there is nothing in the world so undesirable as any acquaintance between you and me."

Wrayson was staggered, the words were so earnestly spoken, and the look which accompanied them was so eloquent. He was never sure, when he thought it over afterwards, what manner of reply he might not have made to an appeal, the genuineness of which was absolutely convincing. But before he could frame an answer, the Baroness intervened.

"Louise," she said softly, "do you not think that this place is a little public for intimate conversation, and will you not introduce to me your friend?"

Wrayson, who had been afraid of dismissal, turned at once, almost eagerly, towards the Baroness. She smiled at him graciously. Louise hesitated for a moment. There was no smile upon her lips. She bowed, however, to the inevitable.

"This is Mr. Wrayson," she said quietly; "the Baroness de Sturm."

The Baroness raised her eyebrows, and she bestowed upon Wrayson a comprehending look. The graciousness of her manner, however, underwent no abatement.

"I fancy," she said, "that I have heard of you somewhere lately, or is it another of the same name? Will you not sit down and take your coffee with us - and a cigarette - yes?"

"We are keeping Mr. Wrayson from his friends, no doubt," Louise said coldly. "Besides - do you see the time, Amy?"

But Wrayson had already drawn up a chair to the table.

"I am quite alone," he said. "If I may stay, I shall be delighted."

"Why not?" the Baroness asked, passing her cigarette

case. "You can solve for us the problem we were just then discussing. Is it *comme-il-faut*, Mr. Wrayson, for two ladies, one of whom is almost middle-aged, to visit a music-hall here in London unescorted?"

Wrayson glanced from Louise to her friend.

"May I inquire," he asked blandly, "which is the lady who is posing as being almost middle-aged?"

The Baroness laughed at him softly, with a little contraction of the eyebrows, which she usually found effective.

"We are going to be friends, Mr. Wrayson," she declared. "You are sitting there in fear and trembling, and yet you have dared to pay a compliment, the first I have heard for, oh! so many months. Do not be afraid. Louise is not so terrible as she seems. I will not let her send you away. Now you must answer my question. May we do this terrible thing, Louise and I?"

"Assuredly not," he answered gravely, "when there is a man at hand who is so anxious to offer his escort as I."

The Baroness clapped her hands.

"Do you hear, Louise?" she exclaimed.

"I hear," Louise answered dryly.

The Baroness made a little grimace.

"You are in an impossible humour, my dear child," she declared.

"Nevertheless, I declare for the music-hall, and for the escort of your friend, Mr. Wrayson, if he really is in earnest."

"I can assure you," he said, "that you would be doing me a great kindness in allowing me to offer my services."

The Baroness beamed upon him amiably, and rose to her feet.

"You have come," she avowed, "in time to save me from despair. I am not used to go about so much unescorted, and I am not so independent as Louise. See," she added, pushing a gold purse towards him, "you shall pay our bill while we put on our cloaks. And will you ask afterwards for my carriage, and we will meet in the portico?"

"With pleasure!" Wrayson answered, rising to his feet as they left the table. "I will telephone for a box to the Alhambra. There is a wonderful new ballet which every one is going to see."

He called the waiter and paid the bill from a remarkably well-filled purse. As he replaced the change, it was impossible for him to avoid seeing a letter addressed and stamped ready for posting, which occupied one side of the gold bag. The name upon the envelope struck him as being vaguely familiar; what had he heard lately of Madame de Melbain? It was associated somehow in his mind with a recent event. It lingered in his memory for days afterwards.

Louise and the Baroness left the room in silence. In the cloak-room the latter watched her friend curiously as

E. Phillips Oppenheim

she arranged her wrap.

"So that is Mr. Wrayson," she remarked.

"Yes!" Louise answered deliberately. "I wish that you had let him go!"

The Baroness laughed softly.

"My dear child," she protested, "why? He seems to me quite a personable young man, and he may be useful! Who can tell?"

Louise shrugged her shoulders. She stood waiting while the Baroness made somewhat extensive use of her powder-puff.

"You forget," she said quietly, "that I am already in Mr. Wrayson's debt pretty heavily."

The Baroness looked quickly around. She considered her young friend a little indiscreet.

"I find you amusing, *ma chère*," she remarked. "Since when have you developed scruples?"

Louise turned towards the door.

"You do not understand," she said. "Come!"

CHAPTER IX

A BOX AT THE ALHAMBRA

The Baroness lowered her lorgnettes and turned towards Wrayson.

"There is a man" she remarked, "in the stalls, who finds us apparently more interesting than the performance. I do not see very well even with my glasses, but I fancy, no! I am quite sure, that his face is familiar to me."

Wrayson leaned forward from his seat in the back of the box and looked downward. There was no mistaking the person indicated by the Baroness, nor was it possible to doubt his obvious interest in their little party. Wrayson frowned slightly as he returned his greeting.

"Ah, then, you know him," the Baroness declared. "It is a friend, without doubt."

"He belongs to my club," Wrayson answered. "His name is Heneage. I beg your pardon! I hope that wasn't my fault."

The Baroness had dropped her lorgnettes on the floor. She stooped instantly to discover them, rejecting almost peremptorily Wrayson's aid. When she sat up again she pushed her chair a little further back.

"It was my clumsiness entirely," she declared. "Ah! it is more restful here. The lights are a little trying in front. You are wiser than I, my dear Louise, to have chosen a seat back there."

She turned towards the girl as she spoke, and Wrayson fancied that there was some subtle meaning in the swift glance which passed between the two. Almost involuntarily he leaned forward once more and looked downwards. Heneage's inscrutable face was still upturned in their direction. There was nothing to be read there, not even curiosity. As the eyes of the two men met, Heneage rose and left his seat.

"You know my friend, perhaps?" Wrayson remarked. "He is rather an interesting person."

The Baroness shrugged her shoulders.

"We are cosmopolitans, Louise and I," she remarked. "We wander about so much that we meet many people whose names even we do not remember. Is it not so, *chérie*?"

Louise assented carelessly. The incident appeared to have interested her but slightly. She alone seemed to be taking an interest in the performance, which from the first she had followed closely. More than once Wrayson had fancied that her attention was only simulated, in order to avoid conversation.

"This ballet," she remarked, "is wonderful. I don't believe that you people have seen any of it - you especially, Amy."

The Baroness glanced towards the stage.

"My dear Louise," she said, "you share one great failing with the majority of your country-people. You cannot do more than one thing at a time. Now I can watch and talk. Truly, the dresses are ravishing. Doucet never conceived anything more delightful than that blend of greens! Tell me about your mysterious-looking friend, Mr. Wrayson. Is he, too, an editor?"

Wrayson shook his head.

"To tell you the truth," he said, "I know very little about him. He is one of those men who seldom talk about themselves. He is a barrister, and he has written a volume of travels. A clever fellow, I believe, but possibly without ambition. At any rate, one never hears of his doing anything now."

"Perhaps," the Baroness remarked, with her eyes upon the stage, "he is one of those who keep their own counsel, in more ways than one. He does not look like a man who has no object in life."

Wrayson glanced downwards at the empty stall.

"Very likely," he admitted carelessly, "and yet, nowadays, it is a little difficult, isn't it, to do anything really worth doing, and not be found out? They say that the press is lynx-eyed."

Louise leaned a little forward in her chair.

"And you," she remarked, "are an editor! Do you feel

quite safe, Amy? Mr. Wrayson may rob us of our most cherished secrets."

Her eyes challenged his, her lips were parted in a slight smile. Underneath the levity of her remark, he was fully conscious of the undernote of serious meaning.

"I am not afraid of Mr. Wrayson," the Baroness answered, smiling. "My age and my dressmaker are the only two things I keep entirely to myself, and I don't think he is likely to guess either."

"And you?" he asked, looking into her companion's eyes.

"There are many things," she answered, in a low tone, "which one keeps to oneself, because confidences with regard to them are impossible. And yet -"

She paused. Her eyes seemed to be following out the mystic design painted upon her fan.

"And yet?" he reminded her under his breath.

"Yet," she continued, glancing towards the Baroness, and lowering her voice as though anxious not to be overheard, "there is something poisonous, I think, about secrets. To have them known without disclosing them would be very often - a great relief."

He leaned a little towards her.

"Is that a challenge?" he asked, "if I can find out?"

The colour left her face with amazing suddenness. She

drew away from him quickly. Her whisper was almost a moan.

"No! for God's sake, no!" she murmured. "I meant nothing. You must not think that I was speaking about myself."

"I hoped that you were," he answered simply.

The Baroness turned in her chair as though anxious to join in the conversation. At that moment came a knock at the door of the box. Wrayson rose and opened it. Heneage stood there and entered at once, as though his coming were the most natural thing in the world.

"Thought I recognized you," he remarked, shaking hands with Wrayson. "I believe, too, I may be mistaken, but I fancy that I have had the pleasure of meeting the Baroness de Sturm."

The Baroness turned towards him with a smile. Nevertheless, Wrayson noticed what seemed to him a strange thing. The slim-fingered, bejeweled hand which rested upon the ledge of the box was trembling. The Baroness was disturbed.

"At Brussels, I believe," she remarked, inclining her head graciously.

"At Brussels, certainly," he answered, bowing low.

She turned to Louise.

"Louise," she said, "you must let me present Mr. Heneage - Miss Deveney. Mr. Heneage has a cousin, I believe, of the same name, in the Belgian Legation. I remember seeing you dance with him at the Palace."

The two exchanged greetings. Heneage accepted a chair and spoke of the performance. The conversation became general and of stereotyped form. Yet Wrayson was uneasily conscious of something underneath it all which he could not fathom. The atmosphere of the box was charged with some electrical disturbance. Heneage alone seemed thoroughly at his ease. He kept his seat until the close of the performance, and even then seemed in no hurry to depart. Wrayson, however, took his cue from the Baroness, who was obviously anxious for him to go.

"Goodnight, Heneage!" he said. "I may see you at the club later."

Heneage smiled a little oddly as he turned away.

"Perhaps," he said.

It was not until they were on their way out that Wrayson realized that she was slipping away from him once more. Then he took his courage into his hands and spoke boldly.

"I wonder," he said, "if I might be allowed to see you ladies home. I have something to say to Miss Fitzmaurice," he added simply, turning to the Baroness.

"By all means," she answered graciously, "if you don't mind rather an uncomfortable seat. We are staying in Battersea. It seems a long way out, but it is quiet, and Louise and I like it."

"In Battersea?" Wrayson repeated vaguely.

The Baroness looked over her shoulder. They were standing on the pavement, waiting for their electric brougham.

"Yes!" she answered, dropping her voice a little, "in Frederic Mansions. By the bye, we are neighbours, I believe, are we not?"

"Quite close ones," Wrayson answered. "I live in the next block of flats."

The Baroness looked again over her shoulder.

"Your friend, Mr. Heneage, is close behind," she whispered, "and we are living so quietly, Louise and I, that we do not care for callers. Tell the man 'home' simply."

Wrayson obeyed, and the carriage glided off. Heneage had been within a few feet of them when they had started, and although his attention appeared to be elsewhere, the Baroness' caution was obviously justified. She leaned back amongst the cushions with a little sigh of relief.

"Mr. Wrayson," she inquired, "may I ask if Mr. Heneage is a particular friend of yours?"

Wrayson shook his head.

"I do not think that any man could call himself Heneage's particular friend," he answered. "He is exceedingly reticent about himself and his doings. He is a man whom none of us know much of."

The Baroness leaned a little forward.

"Mr. Heneage," she said slowly, "is associated in my mind with days and events which, just at present, both Louise and I are only anxious to forget. He may be everything that he should be. Perhaps I am prejudiced. But if I were you, I would have as little to do as possible with that man."

"We do not often meet," Wrayson answered, "and ours is only a club acquaintanceship. It is never likely to be more."

"So much the better," the Baroness declared. "Don't you agree with me, Louise?"

"I do not like Mr. Heneage," the girl answered. "But then, I have never spoken a dozen words to him in my life."

"You have known him intimately?" Wrayson asked the Baroness.

She shrugged her shoulders and looked out of the window.

"Never that, quite," she answered. "I know enough of him, however, to be quite sure that the advice which I have given you is good."

The carriage drew up in the Albert Road, within a hundred yards or so of Wrayson's own block of flats. The Baroness alighted first.

"You must come in and have a whisky and soda," she said to Wrayson.

"If I may," he answered, looking at Louise.

The Baroness passed on. Louise, with a slight shrug of the shoulders, followed her.

CHAPTER X

OUTCAST

The room into which a waiting man servant showed them was large and handsomely furnished. Whisky and soda, wine and sandwiches were upon the sideboard. The Baroness, stopping only to light a cigarette, moved towards the door.

"I shall return" she said, "in a quarter of an hour."

She looked for a moment steadily at her friend, and then turned away. Louise strolled to the sideboard and helped herself to a sandwich.

"Come and forage, won't you?" she asked carelessly. "There are some *pâté* sandwiches here, and you want whisky and soda, of course - or do you prefer brandy?"

"Neither, thanks!" Wrayson answered firmly. "I want what I came for. Please sit down here and answer my questions."

She laughed a little mockingly, and turning round, faced him, her head thrown back, her eyes meeting his unflinchingly. The light from a rose-shaded electric lamp glittered upon her hair. She was wearing black again, and something in her appearance and attitude almost took his breath away. It reminded him of the moment when he had seen her first.

"First," she said, "I am going to ask you a question. Why did you do it?"

"Do what?" he asked.

She gave vent to a little gesture of impatience. He must know quite well what she meant.

"Why did you give evidence at the inquest and omit all mention of me?"

"I don't know," he answered bluntly.

"You have committed yourself to a story," she reminded him, "which is certainly not altogether a truthful one. You have run a great risk, apparently to shield me. Why?"

"I suppose because I am a fool," he answered bitterly.

She shook her head.

"No!" she declared, "that is not the reason."

He moved a step nearer to her.

"If I were to admit my folly," he said, "what difference would it make - if I were to tell you that I did it to save you - the inconvenience of an examination into the motive for your presence in Morris Barnes' rooms that night - what then?"

"It was generous of you," she declared softly. "I ought

to thank you."

"I want no thanks," he answered, almost roughly. "I want to know that I was justified in what I did. I want you to tell me what you were doing there alone in the rooms of such a man, with a stolen key. And I want you to tell me what you know about his death."

"Is that all?" she asked.

"Isn't it enough?" he declared savagely. "It is enough to be making an old man of me, anyhow."

"You have a right to ask these questions," she admitted slowly, "and I have no right to refuse to answer them."

"None at all," he declared. "You shall answer them."

There was a moment's silence. She leaned a little further back against the sideboard. Her eyes were fixed upon his, but her face was inscrutable.

"I cannot," she said slowly. "I can tell you nothing."

Wrayson was speechless for a moment. It was not only the words themselves, but the note of absolute finality with which they were uttered, which staggered him. Then he found himself laughing, a sound so unnatural and ominous that, for the first time, fear shone in the girl's eyes.

"Don't," she cried, and her hands flashed towards him for a moment as though the sight of him hurt her. "Don't be angry! Have pity on me instead."

His nerves, already overwrought, gave way.

"Pity on a murderess, a thief!" he cried. "Not I! I have suffered enough for my folly. I will go and tell the truth to-morrow. It was you who killed him. You did it in the cab and stole back to his rooms to rob - afterwards. Horrible! Horrible!"

Her face hardened. His lack of self-control seemed to stimulate her.

"Have it so," she declared. "I never asked you for your silence. If you repent it, go and make the best bargain you can with the law. They will let you off cheaply in exchange for your information!"

He walked the length of the room and back. Anything to escape from her eyes. Already he hated the words which he had spoken. When he faced her again he was master of himself.

"Listen," he said; "I was a little overwrought. I spoke wildly. I have no right to make such an accusation. But - "

She held out her hand as though to stop him, but he went steadily on.

"But I have a right to demand that you tell me the truth as to what you were doing in Barnes' rooms that night, and what you know of his death. Remember that but for me you would have had to tell your story to a less sympathetic audience."

"I never forget it," she answered, and for the first time her change to a more natural tone helped him to believe in himself and his own judgment. "If you want me to tell you how grateful I am, I might try, but it

E. Phillips Oppenheim

would be a very hard task."

"All that I ask of you," he pleaded, "is that you tell me enough to convince me that my silence was justified. Tell me at least that you had no knowledge of or share in that man's death!"

"I cannot do that," she answered.

He took a quick step backwards. The horror once more was chilling his blood, floating before his eyes.

"You cannot!" he repeated hoarsely.

"No! I knew that the man was in danger of his life," she went on, calmly. "On the whole, I think that he deserved to die. I do not mind telling you this, though. I would have saved him if I could."

He drew a great breath of relief.

"You had nothing to do with his actual death, then?"

"Nothing whatever," she declared.

"It was all I asked you, this," he cried reproachfully. "Why could you not have told me before?"

She shook her head.

"You asked me other things," she answered calmly. "So much of the truth you shall know, at any rate. I have pleaded not guilty to the material action of drawing that cord around the worthless neck of the man whom you knew as Morris Barnes. I plead guilty to knowing why he was murdered, even if I do not know the actual person who committed the deed, and I admit that I was in his rooms for the purpose of robbery. That is all I can tell you."

He drew a little nearer to her.

"Enough! Do you know what it is that you have said? What are you? Who are you?"

She shrugged her shoulders. Somehow, from her side at least, the tragical note which had trembled throughout their interview had passed away. She helped herself to soda water from a siphon on the sideboard.

"You appear, somewhat to my surprise," she remarked, "to know that. I wonder at poor little Edith giving me away."

"All that I know is that you are living here under a false name," he declared.

She shook her head.

"My mother's," she told him. "The discarded daughter always has a right to that, you know."

Her eyes mocked him. He felt himself helpless. This was the opportunity for which he had longed, and it had come to him in vain. He recognized the fact that his defeat was imminent. She was too strong for him.

"I am disappointed," he said, a little wearily. "You will not let me believe in you."

"Why should you wish to?" she asked quickly

Almost immediately she bit her lip, as though she regretted the words, which had escaped her almost involuntarily. But he was ready enough with his answer.

"I cannot tell you that," he said gravely. "I never thought of myself as a particularly emotional person. In fact, I have always rather prided myself on my common sense. That night I think that I went a little mad. Your appearance, you see, was so unusual."

She nodded.

"I must have been rather a shock to you," she admitted.

She watched him closely. The fire in his eyes was not yet quenched.

"Yes!" he said, "you were a shock. And the worst of it is - that you remain one!"

"Ah!"

"You mean to keep me at arm's length," he said slowly, "to tell me as little as possible, and get rid of me. I am not sure that I am willing."

She only raised her eyebrows. She said nothing.

"You have told me nothing of the things I want to know," he cried passionately. "Who and what are you? What place do you hold in the world?"

"None," she answered quietly. "I am an outcast."

He glanced around him.

"You are rich!"

"On the contrary," she assured him, "I am nearly a pauper."

"How do you live, then?" he asked breathlessly.

She shrugged her shoulders.

"Why do you ask me these questions?" she said. "I cannot answer them. Whatever my life may be, I live it to myself."

He leaned a little towards her. His breath was coming quickly, and she, too, caught something of the nervous excitement of his manner.

"There are better things," he began.

"Not for me," she interrupted quickly. "I tell you that I am an outcast. Of you, I ask only that you go away - now - before the Baroness returns, and do your best to blot out the memory of that one night from your life. Remember only that you did a generous action. Remember that, and no more."

"Too late," he answered; "I cannot do it."

"You are a man," she answered, "and you say that?"

"It is because I am a man, and you are what you are, that I cannot," he answered slowly.

There was a moment's breathless silence. Only he fancied that her face had somehow grown softer.

E. Phillips Oppenheim

"You must not talk like that," she said. "You do not know what you are saying - who or what I am. Listen! I think I hear the Baroness."

She leaned a little forward, and the madness fired his blood. Half stupefied, she yielded to his embrace, her lips rested upon his, her frightened eyes were half closed. His arms held her like a vise, he could feel her heart throbbing madly against his. How long they remained like it he never knew - who can measure the hours spent in Paradise! She flung him from her at last, taking him by surprise with a sudden burst of energy, and before he could stop her she had left the room. In her place, the Baroness was standing upon the threshold, dressed in a wonderful blue wrapper, and with a cigarette between her teeth. She burst into a little peal of laughter as she looked into his distraught face.

"For an Englishman," she remarked, "you are a little rapid in your love affairs, my dear Mr. Wrayson, is it not so? So she has left you *planté là*!"

"I - was mad," Wrayson muttered.

The Baroness helped herself to whisky and soda.

"Come again and make your peace, my friend," she said. "You will see no more of her to-night."

Wrayson accepted the hint and went.

CHAPTER XI

FALSE SENTIMENT

With his nerves strung to their utmost point of tension Wrayson walked homeward with the unseeing eyes and mechanical footsteps of a man unable as yet fully to collect his scattered senses. But for him the events of the evening were not yet over. He had no sooner turned the key in the latch of his door and entered his sitting-room, than he became aware of the fact that he had a visitor. The air was fragrant with tobacco smoke; a man rose deliberately from the easy-chair, and, throwing the ash from his cigarette into the fire, turned to greet him. Wrayson was so astonished that he could only gasp out his name.

"Heneage!" he exclaimed.

Heneage nodded. Of the two, he was by far the more at his ease.

"I wanted to see you, Wrayson," he said, "and I persuaded your housekeeper - with some difficulty - to let me wait for your arrival. Can you spare me a few minutes?"

"Of course," Wrayson answered. "Sit down. Will you have anything?"

E. Phillips Oppenheim

Heneage shook his head.

"Not just now, thanks!"

Wrayson took off his hat and coat, threw them upon the table, and lit a cigarette.

"Well," he said, "what is it?"

"I have come," Heneage said quietly, "to offer you some very good advice. You are run down, and you look it. You need a change. I should recommend a sea voyage, the longer the better. They say that your paper is making a lot of money. Why not a voyage round the world?"

"What the devil do you mean?" Wrayson asked.

Heneage flicked off the ash from his cigarette, and looked for a moment thoughtfully into the fire.

"Three weeks ago last Thursday, I think it was," he began, reflectively, "I had supper with Austin at the Green Room Club, after the theatre. He persuaded me, rather against my will, I remember, for I was tired that night, to go home with him and make a fourth at bridge. Austin's flat, as you know, is just below here, on the Albert Road."

Wrayson stopped smoking. The cigarette burned unheeded between his fingers. His eyes were fixed upon his visitor.

"Go on," he said.

"We played five rubbers," Heneage continued, still

looking into the fire; "it may have been six. I left somewhere in the small hours of the morning, and walked along the Albert Road on the unlit side of the street. As I passed the corner here, I saw a hansom waiting before your door, and you - with somebody else, standing on the pavement."

"Anything else?" Wrayson demanded.

"No!" Heneage answered. "I saw you, I saw the lady, and I saw the cab. It was a cold morning, and I am not naturally a curious person. I hurried on."

Wrayson picked up the cigarette, which had fallen from his fingers, and sat down. He could scarcely believe that this was not a dream - that it was indeed Stephen Heneage who sat opposite to him, Heneage the impenetrable, whose calm, measured words left no indication whatever as to his motive in making this amazing revelation.

"You are naturally wondering," Heneage continued, "why, having seen what I did see, I kept silence. I followed your lead, because I fancied, in the first place, that the presence of that young lady was a personal affair of your own, and that she could have no possible connection with the tragedy itself. You were evidently disposed to shield her and yourself at the same time. I considered your attitude reasonable, if a little dangerous. No man is obliged to give himself away in matters of this sort, and I am no scandal-monger. The situation, however, has undergone a change."

Wrayson looked up quickly.

"What do you mean?" he asked.

"To-night," Heneage said calmly, "I recognized your nocturnal visitor with the Baroness de Sturm.

"And what of that?" Wrayson demanded.

Heneage, who was leaning back in his chair, looking into the fire with half closed eyes, straightened himself, and turned directly towards his companion.

"How much do you know about the Baroness de Sturm?" he asked.

"Nothing at all," Wrayson answered. "I met her for the first time to-night."

Heneage looked back into the fire.

"Ah!" he murmured. "I thought that it might be so. The young lady is perhaps an old friend?"

"I cannot discuss her," Wrayson answered. "I can only say that I will answer for her innocence as regards any complicity in the murder of Morris Barnes."

Heneage nodded sympathetically.

"Still," he remarked, "the man was murdered."

"I suppose so," Wrayson admitted.

"And in a most mysterious manner," Heneage continued. "You have gathered, I dare say, from your knowledge of me, that these affairs always interest me immensely. I am almost as great a crank as the

Colonel. I have been thinking over this case a great deal, but I must confess that up to to-night I have not been able to see a gleam of daylight. I had dismissed the young lady from my mind. Now, however, I cannot do so."

"Simply because you saw her with the Baroness de Sturm?" Wrayson asked.

"They are living together," Heneage reminded him, "a condition which naturally makes for a certain amount of intimacy."

"Do you know anything against the Baroness?" Wrayson demanded.

"Against her?" Heneage repeated thoughtfully. "Well, that depends."

"Do you mean to insinuate that she is an adventuress?" Wrayson asked bluntly.

"Certainly not," Heneage replied. "She is a representative of one of the oldest families in Europe, a *persona grata* at the Court of her country, and an intimate friend of Queen Helena's. She is by no means an adventuress."

"Then why," Wrayson asked, "should you attach such significance to the fact of her friendship with Miss Deveney?"

"Because," Heneage remarked, lighting another cigarette, "I happen to know that the Baroness is at present under the strictest police surveillance!"

Wrayson started. Heneage's first statement had reassured him: his later one was simply terrifying. He stared at his visitor in dumb alarm.

"I came to know of this in rather a curious way," Heneage continued. "My information, in fact, came direct from her own country. She is being watched with extraordinary care, in connection with some affair of which I must confess that I know nothing. She is staying in London, a city which I happen to know she detests, without any ostensible reason. Of all parts, she has chosen Battersea as a place of residence. It is her companion whom I saw leaving your flat at three o'clock on the morning of Barnes' murder. I am bound to say, Wrayson, that I find these facts interesting."

"Why have you come to me?" Wrayson asked. "What are you going to do about them?"

"I am going to set myself the task of solving the mystery of Morris Barnes' death," Heneage answered calmly. "If I succeed, I am very much afraid that, directly or indirectly, the presence of Miss Deveney in the flats that night will become known."

"And you advise me, therefore," Wrayson remarked, "to take a voyage - in plain words, to clear out."

"Exactly," Heneage agreed.

Wrayson threw his cigarette angrily into the fire.

"What the devil business is it of yours?" he demanded.

Heneage looked at him steadily.

"Wrayson," he said, "I am sorry that you should use that tone with me. I am no moralist. I admit frankly that I take this matter up because my personal tastes prompt me to. But murder, however great the provocation, is an indefensible thing."

"I am not seeking to justify it," Wrayson declared.

"I am glad to hear that," Heneage answered. "I cannot believe, either, that you would shield any one directly or indirectly connected with such a crime. I am going to ask you, therefore, to tell me what Miss Deveney was doing in these flats on that particular evening."

Wrayson was silent. In the light of what he had just been told about the Baroness, he knew very well how Heneage would regard the truth. Of course, she was innocent, innocent of the deed itself and of all knowledge of it. But Heneage did not know her; he would be hard to convince. So Wrayson shook his head.

"I can tell you nothing," he said. "I admit frankly my sympathies are not with you. I should not say a word likely to bring even inconvenience upon Miss Deveney."

"Dare you tell me," Heneage asked calmly, "that her visit was to you? No! I thought not," he added, as Wrayson remained silent. "I believe that that young lady could solve the mystery of Morris Barnes' death, if she chose."

Then Wrayson had an idea. At any rate, the disclosure would do no harm.

E. Phillips Oppenheim

"Do you know who Miss Deveney is?" he asked.

Heneage looked across at him quickly.

"Do you?"

"Yes! She is the eldest daughter of the Colonel!"

"Our Colonel?" Heneage exclaimed.

Wrayson nodded.

"Her real name is Miss Fitzmaurice," he said. "Her mother's name was Deveney."

Heneage looked incredulous.

"Are you sure about this?" he asked.

"Absolutely," Wrayson answered. "I saw her picture the day of the garden party, and I recognized her at once. There is no doubt about it whatever. She and the Baroness were schoolfellows in Brussels. There is no mystery about their friendship at all."

Heneage was thoughtful for several moments.

"This is interesting," he said at last, "but it does not, of course, affect the situation."

"You mean that you will go on just the same?" Wrayson demanded.

"Certainly! And it rests with you to say whether you will be on my side or theirs," Heneage declared. "If you are on mine, you will tell me what Miss Deveney was doing in these flats on that night of all others. If you are on theirs, you will go and warn them that I am determined to solve the mystery of Morris Barnes' death - at all costs."

"I had no idea," Wrayson remarked quietly, "that you were ambitious to shine as an amateur policeman."

"We all have our hobbies," Heneage answered. "Take the Colonel, for instance, the most harmless, the most good-natured man who ever lived. Nothing in the world fascinates him so much as the details of a tragedy like this, however gruesome they may be. I have seen him handle a murderer's knife as though he loved it. His favourite museum is the professional Chamber of Horrors in Scotland Yard. My own interests run in a slightly different direction. I like to look at an affair of this sort as a chess problem, and to set myself to solve it. I like to make a silent study of all the characters around, to search for motives and dissect evidence. Human nature has its secrets, and very wonderful secrets too."

"I once," Wrayson said thoughtfully, "saw a man tracked down by bloodhounds. My sympathies were with the man."

Heneage nodded.

"Your view of life," he remarked, "was always a sentimental one."

"No correct view," Wrayson declared, "can ignore sentiment."

"Granted; but it must be true sentiment, not false,"

E. Phillips Oppenheim

Heneage said. "This sentiment which interferes with justice is false sentiment."

"Justice is altogether an arbitrary, a relative phrase," Wrayson declared. "I know no more about the case of Morris Barnes than you do. I knew the man by sight and repute, and I knew the manner of his life, and it seems to me a likely thing that there is more human justice about his death than in the punishing the person who compassed it."

"There are cases of that sort," Heneage admitted. "That is the advantage of being an amateur, like myself. My discoveries, if I make any, are my own. I am not bound to publish them."

Wrayson smiled a little bitterly.

"You would be less than human if you didn't," he said.

Heneage rose to his feet and began putting on his coat. Wrayson remained in his seat, without offering to help him.

"So I may take it, I suppose," he said, as he moved towards the door, "that my visit to you is a failure?"

"I have not the slightest idea of running away, if that is what you mean," Wrayson answered. "I am obliged to you for your warning, but what I did I am prepared to stand by."

"I am sorry," Heneage answered. "Good night!"

CHAPTER XII

TIDINGS FROM THE CAPE

Wrayson paused for a moment in his work to answer the telephone which stood upon his table.

"What is it?" he asked sharply.

His manager spoke to him from the offices below.

"Sorry to disturb you, sir, but there is a young man here who won't go away without seeing you. His name is Barnes, and he says that he has just arrived from South Africa."

It was a busy morning with Wrayson, for in an hour or so the paper went to press, but he did not hesitate for a moment.

"I will see him," he declared. "Bring him up yourself."

Wrayson laid down the telephone. Morris Barnes had come from South Africa. It was a common name enough, and yet, from the first, he was sure that this was some relative. What was the object of his visit? The ideas chased one another through his brain. Was he, too, an avenger?

E. Phillips Oppenheim

There was a knock at the door, and the clerk from downstairs ushered in his visitor. Wrayson could scarcely repress a start. It was a younger edition of Morris Barnes who stood there, with an ingratiating smile upon his pale face, a trifle more Semitic in appearance, perhaps, but in other respects the likeness was almost startling. It extended even to the clothes, for Wrayson recognized with a start a purple and white tie of particularly loud pattern. The cut of his coat, the glossiness of his hat and boots, too, were all strikingly reminiscent of the dead man.

His visitor was becoming nervous under Wrayson's close scrutiny. His manner betrayed a curious mixture of diffidence and assurance. He seemed overanxious to create a favourable impression.

"I took the liberty of coming to see you, Mr. Wrayson" he said, twisting his hat round in his hand. "My name is Barnes, Sydney Barnes. Morris Barnes was my brother."

Wrayson pointed to a chair, into which his visitor subsided with exaggerated expressions of gratitude. He had very small black eyes, set very close together, and he blinked continually. The more Wrayson studied him, the less prepossessing he found him.

"What can I do for you, Mr. Barnes?" he asked quietly.

"I have just come from Cape Town," the young man said. "Such a shock it was to me - about my poor brother! Oh! such a shock!"

"How did you hear about it?" Wrayson asked.

"Just a newspaper - I read an account of it all. It did give me a turn and no mistake. Directly I'd finished, I went and booked my passage on the *Dunottar Castle*. I had a very fair berth over there - two quid a week, but I felt I must come home at once. Fact is," he continued, looking down at his trousers, "I had no time to get my own togs together. I was so anxious, you see. That's why I'm wearing some of poor Morris's."

"Are you the only relative?" Wrayson asked.

"'Pon my sam, I am," the other answered with emphasis. "We hadn't a relation in the world. Father and mother died ten years ago, and Morris and I were the only two. Anything that poor Morris possessed belongs to me, sure! There's no one else to claim a farthing's worth. You must know that yourself, Mr. Wrayson, eh?"

"If, as you say, you are the only relative, your brother's effects, of course, belong to you," Wrayson answered.

"It's a sure thing," the young man declared. "I've been to the landlord of the flat, and he gave me up the keys at once. There's only one quarter's rent owing. Pretty stiff though - isn't it? Fifty pounds!"

"Your brother's was a furnished flat, I believe," Wrayson answered. "That makes a difference, of course."

The young man's face fell.

"Then the furniture wasn't his?" he remarked.

Wrayson shook his head.

"No! the furniture belongs to the landlord. There will be an inventory, of course, and you will be able to find out if anything was your brother's."

It was obvious that Mr. Sydney Barnes had not as yet entered upon the purpose of his visit. He fidgeted for a moment or two with his hat, and looked up at Wrayson, only to look nervously away again. To set him more at his ease, Wrayson lit a cigarette and passed the box over.

"Thank you, Mr. Wrayson! Thank you, sir!" his visitor exclaimed. "You see I'm a smoker," he added, holding up his yellow-stained forefinger. "That is, I smoke when I can afford to. Things have been pretty dicky out in South Africa lately, you know. Terrible hard it has been to make a living."

"Your brother was supposed to have done pretty well out there," Wrayson remarked, more for the sake of keeping the conversation alive than anything. The effect of his words, however, was electrical. Mr. Sydney Barnes leaned over from his chair, and his little black eyes twinkled like polished beads.

"Mr. Wrayson," he declared, "a week before he sailed for England, Morris was on his uppers! He was caught in Johannesburg when the war broke out, and he had to stay there. When he turned up in Cape Town again, his own mother wouldn't have known him. He was in rags - he'd come down on a freight - he hadn't a scrap of luggage, or a copper to his name. That was Morris when he came to me in Cape Town!"

Wrayson was listening attentively; he almost feared to let his visitor see how interested he was.

"He was fair done in!" the young man continued. "He never had the pluck of a chicken, and the night he found me in Cape Town he cried like a baby. He had lost everything, he said. It was no use staying in the country any longer. He was wild to get back to England. And yet, do you know, sir, all the time I had the idea that he was keeping something back from me. And he was! He was, too! The - !"

He stopped short. The vindictiveness of his countenance supplied the epithet.

"You'll excuse me if I'm a bit excited, Mr. Wrayson," he continued. "I'll leave you to judge how I've been served when you hear all. He got over me, and I lent him nearly half of my savings, and he started back to England. He took this flat at two hundred pounds a year the very week he got back, and he's lived, from what I can hear, like a lord ever since. Will you believe this, sir! He sent back the money he borrowed from me a quid at a time, and wrote me to say he was saving it with great difficulty - out of his salary of three pounds a week. When he'd paid back the lot, I never heard another line from him. I was doing rotten myself, and he knew well enough that I should have been over first steamer if I'd known about his two hundred a year flat, and all the rest of it. What do you think of my brother, sir, eh? What do you think of him? Treated me nicely, didn't he? Nine pounds ten it was I lent him, and nine pounds ten was all I had back, and here he was living like a duke, and lying to me about his three pounds a week; and there was I hawkering groceries on a barrow, selling sham diamonds, any blooming thing to get a mouthful to eat. Nice sort of brother that, eh? What?"

Wrayson repressed an inclination to smile. There was something grimly humourous about his visitor's indignation.

"You must remember," he said, "that your brother is dead, and that his death itself was a terrible one. Besides, even if you have had to wait for a little time, you are his heir now."

The young man was breathing hard. The perspiration stood out in little beads upon his forehead. He showed his teeth a little. He was becoming more and more unpleasant to look upon as his excitement increased.

"Look here, Mr. Wrayson!" he exclaimed. "I'm coming to that. I've been through his things. Clothes! I never saw such a collection. All from a West End tailor, too! And boots! Patent, with white tops; pumps, everything slap up! Heaven knows what he must have spent upon his clothes. Bills from restaurants, too; why, he seems to have thought nothing of spending a quid or two on a dinner or a supper. Photographs of ladies, little notes asking him to tea; why, between you and me, Mr. Wrayson, sir, he was living like a prince! And look here!"

He rose to his feet and planked down a bank-book on the desk in front of Wrayson.

"Look here, sir," he declared. "Every three months, within a day or two, cash - five hundred pounds. Here you are. Here's the last: March 27 - cash, £500! Look back! January 1 - By cash £500! October 2 - cash, £500! There you are, right back to the very day he arrived in England. And he left South Africa with ten bob of mine in his pocket, after he'd paid his passage! and from what I can hear, he never did a day's work after he landed. And me over there working thirteen and fourteen hours a day, and half the time stony-broke! There's a brother for you! Cain was a fool to him!"

"But you must remember that after all you are going to reap the benefit of it now," Wrayson remarked.

"Ah! but am I?" the young man exclaimed fiercely. "That's what I want to know. Look here! I've been through every letter and every scrap of paper I can find, I've been to the bank and to his few pals, and strike me dead if I can find where that five hundred pounds came from every three months! It was in gold always; he must have gone and changed it somewhere - five hundred golden sovereigns every three months, and I can't find where they came from!"

"Have you been to a solicitor?" Wrayson asked.

"Not yet," the young man answered. "I don't see what good he'll be when I do. Morris was always one of the close sort, and I can't fancy him spending much over lawyers."

"What made you come to me?" Wrayson inquired.

"Well, the caretaker at the flat told me that you and Morris used to speak now and then, and I'm trying every one. I'm afraid he wasn't quite classy enough for you to have palled up with, but I thought he might have let something slip perhaps."

Wrayson shook his head.

"He never spoke to me of his affairs," he said. "He always seemed to have plenty of money, though."

"Doesn't the bank-book prove it?" the young man exclaimed excitedly. "Every one who knew anything about him says the same. There was I half starved in Cape Town, and here was he spending two thousand a year. Beast, he was! I'll find out where it came from if it takes me a lifetime."

Wrayson leaned back in his chair. Nothing since the events of that night itself had appealed to him more than the coming of this young man and his strange story.

"I am sorry that I have no information to give you," he said. "On the other hand, if I can help you in any other way I shall be very glad."

"What should you advise me to do?" the young man asked.

"I should like to think the matter over carefully," Wrayson answered. "What are your engagements for to-day? Can you lunch with me?"

"I have no engagements," his visitor answered eagerly. "When and what time?"

Wrayson repressed a smile.

"I shall be ready in twenty minutes," he answered. "We will go out together if you don't mind waiting."

"I'm on," Mr. Sydney Barnes declared, crossing his

legs. "Don't you hurry on my account. I'll wait as long as you like."

E. Phillips Oppenheim

CHAPTER XIII

SEARCHING THE CHAMBERS

Wrayson took his guest to a popular restaurant, where there was music and a five-course luncheon for three and six. Their conversation during the earlier part of the meal was limited, for Mr. Sydney Barnes showed himself possessed of an appetite which his host contemplated with respectful admiration. His sallow cheeks became flushed and his nervousness had subsided, long before the arrival of the coffee.

"I say, this is all right, this place is," he said, leaning back in his chair with a large cigar between his teeth. "Jolly expensive, I suppose, isn't it?"

Wrayson smiled.

"It depends," he answered. "I don't suppose your brother would have found it so. A bachelor can do himself pretty well on two thousand a year."

"I only hope I get hold of it," Mr. Sydney Barnes declared fervently. "This is the way I should like to live, this is."

"I hope you will," Wrayson answered. "An income of that sort could scarcely disappear into thin air, could it? By the bye, Mr. Barnes, that reminds me of a very important circumstance which, up to now, we have not mentioned. I mean the way your brother met with his death."

The young man nodded thoughtfully.

"Ah!" he remarked, "he was murdered, wasn't he? Some one must have owed him a nasty grudge. Morris always was a one to make enemies."

"I don't know whether the same thing has occurred to you," Wrayson continued, "but I can't help wondering whether there may not have been some connection between his death and that mysterious income of his."

"I've thought of that myself," the young man declared. "All the same, I can't see what he could have carried about with him worth two thousand a year."

"Exactly," Wrayson answered, "but you see the matter stands like this. He was in receipt of about £500 every three months, as his bank-book proves. This sum would represent five per cent interest on forty thousand pounds. Now, considering your brother's position when he left you at Cape Town, and the fact that you cannot discover at his bankers or elsewhere any documents alluding to property or shares of any sort, one can scarcely help dismissing the hypothesis that this payment was the result of dividends or interest. At any rate, let us put that out of the question for the moment. Your brother received five hundred pounds every three months from some one. People don't give money away for nothing nowadays, you know. From whom and for what services did he receive that money?"

Mr. Sydney Barnes looked puzzled.

"Ask me another," he remarked facetiously.

"You do not know of any secrets, I suppose, which your brother may have stumbled into possession of?"

"Not I! He went about with his eyes open and his mouth closed, but I never heard of his having that sort of luck."

"He could not have had any adventures on the steamer, for he came back steerage," Wrayson continued thoughtfully, "and he was in funds almost from the moment he landed in England. I am afraid, Mr. Barnes, that he must have been deceiving you in Cape Town."

"If I could only have a dozen words with him!" the young man muttered savagely.

"It would be useful," Wrayson admitted, "but, unfortunately, it is out of the question. Either he was deceiving you, or he was in possession of something which turned out far more valuable than he had imagined."

"If so, where is it?" Mr. Sydney Barnes demanded. "If it was worth that to him, it may be to me."

"Exactly," Wrayson remarked, "but the question of your brother's murder comes in there. People don't commit a crime like that for nothing, you know. If it was information which your brother had, it died with him. If it was documents, they were probably stolen by the person who killed him."

"Come, that's cheerful," the young man declared ruefully. "If you're guessing right, where do I come in?"

"I'm afraid you don't come in," Wrayson answered; "but remember I am only following out a surmise. Have you looked through your brother's papers carefully?"

"I've gone through 'em all," Mr. Sydney Barnes answered, "but, of course, I was looking for scrip or a memorandum of investments, or something of that sort. Perhaps if a clever chap like you were to go through them, you might come across a clue."

"It seems hard to believe that he shouldn't have left something of the sort behind him," Wrayson answered. "It might be only an address, or a name, or anything."

"Will you come round with me and see?" Mr. Barnes demanded eagerly. "It wouldn't take you long. You're welcome to see everything there is there."

Wrayson called for the bill.

"Very well" he said, "we will take a hansom round there at once."

They left the place a few minutes later, and drove to Battersea.

"There's a quarter to run, the landlord says, so I'm staying here," Barnes explained, as he unlocked the front door. "I can't afford a servant or anything of that sort of course, but I shall just sleep here."

The rooms had a ghostly and unkempt appearance. The atmosphere of the sitting-room was stuffy and redolent of stale tobacco smoke. Wrayson's first action was to throw open the window.

"There isn't a sign of a paper anywhere, except in that desk," the young man remarked. "You'll find things in a mess, but whatever was there is there now. I've destroyed nothing."

Wrayson seated himself before the desk, and began a careful search. There were restaurant bills without number, and a variety of ladies' cards, more or less soiled. There were Empire and Alhambra programmes, a bundle of racing wires, and an account from a bookmaker showing a small debit balance. There were other miscellaneous bills, a plaintive epistle from a lady signing herself Flora, and begging for the loan of a fiver for a week, and an invitation to tea from a spinster who called herself Poppy. Amongst all this mass of miscellaneous documents there were only three which Wrayson laid on one side for further consideration. One of these was a note, dated from the Adelphi a few days before the tragedy, and written in a stiff, legal hand. It contained only a few lines:

"DEAR SIR, -

"My client will be happy to meet you at any time on Thursday you may be pleased to appoint, either here or at your own address. Please reply, making an appointment, by return of post.

"Yours faithfully,

"W. BENTHAM."

The second document was also in the shape of a letter from a firm of private detective agents and was dated only a day earlier than the lawyer's letter. It ran as follows:

"MY DEAR SIR, -

"In reply to your inquiry, our charges for watching a single person in London only are three guineas a day, including all expenses. For that sum we can guarantee that the person with whose movements you desire to keep in touch will be closely shadowed from roof to roof, so long as the person remains within seven miles of Charing Cross. A daily report will be made to you, and should legal proceedings ensue from any information procured by us, you may rely upon any witness whom we might place in the box.

"Trusting to hear from you,

"We are, yours sincerely,

"McKENNA & FOULDS."

The third document which Wrayson had preserved was the Cunard sailing list for the current month, the plan of a steamer which sailed within a week of the murder, and a few lines from the steamship office respecting accommodation.

"These, at any rate, will give you something to do," Wrayson remarked. "You can go to the lawyer and find out who his client was who desired to see your brother. There is a chance there! You can go to McKenna & Foulds and find out who it was whom he wanted

E. Phillips Oppenheim

shadowed, and you can go to the Cunard office and see whether he really intended sailing for America."

Mr. Sydney Barnes looked a little doubtful.

"I suppose," he suggested timidly, "you couldn't spare the time to go round to these places with me? You see, I'm not much class over here, even in Morris's togs. They'd take more notice of you, being a gentleman. Good God! what's that?"

Both men had started, for the sound was unexpected. Some one was fitting a latch-key into the door!

CHAPTER XIV

THE DEAD MAN'S BROTHER

At the sight of the two men who awaited her entrance, the Baroness stopped short. Whatever alarm or surprise she may have felt at their presence was effectually concealed from them by the thick veil which she wore, through which her features were undistinguishable. As though purposely, she left to them the onus of speech.

Wrayson took a quick step towards her.

"Baroness!" he exclaimed. "What are you - I beg your pardon, but what are you doing here?"

She raised her veil and looked at them both attentively. In her hand she still held the latch-key by means of which she entered.

"Do you know," she answered quietly, "I was just going to ask you the same thing."

"Our presence is easily explained," Wrayson answered. "This is Mr. Sydney Barnes, the brother of the Mr. Barnes who used to live here. He is keeping the flat on for a short time."

The Baroness was surprised, and showed it. Without a

E. Phillips Oppenheim

moment's hesitation, however, she accepted Wrayson's words as an introduction to the young man, and held out her hand to him with a brilliant smile.

"I am very glad to meet you, Mr. Barnes," she said, "even under such painful circumstances. I knew your brother very well, and I have heard him speak of you."

Mr. Sydney Barnes did not attempt to conceal his surprise. He shook hands with the Baroness, however, and regarded her with undisguised admiration.

"Well, this licks me!" he exclaimed frankly. "Do you mean to say that you were a friend of Morris's?"

"Certainly," the Baroness answered. "Why not?"

"Oh! I don't know," the young man declared. "I'm getting past being surprised at anything. I suppose it's the oof that makes the difference. A friend of Morris's, you said. Why, perhaps - " He hesitated, and glanced towards Wrayson.

"There is no harm in asking the Baroness, at any rate," Wrayson said. "The fact of the matter is," he continued, turning towards her, "that Mr. Sydney Barnes here finds himself in a somewhat extraordinary position. He is the sole relative and heir of his brother, and he has come over here from South Africa, naturally enough, to take possession of his effects. Now there is no doubt, from his bank-book, and his manner of life, that Morris Barnes was possessed of a considerable income. According to his bank-book it was £2,000 a year."

The Baroness nodded thoughtfully.

"He told me once that he was worth as much as that," she remarked,

"Exactly, but the curious part of the affair is that, up to the present, Mr. Sydney Barnes has been unable to discover the slightest trace of any investments or any sum of money whatever. Now can you help us? Did Morris Barnes ever happen to mention to you in what direction his capital was invested? Did he ever give you any idea at all as to the source of his income?"

The Baroness stood quite still, as though lost in thought. Wrayson watched her with a curious sense of fascination. He knew very well that the subtle brain of the woman was occupied in no fruitless attempt at reminiscence; he was convinced that the Baroness had never exchanged a single word with Morris Barnes in her life. She was thinking her way through this problem - how best to make use of this unexpected tool. Their eyes met and she smiled faintly. She judged rightly that Wrayson, at any rate, was not deceived.

"I cannot give you any definite information," she said at last, "but - "

She hesitated, and the young man's eagerness escaped all bounds.

"But what?" he cried, leaning breathlessly towards her. "You know something! What is it? Go on! Go on!"

"I think that if I can remember it," she continued, "I can tell you the name of the solicitor whom he employed."

The young man dashed his fist upon the table. He was

pale almost to the lips.

"By God! you must remember it," he cried. "Don't say you've forgotten. It's most important. Two thousand a year! - pounds! Think!"

She turned towards Wrayson. She wished to conciliate him, but the young man was not a pleasant sight.

"It was something like Benton," she suggested.

Wrayson glanced downward at one of the three documents which he had preserved.

"Bentham!" he exclaimed. "Was that it?"

The face of the Baroness cleared at once.

"Of course it was! How stupid of me to have forgotten. His offices are somewhere in the Adelphi."

Barnes caught up his hat.

"Where is that?" he exclaimed. "I'm off."

Wrayson held out his hand.

"Wait a moment," he said. "There is no hurry for an hour or so. This affair may not be quite so simple, after all."

"Why not?" the young man demanded fiercely. "It's my money, isn't it? I can take out letters of admini-stration. It belongs to me. He'll have to give it up."

"In the long run I should say that he will - if he has it,"

Wrayson answered. "But before you go to him, remember this. He has seen the account of your brother's death. He did not appear at the inquest. He has taken no steps to discover his next of kin. Both of these proceedings were part of his natural duty."

"Mr. Wrayson is quite right," the Baroness remarked. "Mr. Bentham has not behaved as an honest man. He will have to be treated firmly but carefully. You are a little excited just now. Wait for an hour or so, and perhaps Mr. Wrayson will go with you."

Barnes turned towards him eagerly, and Wrayson nodded.

"Yes! I'll go," he said. "I know Mr. Bentham slightly. He once paid me rather a curious visit. But never mind that now."

"Was it in connection with this affair?" the Baroness asked him quietly.

Wrayson affected not to hear. He passed his cigarette case to Barnes, who was stamping up and down the room, muttering to himself.

"Look here, you'd better have a smoke and calm down, young man," he said. "It's no use going to see Bentham in a state like this."

The young man threw himself into a chair. Suddenly he sat up again, and addressed the Baroness.

"I say," he exclaimed, "how is it that you have a key to this flat? What did you come here for this afternoon?" The Baroness laughed softly.

"Well, I got the key from the landlord a few days ago. I told him that I might take the flat, and he told me to come in and look at it and return the key - which you see I haven't done. To be quite honest with you, though, I had another reason for coming here."

The young man looked at her with mingled suspicion and admiration. She had raised her veil now, and even Wrayson was aware that he had scarcely realized how beautiful a woman she was. Her tailor-made gown of dark green cloth fitted her to perfection; she was turned out with all that delightful perfection of detail which seems to be the Frenchwoman's heritage. Her smile, half pathetic, half appealing, was certainly sufficient to turn the head of a dozen young men such as Sydney Barnes.

"I have told you," she continued, "that your brother and I used to be very good friends. I wrote him now and then some rather foolish letters. He promised to destroy them, but - men are so foolish, you know, sometimes - I was never quite sure that he had kept his word, and I meant to take this opportunity of looking for myself that he had not left them about. You do not blame me, Mr. Sydney? You are not cross?"

He kept his eyes upon her as though fascinated.

"No!" he said. "No! I mean of course not."

"These letters," she continued, "you have not seen them, Mr. Sydney? No? Or you, Mr. Wrayson?"

"We have not come across any letters at all answering to that description," Wrayson assured her.

The Baroness glanced across at Barnes, who was certainly regarding her in somewhat peculiar fashion.

"Why does Mr. Sydney look at me like that?" she asked, with a little shrug of the shoulders. "He does not think that I came here to steal? Why, Mr. Sydney," she added, "I am very, very much richer than ever your brother was."

"Richer - than he was! Richer than two thousand a year!" he gasped.

The Baroness laughed softly but heartily. She stole a sidelong glance at Wrayson.

"Why, my dear young man," she said, "it costs me - oh! quite as much as that each year to dress."

Barnes looked at her as though she were something holy. When he spoke, there was awe in his tone. The problem which had formed itself in his thoughts demanded expression.

"And you say that you were a pal - I mean a friend of Morris's? You wrote him letters?"

The Baroness smiled.

"Why not?" she exclaimed. "Women have queer tastes, you know. We like all sorts of men. I think I must ask Mr. Wrayson to bring you in to tea one afternoon. Would you like to come?"

"Yes!" he answered.

She nodded a farewell and turned to Wrayson.

"As for you," she said under her breath, "you had better come soon if you want to make your peace with Louise."

"May I come this afternoon?" he asked.

She nodded, and held out her exquisitely gloved hand.

"I knew you were going to be an ally" she murmured under her breath. "Don't let the others get hold of him."

She was gone before Wrayson could ask for an explanation. The others! If only he could discover who they were.

He turned back into the room.

"Do you mind coming down into my flat for a moment, Barnes?" he asked. "I want to telephone to the office before I go out with you again."

The young man followed him heavily. He seemed a little dazed. In Wrayson's sitting-room, he stood looking about him as though appraising the value of the curios, pictures, and engravings with which the apartment was crowded. Wrayson, while waiting for his call, watched him curiously. In his present state his vulgarity was perhaps less glaringly apparent, but his lack of attractiveness was accentuated. His ears seemed to have grown larger, his pinched, Semitic features more repulsive, and his complexion sallower. He was pitchforked into a world of which he knew nothing, and he seemed stunned by his first contact with it. Only one thing remained - the greed in his eyes. They seemed to have grown narrower and brighter with desire.

He did not speak until they were in the cab. Then he turned to Wrayson.

"I say," he exclaimed, "what was her name?"

Wrayson smiled.

"The Baroness de Sturm," he answered.

"Baroness! Real Baroness! All O.K., I suppose?"

"Without a doubt," Wrayson answered.

"And Morris knew her - she wrote letters to him," he continued, "a woman - like that."

He was silent for several moments. It was obvious that his opinion of his brother was rising rapidly. His tone had become almost reverential.

"I've got to find where that money is," he said abruptly. "If I go through fire and water to get it, I'll have it! I'll keep on Morris's flat. I'll go to his tailor! I'll - you're laughing at me. But I mean it! I've had enough of grubbing along on nothing a week, and living in the gutters. I want a bit of Morris's luck."

Wrayson put his head out of the cab. The young man's face was not pleasant to look at.

"We are there," he said. "Come along."

CHAPTER XV

THE LAWYER'S SUGGESTION

The offices of Mr. Bentham were situated at the extreme end of a dingy, depressing looking street which ran from the Adelphi to the Embankment Gardens. It was a street of private hotels which no one had ever heard of, and where apparently no one ever stayed. A few cranky institutions, existing under the excuse of charity, had their offices there, and a firm of publishers, whose glory was of the past, still dragged out their uncomfortable and profitless existence in a building whose dusty windows and smoke-stained walls sufficiently proclaimed their fast approaching extinction. They found the name of Mr. Bentham upon a rusty brass plate outside the last building in the street, with the additional intimation that his offices were upon the first floor. There they found him, without clerks, without even an errand boy, in a large bare apartment overlooking the embankment. The room was darkened by the branches of one of a row of elm trees, and the windows themselves were curtainless. There was no carpet upon the floor, no paper upon the walls, no rows of tin boxes, none of the usual surroundings of a lawyer's office. The solicitor, who had bidden them enter, did not at first offer them any salutation. He paused in a letter which he was writing and his eyes rested for a moment upon Wrayson, and for a second or two longer upon his companion.

"Good afternoon, Mr. Bentham!" Wrayson said. "My name is Wrayson - you remember me, I daresay."

"I remember you certainly, Mr. Wrayson," the lawyer answered. His eyes were resting once more upon Sydney Barnes.

"This," Wrayson explained, "is Mr. Sydney Barnes, a brother of the Mr. Morris Barnes, who was, I believe, a client of yours."

"Scarcely," the lawyer murmured, "a client of mine, although I must confess that I was anxious to secure him as one. Possibly if he had lived a few more hours, the epithet would have been in order."

Wrayson nodded.

"From a letter which we found in Mr. Barnes' desk," he remarked, "we concluded that some business was pending between you. Hence our visit."

Mr. Bentham betrayed no sign of interest or curiosity of any sort.

"I regret," he said, "that I cannot offer you chairs. I am not accustomed to receive my clients here. If you care to be seated upon that form, pray do so."

Wrayson glanced at the form and declined. Sydney Barnes seemed scarcely to have heard the invitation. His eyes were glued upon the lawyer's face.

"Will you tell me precisely," Mr. Bentham said, "in

what way I can be of service to you?"

"I want to know where my brother's money is," Barnes declared, stepping a little forward. "Two thousand a year he had. We've seen it in his bank-book. Five hundred pounds every quarter day! And we can't find a copper! You were his lawyer, or were going to be. You must have known something about his position."

Mr. Bentham looked straight ahead with still, impassive face. No trace of the excitement in Sydney Barnes' face was reflected in his features.

"Two thousand a year," he repeated calmly. "It was really as much as that, was it? Your brother had, I believe, once mentioned the amount to me. I had no idea, though, that it was quite so large."

"I am his heir," the young man declared feverishly. "I'll take my oath there's no one else. I'm going to take out letters of administration. He hadn't another relation on God's earth."

Mr. Bentham regarded the young man thoughtfully.

"Have you any idea, Mr. Barnes," he asked, "as to the source of this income?"

"Of course I haven't," Barnes answered. "That's why we're here. You must know something about it."

"Your brother was not my client," the lawyer said slowly. "If his death had not been quite so sudden, I think that he might have been. As it is, I know very little of his affairs. I am afraid that I can be of very little use to you."

"You must know something," Barnes declared doggedly. "You must tell us what you do know."

"Your brother was," Mr. Bentham said, "a very remarkable man. Has it never occurred to you, Mr. Barnes, that this two thousand a year might have been money received in payment of services rendered - might have been, in short, in the nature of a salary?"

"Not likely," Barnes answered, contemptuously. "Morris did no work at all. He did nothing but just enjoy himself and spend money."

"Nothing but enjoy himself and spend money," Mr. Bentham repeated. "Ah! Did you see a great deal of your brother during the last few years?"

"I saw nothing of him at all. I was out in South Africa. I have only just got back. Not but that I'd been here long ago," the young man added, with a note of exasperation in his tone, "if I'd had any idea of the luck he was in. Why, I lent him a bit to come back with, though I was only earning thirty bob a week, and the brute only sent it me back in bits, and not a farthing over."

"That was not considerate of him," Mr. Bentham agreed - "not at all considerate. Your brother had the command of considerable sums of money. In fact, Mr. Barnes, I may tell you, without any breach of confidence, I think that if he had kept his appointment with me on the night when he was murdered, I was prepared, on behalf of my client, to hand him a cheque for ten thousand pounds!"

E. Phillips Oppenheim

Barnes struck the table before him with his clenched fist.

"For what?" he cried, hysterically. "Ten thousand pounds for what?"

"Your brother," Mr. Bentham said calmly, "was possessed of securities which were worth that much or even more to my client."

"And where are they now?" Barnes gasped.

"I do not know," Mr. Bentham answered. "If you can find them, I think it very likely that my client might make you a similar offer."

It was the first ray of hope. Barnes moistened his dry lips with his tongue, and drew a long breath.

"Securities!" he muttered. "What sort of securities?"

"There, unfortunately," Mr. Bentham said, "I am unable to help you. I am an agent only in the matter. They were securities which my client was anxious to buy, and your brother was not unwilling to sell for cash, notwithstanding the income which they were bringing him in."

"But how can I look for them, if I don't know what they are?" Barnes protested.

"There are difficulties, certainly," the lawyer admitted, carefully polishing his spectacles with the corner of a silk handkerchief; "but, then, as you have doubtless surmised, the whole situation is a difficult one."

"You can get to know," Barnes exclaimed. "Your client would tell you."

Mr. Bentham sighed gently.

"Of course," he said, "I am only quoting my own opinion, but I do not think that my client would do anything of the sort. These securities happen to be of a somewhat secret nature. Your brother was in a position to make an exceedingly clever use of them. It appears incidentally to have cost him his life, but there are risks, of course, in every profession."

Barnes stared at him with wide-open eyes. He seemed, for the moment, struck dumb. Wrayson, who had been silent during the greater part of the conversation, turned towards the lawyer.

"You believe, then," he asked, "that Morris Barnes was murdered for the sake of these securities?"

"I believe - nothing," the lawyer answered. "It is not my business to believe. Mr. Morris Barnes was in the receipt of an income of two thousand a year, which we might call dividend upon these securities. My client, through me, made Mr. Barnes a cash offer to buy them outright, and although I must admit that Mr. Barnes had not closed with us, yet I believe that he was on the point of doing so. He had doubtless had it brought home to him that there was a certain amount of danger associated with his position generally. The night on which my client arrived in England was the night upon which Mr. Morris Barnes was murdered. The inference to be drawn from this circumstance I can leave, I am sure, to the common sense of you two gentlemen."

E. Phillips Oppenheim

"First, then," Wrayson said, "it would appear that he was murdered by the people who were paying him two thousand a year, and who were acting in opposition to your client!"

Mr. Bentham shrugged his shoulder gently.

"It does not sound unreasonable," he admitted.

"And secondly," Wrayson continued, "if that was so, he was probably robbed of these securities at the same time."

"Now that, also," Mr. Bentham said smoothly, "sounds reasonable. But, as a matter of fact," he continued, looking down upon the table, "there are certain indications which go to disprove it. My personal opinion is that the assassin - granted that there was an assassin, and granted that he was acting on behalf of the parties we have referred to - met with a disappointment."

"In plain words," Wrayson interrupted, "you mean that the other side have not possessed themselves of the securities?"

"They certainly have not," Mr. Bentham declared. "They still remain - the property by inheritance of this young gentleman here - Mr. Sydney Barnes, I believe."

His tone was so even, so expressionless, that its slightest changes were noticeable. It seemed to Wrayson that a faint note of sarcasm had crept into these last few words. Mr. Barnes himself, however, was quite oblivious of it. His yellow-stained fingers were spread out upon the table. He leaned over towards the lawyer. His under lip protruded, his deep-set eyes seemed closer than ever together. He was grimly, tragically in earnest.

"Look here," he said. "What can I do to get hold of 'em? I don't care what it is. I'm game! I'll deal with your man - the cash client. I'll give you a commission, see! Five per cent on all I get. How's that? I'll play fair. Now chuck away all this mystery. What were these securities? Where shall I start looking for them?"

Mr. Bentham regarded him with stony face. "There are certain points," he said, "upon which I cannot enlighten you. My duty to my client forbids it. I cannot describe to you the nature of those securities. I cannot suggest where you should look for them. All that I can say is that they are still to be found, and that my client is still a buyer."

The young man turned to Wrayson. His face was twitching with some emotion, probably anger.

"Did you ever hear such bally rot!" he exclaimed. "He knows all about these securities all right. They belong to me. He ought to be made to tell."

Wrayson shrugged his shoulders.

"It does seem rather a wild-goose chase, doesn't it?" he remarked. "Can't you tell him a little more, Mr. Bentham?"

Mr. Bentham sighed, as though his impotence were a matter of sincere regret to him.

"The only advice I can offer Mr. Barnes," he said, "is

that he induce you to aid him in his search. Between you, I should never be surprised to hear of your success."

"And why," Wrayson asked, "should you consider me such a useful ally?"

Mr. Bentham looked at him steadily for a moment.

"You appear to me," he said, "to be a young man of intelligence - and you know how to keep your own counsel. I should consider Mr. Barnes very fortunate if you could make up your mind to aid him in his search."

"It is not my affair," Wrayson answered stiffly. "I could not possibly pledge myself to enter upon such a wild-goose chase."

Mr. Bentham turned over some papers which lay upon the table before him. He had apparently had enough of the conversation.

"You must not call it exactly that, Mr. Wrayson," he said. "Mr. Barnes' success in his quest would probably result in an act of justice to society. To you personally, I should imagine it would be expressly interesting."

"What do you mean?" Wrayson asked, quickly.

The lawyer looked at him calmly.

"It should solve the mystery of Morris Barnes' murder!" he answered.

Wrayson touched his companion on the shoulder.

"I think that we might as well go," he said. "Mr. Bentham does not mean to tell us anything more."

Barnes moved slowly towards the door, but with reluctance manifested in his sullen face and manner.

"I don't know how I'm going to set about this job," he said, turning once more towards the lawyer. "I shall do what I can, but you haven't seen the last of me, yet, Mr. Bentham. If I fail, I shall come back to you."

The lawyer shrugged his shoulders. He was already absorbed in other work.

CHAPTER XVI

A DINNER IN THE STRAND

Wrayson was conscious, from the moment they left Mr. Bentham's office, of a change in the deportment of the young man who walked by his side. A variety of evil passions had developed one at least more tolerable - he was learning the lesson of self-restraint. He did not speak until they reached the corner of the street.

"Where can we get a drink?" he asked, almost abruptly. "I want some brandy."

Wrayson took him to a bar close by. They sat in a quiet corner.

"I want to ask you something," he said, leaning halfway over the little table between them. "How much do you know about the lady who came into my brother's flat when we were there?"

The direct significance of the question startled Wrayson. This young man was beginning to think.

"How much do I know of her?" he repeated. "Very little."

"She is really a Baroness - not one of these faked-up ones?"

"She is undoubtedly the Baroness de Sturm," Wrayson answered, a little stiffly.

"And she has plenty of coin?"

"Certainly," Wrayson answered. "She is a great lady, I believe, in her own country."

Barnes struck the table softly with the flat of his hand. His eyes were searching for his answer in Wrayson's face, almost before the words had left his lips.

"Do you believe then," he asked, "that a woman like that wrote love-letters to Morris? You knew Morris. He was what those sort of people call a bounder. Same as me! If he knew her at all it was a wonder. I can't believe in the love-letters."

Wrayson shrugged his shoulders.

"The whole affair," he declared, "everything connected with your brother, is so mysterious that I really don't know what to say."

"You knew Morris," the young man persisted. "You know the Baroness. Set 'em down side by side. They don't go, eh? You know that. Morris could tog himself up as much as he liked, and he was always a good 'un at that when he had the brass, but he'd never be able to make himself her sort. And if she's a real lady, and wasn't after the brass, then I don't believe that she ever wrote him love-letters. What?"

E. Phillips Oppenheim

Wrayson said nothing. The young man held out his empty glass to a waiter.

"More brandy," he ordered briefly. "Look here, Mr. Wrayson," he added, adopting once more his mysterious manner, "those love-letters don't go! What did the Baroness want in my brother's flat? She struck me dumb when I first saw her. I admit it. I'd have swallowed anything. More fool me! I tell you, though, I'm not having any more. Will you come along with me to her house now, and see if we can't make her tell us the truth?"

Wrayson shook his head deliberately.

"Mr. Barnes," he said, "I am sorry to disappoint you, and I sympathize very much with your position, but you mustn't take it for granted that I am, shall we say, your ally in this matter. I haven't either the time or the patience to give to investigations of this sort. I have done what I could for you, and I will give you what advice I can, or help you in any way, if you care to come and see me. But you mustn't count on anything else."

Barnes' face dropped. He was obviously disappointed.

"You won't come and see the Baroness with me even?" he asked.

"I think not," Wrayson answered. "To tell you the truth, I don't think that it would be of any use. Even if your suspicions are correct - and you scarcely know what you suspect, do you? - the Baroness is much too clever a woman to allow herself to be pumped by either you or me."

Wrayson felt himself subjected for several moments to the scrutinizing stare of those blinking, unpleasant eyes.

"You're not taking her side against me, are you?" Barnes asked distrustfully.

"Certainly not," Wrayson answered impatiently. "You must be reasonable, my young friend. I have done what I can to put you in the way of helping yourself, but I am a busy man. I have my own affairs to look after, and I can't afford to play the part of a twentieth-century Don Quixote."

"I understand," the young man said slowly. "You are going to turn me up."

"You are putting a very foolish construction upon what I have said," Wrayson answered irritably. "I have gone out of my way to help you, but, frankly, I think that yours is a wild-goose chase."

Barnes rose to his feet and finished his brandy.

"I don't believe it," he declared. "I'm going to have that two thousand a year, if I have to take that man Bentham by the throat and strangle the truth out of him. If I can't find out without, I'll make him tell me the truth if I swing for it. By God, I will!"

They left the place together and walked towards the corner of the street.

"I shouldn't do anything rash, if I were you," Wrayson said. "I fancy you'd find Bentham a pretty tough sort to tackle. You must excuse me now. I am going into the club for a few minutes."

"How are you, Wrayson?" a quiet voice asked behind.

Wrayson turned round abruptly. It was Stephen Heneage who had greeted him - the one man whom, at that moment, he was least anxious to meet of any person in the world. Already he could see that Heneage was taking quiet but earnest note of his companion.

Wrayson nodded a little abruptly and left Barnes without any further farewell.

"Coming round to the club?" he asked.

Heneage assented, and glanced carelessly behind at Barnes, who was walking slowly in the opposite direction.

"Who's your friend?" he asked. "You shook him off a little suddenly, didn't you?"

"He is not a friend," Wrayson answered, "and I was trying to get rid of him when you came up. He is nobody of any account."

Heneage shook his head thoughtfully.

"It won't do, Wrayson," he said. "That young man possessed a cast of features which are positively unmistakable."

"What do you mean?" Wrayson demanded.

"I mean that he was a relation, and a near relation, too, I should imagine, of our deceased friend Morris

Barnes," Heneage answered coolly. "I shall be obliged to make that young man's acquaintance."

"Damn you and your prying!" Wrayson exclaimed angrily. "I wish - "

He stopped abruptly. Heneage was already retracing his steps.

Wrayson, after a moment's indecision, went on to the club, and made his way at once to the billiard-room. The Colonel was sitting in his usual corner chair, watching a game of pool, beaming upon everybody with his fatherly smile, encouraging the man who met with ill luck, and applauding the successful shots. He was surrounded by his cronies, but he held out his hand to Wrayson, who leaned against the wall by his side and waited for his opportunity.

"Colonel," he said at last in his ear, taking advantage of the applause which followed a successful shot, "I want half an hour's talk with you, quite by ourselves. Can you slip away and come and dine with me somewhere?"

The Colonel looked dubious.

"I'm afraid they won't like it," he answered. "Freddy and George are here, and Tempest's coming in later."

"I can't help it," Wrayson answered. "You can guess what it's about. It's a serious matter."

The Colonel sighed.

"We might find an opportunity later on," he suggested.

"It won't do," Wrayson answered. "I want to get right away from here. I wouldn't bother you if it wasn't necessary."

"I'm sure you wouldn't," the Colonel admitted. "We'll slip away quietly when this game is over. It won't be long. Good shot, Freddy! Sixpence, you divide!"

They found themselves in the Strand about half an hour later.

"Where shall we go?" Wrayson asked. "Somewhere quiet."

"Across the way," the Colonel answered. "We shan't see any one we know there."

Wrayson nodded, and they crossed the street and entered Luigi's. It was early for diners, and they found a small table in a retired corner. Wrayson ordered the dinner, and then leaned across the table towards his guest.

"It's that Barnes matter, Colonel," he said quietly. "Heneage has taken it up and means going into it thoroughly. He saw me letting out your daughter that night."

The Colonel was in the act of helping himself to *hors d'oeuvre* His fork remained suspended for a moment in the air. Then he set it down with trembling fingers. The cheery light had faded from his face. He seemed suddenly older. His voice sounded unnatural.

"Heneage!" he repeated, sharply. "Stephen Heneage! What affair is it of his?"

"None," Wrayson answered. "He likes that sort of thing, that's all. He saw - your daughter with a lady - the Baroness de Sturm, and the seeing them together, after he had watched her come out of the flat that night, seemed to suggest something to him. He warned me that he had made up his mind to solve the mystery of Morris Barnes' murder; he advised me, in fact, to clear out. And now, since then -"

The waiter brought the soup. Wrayson broke off and talked for a moment or two to the *maître d'hôtel*, who had paused at their table. Presently, when they were alone, he went on.

"Since then, a young brother of Barnes has turned up from South Africa. There was some mystery about Morris Barnes and the source of his income. The brother is just as determined to solve this as Heneage seems to be to discover the - the murderer! They will work together, and I am afraid! Not for myself! You know for whom."

The Colonel was very grave. He ate slowly, and he seemed to be thinking.

"There is one man, a solicitor named Bentham," Wrayson continued, "who I believe knows everything. But I do not think that even Heneage will be able to make him speak. His connection with the affair is on behalf of a mysterious client. Young Barnes and I went to see him this afternoon, but beyond encouraging the boy to search for the source of his brother's income, he wouldn't open his mouth."

"A solicitor named Bentham," the Colonel repeated mechanically. "Ah!"

E. Phillips Oppenheim

"Do you know him?" Wrayson asked.

"I have heard of him," the Colonel answered. "A most disreputable person, I believe. He has offices in the Adelphi."

Wrayson nodded.

"And whatever his business is," he continued, "it isn't the ordinary business of a solicitor. He has no clerks - not even an office boy!"

The Colonel poured himself out a glass of wine.

"No clerks - not even an office boy! It all agrees with what I have heard. A bad lot, Wrayson, I am afraid - a thoroughly bad lot. Are you sure that up to now he has kept his own counsel?"

"I am sure of it," Wrayson answered.

The Colonel seemed in some measure to have recovered himself. He looked Wrayson in the face, and though grave, his expression was decidedly more natural.

"Herbert," he asked, sinking his voice almost to a whisper, "who do you believe murdered Morris Barnes?"

"God knows," Wrayson answered.

"Do you believe - that - my daughter had any hand in it?"

"No!" Wrayson declared fiercely.

The Colonel was silent for a moment. He seemed to be contemplating the label on the bottle of claret which reposed in its cradle by their side.

"And yet," he said thoughtfully, "she would necessarily be involved in any disclosures which were made."

"And so should I," Wrayson declared. "And those two, Sydney Barnes and Heneage, mean to bring about disclosures. That is why I felt that I must talk to some one about this. Colonel, can't you get your daughter to tell us the whole truth - what she was doing in Barnes' flat that night, and all the rest of it? We should be forewarned then!"

The Colonel covered his face with his hand for a moment. The question obviously distressed him.

"I can't, Herbert," he said, in a low tone. "You would scarcely think, would you, that I was the sort of man to live on irreconcilable terms with one of my own family? But there it is. Don't think hardly of her. It is more the fault of circumstances than her fault. But I couldn't go to see her - and she wouldn't come to see me."

Wrayson sighed.

"It is like the rest of this cursed mystery, utterly incomprehensible," he declared. "I shall never - "

With his glass half raised to his lips, he paused suddenly in his sentence. His face became a study in the expression of a boundless amazement. His eyes were fastened upon the figures of two people on their way up the room, preceded by the smiling *maître*

E. Phillips Oppenheim

d'hôtel. Some words, or rather an exclamation, broke incoherently from his lips. He set down his glass hurriedly, and a stain of red wine crept unheeded across the tablecloth.

"Look," he whispered hoarsely, - "look!"

CHAPTER XVII

A CONFESSION OF LOVE

The Colonel turned bodily round in his chair. The couple to whom Wrayson had drawn his attention were certainly incongruous enough to attract notice anywhere. The man was lank, elderly, and of severe appearance. He was bald, he had slight side-whiskers, he wore spectacles, and his face was devoid of expression. He was dressed in plain dinner clothes of old-fashioned cut. The tails of his coat were much too short, his collar belonged to a departed generation, and his tie was ready made. In a small Scotch town he might have passed muster readily enough as the clergyman or lawyer of the place. As a diner at Luigi's, ushered up the room to the soft strains of "La Mattchiche," and followed by such a companion, he was almost ridiculously out of place. If anything, she was the more noticeable of the two to the casual observer. Her hair was dazzlingly yellow, and arranged with all the stiffness of the coiffeur's art. She wore a dress of black sequins, cut perilously low, and shorn a little by wear of its pristine splendour. Her complexion was as artificial as her high-pitched voice; her very presence seemed to exude perfumes of the patchouli type. She was the sort of person concerning whom the veriest novice in such matters could have made no mistake. Yet her companion seemed wholly

E. Phillips Oppenheim

unembarrassed. He handed her the menu and looked calmly around the room.

"Who are those people?" the Colonel asked. "Rather a queer combination, aren't they?"

"The man is Bentham, the lawyer," Wrayson answered. His eyes were fixed upon the lady, who seemed not at all indisposed to become the object of any stray attention.

"That Bentham!" the Colonel repeated, under his breath. "But what on earth - where the mischief could he pick up a companion like that?"

Wrayson scarcely heard him. He had withdrawn his eyes from the lady with an effort.

"I have seen that woman somewhere," he said thoughtfully - "somewhere where she seemed quite as much out of place as she does here. Lately, too."

"H'm!" the Colonel remarked, leaning back in his chair to allow the waiter to serve him. "She's not the sort of person you'd be likely to forget either, is she?"

"And, by Heavens, I haven't!" Wrayson declared, suddenly laying down his knife and fork. "I remember her now. It was at the inquest - Barnes' inquest. She was one of the two women at whose flat he called on his way home. What on earth is Bentham doing with her?"

"You think," the Colonel remarked quietly, "that there is some connection -"

"Of course there is," Wrayson interrupted. "Does that old fossil look like the sort to take such a creature about for nothing? Colonel, he doesn't know himself - where those securities are! He's brought that woman here to pump her!"

The Colonel passed his hand across his forehead.

"I am getting a little confused," he murmured.

"And I," Wrayson declared, with barely suppressed excitement, "am beginning to see at least the shadow of daylight. If only you had some influence with your daughter, Colonel!"

The Colonel looked at him steadfastly. Wrayson wondered whether it was the light, or whether indeed his friend had aged so much during the last few months.

"I have no influence over my daughter, Wrayson," he said. "I thought that I had already explained that. And, Herbert," he added, leaning over the table, "why don't you let this matter alone? It doesn't concern you. You are more likely to do harm than good by meddling with it. There may be interests involved greater than you know of; you may find understanding a good deal more dangerous than ignorance. It isn't your affair, anyhow. Take my advice! Let it alone!"

"I wish I could," Wrayson answered, with a little sigh. "Frankly, I would if I could, but it fascinates me."

"All that I have heard of it," the Colonel remarked wearily, "sounds sordid enough."

E. Phillips Oppenheim

Wrayson nodded.

"I think," he said, "that it is the sense of personal contact in a case like this which stirs the blood. I have memories about that night, Colonel, which I couldn't describe to you - or any one. And now this young brother coming on the scene seems to bring the dead man to life again. He's one of the worst type of young bounders I ever came into contact with. A creature without sentiment or feeling of any sort - nothing but an almost ravenous cupidity. He's wearing his brother's clothes now - thinks nothing of it! He hasn't a single regret. I haven't heard a single decent word pass his lips. But he wants the money. Nothing else! The money!"

"Do you believe," the Colonel asked, "that he will get it?"

"Who can tell?" Wrayson answered. "That Morris Barnes was in possession of valuables of some sort, everything goes to prove. Just think of the number of people who have shown their interest in him. There is Bentham and his mysterious client, the Baroness de Sturm and your daughter, and - the person who murdered him. Apparently, even though he lost his life, Barnes was too clever for them, for his precious belongings must still be undiscovered."

The Colonel finished his wine and leaned back in his chair.

"I am tired of this subject," he said. "I should like to get back to the club."

Wrayson called for the bill a little unwillingly. He was,

in a sense, disappointed at the Colonel's attitude.

"Very well," he said, "we will bury it. But before we do so, there is one thing I have had it in my mind to say - for some time. I want to say it now. It is about your daughter, Colonel!"

The Colonel looked at him curiously.

"My daughter?" he repeated, under his breath.

Wrayson leaned a little forward. Something new had come into his face. This was the first time he had suffered such words to pass his lips - almost the first time he had suffered such thoughts to form themselves in his mind.

"I never looked upon myself," he said quietly, "as a particularly impulsive person. Yet it was an impulse which prompted me to conceal the truth as to her presence in the flat buildings that night. It was a serious thing to do, and somehow I fancy that the end is not yet."

"Why did you do it?" the Colonel asked. "You did not know who she was. It could not have been that."

"Why did I do it?" Wrayson repeated. "I can't tell you. I only know that I should do it again and again if the need came. If I told you exactly how I felt, it would sound like rot. But I'm going to ask you that question."

"Well?"

The Colonel's grey eyebrows were drawn together. His eyes were keen and bright. So he might have looked in time of stress; but he was not in the least like the genial idol of the Sheridan billiard-room.

"If I came to you to-morrow," Wrayson said, "and told you that I had met at last the woman whom I wished to make my wife, and that woman was your daughter, what should you say?"

"I should be glad," the Colonel answered simply.

"You and she are, for some unhappy reason, not on speaking terms. That - "

"Good God!" the Colonel interrupted, "whom do you mean? Whom are you talking about?"

"About your daughter - whom I shielded - the companion of the Baroness de Sturm. Your daughter Louise."

The Colonel raised his trembling fingers to his forehead. His voice quivered ominously.

"Of course! Of course! God help me, I thought you meant Edith! I never thought of Louise. And Edith has spoken of you lately."

"I found your younger daughter charming," Wrayson said seriously, "but it was of your daughter Louise I was speaking. I thought that you would understand that."

"My daughter - whom you found - in Morris Barnes' flat - that night?"

"Exactly," Wrayson answered, "and my question is

this. I cannot ask you why you and she parted, but at least you can tell me if you know of any reason why I should not ask her to be my wife."

The Colonel was silent.

"No!" he said at last, "there is no reason. But she would not consent. I am sure of that."

"We will let it go at that," Wrayson answered. "Come!"

He had chosen his moment for rising so as to pass down the room almost at the same time as Mr. Bentham and his strange companion. Prolific of smiles and somewhat elephantine graces, the lady's darkened eyes met Wrayson's boldly, and finding there some encouragement, she even favoured him with a backward glance. In the vestibule he slipped a half-crown into the attendant's hand.

"See if you can hear the address that lady gives her cabman," he whispered.

The boy nodded, and hurried out after them. Wrayson kept the Colonel back under the pretence of lighting a fresh cigar. When at last they strolled forward, they met the boy returning. He touched his hat to Wrayson.

"Alhambra, sir!" he said, quietly. "Gone off alone, sir, in a hansom. Gentleman walked."

The Colonel kept silence until they were in the street.

"Coming to the club?" he asked, a little abruptly.

"No!" Wrayson answered.

"You are going after that woman?" the Colonel exclaimed.

"I am going to the Alhambra," Wrayson answered. "I can't help it. It sounds foolish, I suppose, but this affair fascinates me. It works on my nerves somehow. I must go."

The Colonel turned on his heel. Without another word, he crossed the Strand, leaving Wrayson standing upon the pavement. Wrayson, with a little sigh, turned westwards.

CHAPTER XVIII

AN AMATEUR DETECTIVE

Wrayson easily discovered the object of his search. She was seated upon a lounge in the promenade, her ample charms lavishly displayed, and her blackened eyes mutely questioning the passers-by. She welcomed Wrayson with a smile which she meant to be inviting, albeit she was a little suspicious. Men of Wrayson's stamp and appearance were not often such easy victims.

"Saw you at Luigi's, didn't I?" he asked, hat in hand.

She nodded, and made room for him to sit down by her side.

"Did you see the old stick I was with?" she asked. "I don't know why I was fool enough to go out with him. Trying to pump me about poor old Barney, too, all the time. Just as though I couldn't see through him."

"Old Barney!" Wrayson repeated, a little perplexed.

She laughed coarsely.

"Oh! come, that won't do!" she declared. "I'm almost sure you're on the same lay yourself. Didn't I see you at the inquest? - Morris Barnes' inquest, of course? You know whom I mean right enough."

"I know whom you mean now," Wrayson admitted. "Yes! I was there. Queer affair, wasn't it?"

The lady nodded.

"I should like a liqueur," she remarked, with apparent irrelevance. "Benedictine!"

They were seated in front of a small table, and were at times the object of expectant contemplation on the part of a magnificent individual in livery and knee-breeches. Wrayson summoned him and ordered two Benedictines.

"Now I don't mind telling you," the lady continued, leaning over towards him confidentially, "that I'm dead off that old man who came prying round and took me out to dinner, to pump me about poor Barney! He didn't get much out of me. For one thing, I don't know much. But the little I do know I'd sooner tell you than him."

"You're very kind," Wrayson murmured. "He used to come to these places a good deal, didn't he?"

She nodded assent.

"He was always either here or at the Empire. He wasn't a bad sort, Barney, although he was just like all the rest of them, close with his money when he was sober, and chucking it about when he'd had a drop too much. What did you want to know about him in particular?"

"Well, for one thing," Wrayson answered, "where he got his money from."

She shook her head.

"He was always very close about that," she said. "The only story I ever heard him tell was that he'd made it mining in South Africa."

"You have really heard him say that?" Wrayson asked.

"Half a dozen times," she declared.

"That proves, at any rate," he remarked thoughtfully, "that there was some mystery about his income, because I happen to know that he came back from South Africa a pauper."

"Very likely," she remarked. "Barney was always the sort who would rather tell a lie than the truth."

"Did he say anything to you that night about being in any kind of danger?" he asked.

She shook her head.

"No! I don't think so. I didn't take particular notice of what he said, because he was a bit squiffy. I believe he mentioned some thing about a business appointment that night, but I really didn't take much notice."

"You didn't tell them anything about that at the inquest," Wrayson remarked.

"I know I didn't," she admitted. "You see, I was so knocked over, and I really didn't remember anything clearly, that I thought it was best to say nothing at all. They'd only have been trying to ferret things out of me that I couldn't have told them."

"I think that you were very wise," Wrayson said. "You don't happen to remember anything else that he said, I suppose?"

"No! except that he seemed a little depressed. But there's something else about Barney that I always suspected, that I've never heard mentioned yet. Mind you, it may be true or it may not, but I always suspected it."

"What was that?" Wrayson demanded.

"I believe that he was married," she declared impressively.

"Married!"

Wrayson looked incredulous. It certainly did not seem probable.

"Where is his wife then?" he asked. "Why hasn't she turned up to claim his effects? Besides, he lived alone. He was my neighbour, you know. His brother has taken possession of his flat."

The lady rather enjoyed the impression she had made. She was not averse, either, to being seen in so prominent a place in confidential talk with a man of Wrayson's appearance. It might not be directly remunerative, but it was likely to do her good.

"He showed me a photograph once," she continued. "A

baby-faced chit of a girl it was, but he was evidently very proud of it. A little girl of his down in the country, he told me. Then, do you know this? He was never in London for Sunday. Every week-end he went off somewhere; and I never heard of any one who ever saw him or knew where he went to."

"This is very interesting," Wrayson admitted; "but if he was married, surely his wife would have turned up by now!"

"Why should she?" the lady answered. "Don't you see that she very likely has what all you gentlemen seem to be so anxious about - his income?"

"By Jove!" Wrayson exclaimed softly. "Of course, if there was anything mysterious about the source of it, all the more reason for her to keep dark."

"Well, that's what I've had in my mind," she declared, summoning the waiter. "I'll take another liqueur, if you don't mind."

Wrayson nodded. His thoughts were travelling fast.

"Did you tell Mr. Bentham this?" he asked.

"Not I," she answered. "The old fool got about as much out of me as he deserved - and that's nothing."

"I'm sure I'm very much obliged," Wrayson answered, drawing out his pocketbook. "I wonder if I might be allowed - ?"

He glanced at her inquiringly. She nodded. "I'm not proud," she declared.

* * * * *

"As an amateur detective," Wrayson remarked to himself, as he strolled homewards, "I am beginning rather to fancy myself. And yet -"

His thoughts had stolen away. He forgot Morris Barnes and the sordid mystery of which he was the centre. He remembered only the compelling cause which was driving him towards the solution of it. The night was warm, and he walked slowly, his hands behind him, and ever before his eyes the shadowy image of the girl who had brought so many strange sensations into his somewhat uneventful life. Would he ever see her, he wondered, without the light of trouble in her eyes, with colour in her cheeks, and joy in her tone? He thought of her violet-rimmed eyes, her hesitating manner, her air always as of one who walked hand in hand with fear. She was not meant for these things! Her lips and eyes were made for laughter; she was, after all, only a girl. If he could but lift the cloud! And then he looked upwards and saw her - leaning from the little iron balcony, and looking out into the cool night.

He half stopped. She did not move. It was too dark to see her features, but as he looked upwards a strange idea came to him. Was it a gesture or some unspoken summons which travelled down to him through the semi-darkness? He only knew, as he turned and entered the flat, that a new chapter of his life was opening itself out before him.

CHAPTER XIX

DESPERATE WOOING

Wrayson felt, from the moment he crossed the threshold of the room, that he had entered an atmosphere charged with elusive emotion. He was not sure of himself or of her as she turned slowly to greet him. Only he was at once conscious that something of that change in her which he had prophetically imagined was already shining out of her eyes. She was at once more natural and further removed from him.

"I am glad," she said simply. "I wanted to say good-bye to you."

He was stunned for a moment. He had not imagined this.

She nodded.

"Good-bye!" he repeated. "You are going away?"

"To-morrow. Oh! I am glad. You don't know how glad I am."

She swept past him and sank into an easy-chair. She wore a black velveteen evening dress, cut rather high, without ornament or relief of any sort, and her neck

　　　E. Phillips Oppenheim

gleamed like polished ivory from which creeps always a subtle shade of pink. Her hair was parted in the middle and brushed back in little waves, her eyes were full of fire, and her face was no longer passive. Beautiful she had seemed to him before, but beautiful with a sort of impersonal perfection. She was beautiful now in her own right, the beauty of a woman whom nature has claimed for her own, who acknowledges her heritage. The fear-frozen subjectivity in which he had yet found enough to fascinate him had passed away. He felt that she was a stranger.

"Always," she murmured, "I shall think of London as the city of dreadful memories. I should like to be going to set my face eastwards or westwards until I was so far away that even memory had perished. But that is just where the bonds tell, isn't it?"

"There are many who can make the bonds elastic," he answered. "It is only a question of going far enough."

"Alas!" she answered, "a few hundred miles are all that are granted to me. And London is like a terrible octopus. Its arms stretch over the sea."

"A few hundred miles," he repeated, with obvious relief. "Northward or southward, or eastward or westward?"

"Southward," she answered. "The other side of the Channel. That, at least, is something. I always like to feel that there is sea between me and a place which I - loathe!"

"Is London so hateful to you, then?" he asked.

"Perhaps I should not have said that," she answered. "Say a place of which I am afraid!"

He looked across at her. He, too, in obedience to a gesture from her, was seated.

"Come," he said, "we will not talk of London, then. Tell me where you are going."

She shook her head.

"To a little Paradise I know of."

"Paradise," he reminded her, "was meant for two."

"There will be two of us," she answered, smiling.

He felt his heart thump against his ribs.

"Then if one wanted to play the part of intruder?"

She shook her head.

"The third person in Paradise was always very much *de trop*," she reminded him.

"It depends upon the people who are already there," he protested.

"My friend," she said, "is in search of solitude, absolute and complete."

He shook his head.

"Such a place does not exist," he declared confidently. "Your friend might as well have stayed at home."

"She relies upon me to procure it for her," she said.

A rare smile flashed from Wrayson's lips.

"You can't imagine what a relief her sex is to me!" he exclaimed.

"I don't know why," she answered pensively. "Do you know anything about the North of France, Mr. Wrayson?"

"Not much," he answered. "I hope to know more presently."

Her eyes laughed across at him.

"You know what I said about the third person in Paradise?"

"I can't admit your Paradise," he said.

"You are a heretic," she answered. "It is a matter of sex, of course."

"Naturally! Paradise is so relative. It may be the halo thrown round a court in the city or a rose garden in the country, any place where love is!"

"And may I not love my friend!" she demanded.

"You may love me," he answered, the passion suddenly vibrating in his tone. "I will be more faithful than any friend. I will build Paradise for you - wherever you will! I will build the walls so high that no harm or any fear shall pass them."

She waved him back. Something of the old look, which he hated so to see, was in her face.

"You must not talk to me like this, Mr. Wrayson," she said. "Indeed you must not."

"Why not?" he demanded. "If there is a reason I will know it."

She looked him steadily in the eyes.

"Can't you imagine one for yourself?" she asked.

He laughed scornfully.

"You don't understand," he said. "There is only one reason in the world that I would admit - I don't even know that I would accept that. The other things don't count. They don't exist."

She looked at him a little incredulously. She was still sitting, and he was standing now before her. Her fingers rested lightly upon the arms of her chair, she was leaning slightly forward as though watching for something in his face.

"Tell me that there is another man," he cried, "that you don't care for me, that you never could care for me, and I will go away and you shall never see my face again. But nothing short of that will drive me from you."

He spoke quickly, his tone was full of nervous passion. It never occurred to her to doubt him.

"You can be what else you like," he continued, "thief, adventuress - murderess! So long as there is no other man! Come to me and I will take you away from it all."

She laughed very softly, and his pulses thrilled at the sound, for there was no note of mockery there; it was the laugh of a woman who listens to hidden music.

"You are a bold lover," she murmured. "Have you been reading romances lately? Do you know that it is the twentieth century, and I have seen you three times? You don't know what you say. You can't mean it."

"By Heaven, I do!" he cried, and for one exquisite moment he held her in his arms. Then she freed herself with a sudden start. She had lost her composure. Her cheeks were flushed.

"Don't!" she cried, sharply. "Remember our first meeting. I am not the sort of person you imagine. I never can be. There are reasons - "

He swept them aside. Something seemed to tell him that if he did not succeed with her now, his opportunity would be gone forever.

"I will listen to none of them," he declared, standing between her and the door. "They don't matter! Nothing matters! I choose you for my wife, and I will have you. I wouldn't care if you came to me from a prison. Better give in, Louise. I shan't let you escape."

She had indeed something of the look of a beautiful hunted animal as she leaned a little towards him, her eyes riveted upon his, her lips a little parted, her bosom rising and falling quickly. She was taken completely by surprise. She had not given Wrayson credit for such strength of mind or purpose. She had believed entirely in her own mastery over him, for any such assault as he was now making. And she was learning the truth. Love that makes a woman weak lends strength to the man. Their positions were becoming reversed. It was he who was dictating to her.

"I am going away," she said nervously. "You will forget me. You must forget me."

"You shall not go away," he answered, "unless I know where. Don't be afraid. You can keep your secrets, whatever they are. I want to know nothing. Go on exactly with the life you are leading, if it pleases you. I shan't interfere. But you are going to be my wife, and you shall not leave London without telling me about it."

"I am leaving London," she faltered, "to-morrow."

"I was thinking," he remarked, calmly, "of taking a little holiday myself."

She laughed uneasily.

"You are absurd," she declared, "and you must go away. Really! The Baroness will be home directly. I would rather, I would very much rather that she did not find you here."

He held out his arms to her. His eyes were bright with the joy of conquest.

"I will go, Louise," he answered, "but first I will have my answer - and no answer save one will do!"

She bit her lip. She was moved by some emotion, but he was unable, for the moment, to classify it.

"I think," she declared, "that you must be the most persistent man on earth."

"You are going to find me so," he assured her.

"Listen," she said firmly, "I will not marry you!"

He shrugged his shoulders.

"On that point," he answered, "I am content to differ from you. Anything else?"

She stamped her foot.

"I do not care for you! I do not wish to marry you!" she repeated. "I am going away, and I forbid you to follow me."

"No good!" he declared, stolidly. "I am past all that."

She held up her finger, and glanced backward out of the window.

"It is the Baroness," she said. "I must go and open the door."

For one moment she lay passive in his arms; then he could have sworn that her lips returned his kiss. She was there when they heard the turning of a latch-key in the door. With a little cry she slipped away and left him alone. The outer door was thrown open, and the Baroness stood upon the threshold.

CHAPTER XX

STABBED THROUGH THE HEART

The Baroness recognized Wrayson with a little shrug of the shoulders.

"Ah! my dear Mr. Wrayson," she exclaimed, "this is very kind of you. You have been keeping Louise company, I hope. And see what droll things happen! It is your friend, Mr. Barnes, who has brought me home this evening, and who will take a whisky and soda before he goes. Is it not so, my friend?"

She turned around, but there was no immediate response. The Baroness looked over the banisters and beheld her escort in the act of ascending.

"Coming right along," he called out cheerfully. "It was the cabman who tried to stop me. He wanted more than his fare. Found he'd tackled the wrong Johnny this time."

Mr. Sydney Barnes came slowly into view. He was wearing an evening suit, obviously too large for him, a made-up white tie had slipped round underneath his ear, a considerable fragment of red silk handkerchief was visible between his waistcoat and much crumpled white shirt. An opera hat, also too large for him, he

E. Phillips Oppenheim

was wearing very much on the back of his head, and he was smoking a very black cigar, from which he had failed to remove the band. He frowned when he saw Wrayson, but followed the Baroness into the room with a pronounced swagger.

"You two need no introduction, of course," the Baroness remarked. "I am not going to tell you where I found Mr. Barnes. I do not expect to be very much longer in England, so perhaps I am not so careful as I ought to be. Louise, if she knew, would be shocked. Now, Mr. Wrayson, do not hurry away. You will take some whisky and soda? I am afraid that my young friend has not been very hospitable."

"You are very kind," Wrayson said. "To tell you the truth, I was rather hoping to see Miss Fitzmaurice again. She disappeared rather abruptly."

The Baroness shook her finger at him in mock reproach.

"You have been misbehaving," she declared. "Never mind. I will go and see what I can do for you."

She stood for a moment before a looking-glass arranging her hair, and then left the room humming a light tune. Sydney Barnes, with his hands in his pockets, flung himself into an easy-chair.

"I say," he began, "I don't quite see what you're doing here."

Wrayson looked at him for a moment in supercilious surprise.

"I scarcely see," he answered, "how my movements concern you."

Mr. Barnes was unabashed.

"Oh! chuck it," he declared. "You know very well what I'm thinking of. To tell you the truth, I've come to the conclusion that there's some connection between this household and my brothers affairs. That's why I'm palling on to the Baroness. She's a fine woman - class, you know, and all that sort of thing, but what I want is the shino! You tumble?"

Wrayson shrugged his shoulders slightly.

"I wish you every success," he said. "Personally, I think that you are wasting your time here."

"Perhaps so," Barnes answered. "I'm taking my own risks."

Wrayson turned away, and at that moment the Baroness re-entered the room.

"My friend," she said, addressing Wrayson, "I can do nothing for you. Whether you have offended Louise or made her too happy, I cannot say. But she will not come down. You will not see her again to-night."

"I am sorry," Wrayson answered. "She is going away to-morrow, I understand?"

The Baroness sighed.

"Alas!" she declared, "I must not answer any questions. Louise has forbidden it."

Wrayson took up his hat.

"In that case," he remarked, "there remains nothing for me but to wish you good night!"

There was a cab on the rank opposite, and Wrayson, after a moment's hesitation, entered it and was driven to the club. He scarcely expected to find any one there, but he was in no mood for sleep, and the thought of his own empty rooms chilled him. Somewhat to his surprise, however, he found the smoking-room full. The central figure of the most important group was the Colonel, his face beaming with good-nature, and his cheeks just a little flushed. He welcomed Wrayson almost boisterously.

"Come along, Herbert," he cried. "Plenty of room. What'll you have to drink, and have you heard the news?"

"Whisky and soda," Wrayson answered, sinking into an easy-chair, "and I haven't heard any news."

The Colonel took his cigar from his mouth, and leaned forward in his chair. He had the appearance of a man who was striving to appear more grave than he felt.

"You remember the old chap we saw dining at Luigi's to-night - Bentham, I think you said his name was?"

Wrayson nodded.

"Of course! What about him?"

"He's dead!" the Colonel declared.

Wrayson jumped out of his chair.

"Nonsense!" he exclaimed. "You don't mean it, Colonel!"

"Unfortunately, I do," the Colonel answered. "He was found dead on the stairs leading to his office, about ten o'clock to-night. A most interesting case. The murder, presuming it was a murder, appears to have been committed - "

Wrayson was suddenly pale.

"Murder!" he repeated. "Colonel, do you mean this?"

The Colonel, who hated being interrupted, answered a little testily.

"My dear Wrayson," he expostulated, "is this the sort of thing a man invents for fun? Do listen for a moment, if you can, in patience. It is a deeply interesting case. If you remember, it was about nine o'clock when we left Luigi's; Bentham must have gone almost straight to his office, for he was found there dead a very few minutes after ten."

"Who killed him, and why?" Wrayson asked breathlessly.

"That, I suppose, we shall know later," the Colonel answered. "The police will be on their mettle this time, but it isn't a particularly easy case. He was found lying on his face, stabbed through the heart. That is all anybody knows."

The thoughts went rushing through Wrayson's brain.

E. Phillips Oppenheim

He remembered the man as he had seemed only a few hours ago, cold, stonily indifferent to young Barnes' passionate questions, inflexibly silent, a man who might easily kindle hatreds, to all appearance without a soft spot or any human feeling. He remembered the close of their interview, and Sydney Barnes' rash threat. The suggested idea clothed itself almost unconsciously with words.

"I have just seen young Barnes," he said. "He has been at the Empire all the evening."

The Colonel lit another cigar.

"It takes a man of nerve and deliberation," he remarked, "to commit a murder. From what I have heard of him, I should not imagine your young friend to be possessed of either. The lady whom he was entertaining, or rather failing to entertain, at dinner - "

"I have seen her since," Wrayson interrupted shortly. "She went straight to the Alhambra."

The Colonel nodded.

"I would have insured her against even suspicion," he remarked. "She was a large, placid woman, of the flabby order of nerves. She will probably faint when she hears what has happened. She might box a man's ears, but her arm would never drive a dagger home into his heart, especially with such beautiful, almost mathematical accuracy. We must look elsewhere, I fancy, for the person who has paid Bentham's debt to society. Heneage, here, has an interesting theory."

Wrayson looked across and found that his eyes met

Heneage's. He was sitting a little in the background, with a newspaper in his hand, which he was, however, only affecting to read. He was taking note of every word of the conversation. He was obviously annoyed at the Colonel's reference to him, but he did his best to conceal it.

"Scarcely a theory," he remarked, laying down his paper for a moment. "I can hardly call it that. I only remarked that I happened to know a little about Bentham, and that his clients, if he had any, were mostly foreigners, and their business of a shady nature. As a matter of fact, he was struck off the rolls here some years ago. I forget the case now, but I know that it was a pretty bad one."

"So you see," the Colonel resumed, "he was probably in touch with a loose lot, though what benefit his death could have been to any one it is, of course, a little hard to imagine. Makes one think, somehow, of this Morris Barnes affair, doesn't it? I wonder if there is any connection between the two."

Heneage laid down his paper now, and abandoned his attitude of indifferent listener. He was obviously listening for what Wrayson had to say.

"Connection of some sort between the two men there certainly was,"
Wrayson admitted. "We know that."

"Exactly," Heneage remarked. "I speak without knowing very much about the matter, but I am thoroughly convinced of one thing. If you can find the murderer of Morris Barnes, you will solve, at the same time, the mystery of Bentham's death. It is the same affair; part and parcel of the same tangle."

The Colonel was silent for a few moments. He seemed to be reflecting on Heneage's words.

"I believe you are right," he said at last. "I should be curious to know, though, how you arrived at this decision."

Heneage looked past him at Wrayson.

"You should ask Wrayson," he said.

But Wrayson had risen, and was sauntering towards the door.

"I'm off," he remarked, looking backwards and nodding his farewells. "If I stay here any longer, I shall have nightmare. Time you fellows were in bed, too. How's the Malleni fund, Colonel?"

The Colonel's face relaxed. A smile of genuine pleasure lit up his features.

"Going strong," he declared triumphantly. "We shall ship him off for Italy next week with a very tidy little cheque in his pocket. Dear old Dobson gave us ten pounds, and the concert fund is turning out well."

Wrayson lit a cigarette and looked back from the open door.

"You're more at home with philanthropy than horrors, Colonel," he remarked. "Good night, everybody!"

CHAPTER XXI

THE FLIGHT OF LOUISE

The Baroness was looking her best, and knew it. She had slept well the night before, and her eyes were soft and clear. Her maid had been unusually successful with her hair, and her hat, which had arrived only that morning from Paris, was quite the smartest in the room. She was at her favourite restaurant, and her solitary companion was a good-looking man, added to which the caviar was delightfully fresh, and the toast crisp and thin. Consequently the Baroness was in a particularly good temper.

"I really do wish, my dear friend," she said, smiling across at him, "that I could do what you ask. But it is not so simple, not so simple as you think. You say, 'Give me the address of your friend,' You ask me nicely, and I like you well enough to be glad to do it. But Louise she say to me, 'Give no one my address! Let no one know where I am gone.'"

"I'm sure she didn't mean that to apply to me," Wrayson pleaded.

"Ah! but she even mentioned your name," the Baroness declared. "I say to her, 'Not even Mr. Wrayson?' and she answered, 'No! No! No!'"

E. Phillips Oppenheim

"And you promised?" he asked.

"Why, yes! What else could I do?" she replied. "I say to her, 'You are a very foolish girl, Louise. After you have gone you will be sorry. Mr. Wrayson will be angry with you, and I shall make myself very, very agreeable to him, and who knows but he will forget all about you?' But Louise she only shake her head. She knows her own countrymen too well. They are so terribly insularly constant."

"Is that such a very bad quality, Baroness?"

"Ah! I find it so," she admitted. "I do not like the man who can think of only one thing, only one woman at a time. He is so dull, he has no imagination. If he has only one sweetheart, how can he know anything about us? for in a hundred different women there are no two alike."

"That is all very well," Wrayson answered, smiling; "but, you see, if a man cares very much for one particular woman, he hasn't the least curiosity about the rest of her sex."

She sighed gently, and her eyes flashed her regrets. Very blue eyes they were to-day, almost as blue as the turquoises about her throat.

"They say," she murmured, "that some Englishmen are like that. It is so much a pity - when they are nice!"

"I suppose," he suggested, "that yours is the Continental point of view."

She was silent until the waiter, who was filling her

glass with white wine, had departed. Then she leaned over towards him. Her forehead was a little wrinkled, her eyebrows raised. She had the half-plaintive air of a child who is complaining of being unjustly whipped.

"Yes! I think it is," she answered. "The lover, as I know him, is one who could not be unkind to a woman. In his heart he is faithful, perhaps, to one, but for her sake the whole world of beautiful women are objects of interest to him. He will flirt with them when they will. He is always their admirer. In the background there may always be what you call the preference, but that is his secret."

Wrayson smiled across the table.

"This is a very dangerous doctrine, Baroness!" he declared.

"Dangerous?" she murmured.

"For us! Remember that we are a susceptible race."

She flung out her hands and shook her head. Susceptible! She denied it vehemently.

"It is on the contrary," she declared. "You do not lose your heads or your hearts very easily, you Englishmen."

"You do not know us," he protested.

"I know *you*," she answered. "For myself, I admit it. When I am with a man who is nice, I try that I may make him, just a little, no more, but just a little in love with me. It makes things more amusing. It is better for him, and we are not bored. But with you, *mon ami, I* know very well that I waste my time. And so, I ask you instead this question. Tell me why you have invited me to take luncheon with you."

She flashed her question across at him carelessly enough, but he felt that she expected an answer, and that she was not to be deceived.

"I wanted Miss Fitzmaurice's address," he said.

"Naturally. But what else?"

He sighed.

"I want to know more than you will tell me, I am afraid," he said. "I want to know why you and Miss Fitzmaurice are living together in London and leading such an unusual life, and how in Heaven's name you became concerned in the affairs of Morris Barnes."

"Ah!" she said. "You want to know that? So!"

"I do," he admitted.

"And yet," she remarked, "even for that it was not worth while to make love to me! You ask so much, my friend, and you give so little."

"If you - " he began, a little awkwardly.

Her light laugh stopped him.

"Ah, no! my friend, you must not be foolish," she said. "I will tell you what I can for nothing, and that, I am afraid, is very little more than nothing. But as for offering me a bribe, you must not think of that. It would not be *comme-il-faut;* not at all *gentil.*"

"Tell me what you can, then," he begged.

She shrugged her shoulders.

"It is so little," she declared; "only this. We are not adventuresses, Louise and I. We are living together because we were schoolfellows, and because we are both anxious to succeed in a certain undertaking to which, for different reasons, we have pledged ourselves. To succeed we needed some papers which had come into the hands of Mr. Mo rris Barnes. That is why I am civil to that little - what you call bounder, his brother."

"It sounds reasonable enough, this," Wrayson said; "but what about the murder of Morris Baines, on the very night, you know, when Louise was there?"

"It is all a very simple matter," the Baroness answered, quietly, "but yet it is a matter where the death of a few such men would count for nothing. A few ages ago it would not have been a matter of a dozen Morris Barnes, no, nor a thousand! Diplomacy is just as cruel, and just as ruthless, as the battlefield, only it works, down there - underground!"

"It is a political matter, then?" Wrayson asked swiftly.

The Baroness smiled. She took a cigarette from her little gold case and lit it.

"Ah!" she exclaimed, "you must not try to, what you say, pump me! You can call it what you will. Only to

E. Phillips Oppenheim

Louise, as to me, it is very much a personal affair. Shall we talk now, for a little, of other things?"

Wrayson sighed.

"I may not know, then," he begged, "where Louise has gone, or why?"

"It would not be her wish," the Baroness answered, "that I should tell you."

"Very well," Wrayson said, "I will ask you no more questions. Only this. I have told you of this man Bentham."

The Baroness inclined her head. He had told her nothing that was news to her.

"Was he on your side, or opposed to you?"

"You are puzzling me," the Baroness confessed.

"Already," Wrayson explained, "I know as much of the affair as this. Morris Barnes was in possession of something, I do not know whether it was documents, or what possible material shape it had, but it brought him in a considerable income, and both you and some others were endeavouring to obtain possession of it. So far, I believe that neither of you have succeeded. Morris Barnes has been murdered in vain; Bentham the lawyer, who telephoned to me on the night of his death, has shared his fate. To whose account do these two murders go, yours or the others'?"

"I cannot answer that question, Mr. Wrayson," the Baroness said.

"Do you know," Wrayson demanded, dropping his voice a little, "that, but for my moral, if not actual perjury, Louise herself would have been charged with the murder of Morris Barnes?"

"She had a narrow escape," the Baroness admitted.

"She had a narrow escape," Wrayson declared, "but the unfortunate part of the affair is, that she is not even now safe!"

The Baroness looked at him curiously. She was in the act of drawing on her gloves, but her fingers suddenly became rigid.

"What do you mean?" she asked.

"I mean," Wrayson said, "that another person saw her come out of the flats that night. It was a friend of mine, who kept silence at first because he believed that it was a private assignation of my own. Since then events have occurred to make him think differently. He has gone over to the other side. He is spending his time with young Sydney Barnes, and he has set himself to discover the mystery of Morris Barnes' murder. He has even gone so far as to give me warning that I should be better out of England."

"Who is this person?" the Baroness asked calmly.

"His name is Stephen Heneage, and he is a member of my club, the club to which Louise's father also belongs," Wrayson replied.

The Baroness suddenly dropped her veil, but not before Wrayson had seen a sudden change in her face.

He remembered suddenly that Heneage was no stranger to her, he remembered the embarrassment of their meeting at the Alhambra.

"You know him, of course," he repeated. "Heneage is not a man to be trifled with. He has had experience in affairs of this sort, he is no ordinary amateur detective."

"Yes! I know Mr. Stephen Heneage," the Baroness said. "Tell me, does Louise know?"

Wrayson shook his head.

"I have had no opportunity of telling her," he answered. "I might not have thought so seriously of it, but this morning I received a note from Heneage."

"Yes! What did he say?"

"It was only a line or two," Wrayson answered. "He reminded me of his previous warning to me to leave England for a time, and he underlined it. Louise ought to know. I want to tell her!"

"I am glad you did not tell me this before," the Baroness said, as they left the room together, "or it would have spoiled my luncheon. I do not like your friend, Mr. Heneage!"

"You will give me Louise's address?" he asked. "Some one must see her."

"I will send it you," the Baroness promised, "before the day is out."

CHAPTER XXII

THE CHÂTEAU OF ÉTARPE

"One would scarcely believe," Wrayson remarked, leaning back in his chair and drawing in a long deep breath, "that we are within three miles of one of the noisiest and most bustling of French watering places."

"It is incredible," his companion admitted.

They were seated in a garden behind the old inn of the *Lion d'Or*, in the village of St. Étarpe. Before them was a round table, on whose spotless white cloth still remained dishes of fruit and a bottle of wine - not the *vin ordinaire* which had been served with their repast, but something which Wrayson had ordered specially, and which the landlord himself, all smiles and bows, had uncorked and placed before them. Wrayson produced his cigarette case.

"How did you hear of this place?" he asked, watching the smoke curl upwards into the breathless air. "I fancy that you and I are the only guests here."

Wrayson's companion, tall, broad-shouldered, and heavily bearded, was busy filling a pipe from a pouch by his side. His features were unmistakably Saxon, and his cheeks were tanned, as though by much exposure

E. Phillips Oppenheim

to all sorts of weathers. He was still apparently on the right side of middle age, but his manners were grave, almost reserved.

"I was in the neighbourhood many years ago," he answered. "I had a fancy to revisit the place. And you?"

"I discovered it entirely by accident," Wrayson admitted. "I walked out from Chourville this morning, stayed here for some luncheon, and was so delighted that I took a room and went straight back for my bag. There isn't an emperor in Europe who has so beautiful a dining-room as this!"

Together they looked across the valley, a wonderful panorama of vine-clad slopes and meadows, starred with many-coloured wild flowers, through which the river wound its way, now hidden, now visible, a thin line of gleaming quicksilver. Tall poplars fringed its banks, and there were white cottages and farmhouses, mostly built in the shelter of the vine-covered cliffs. To the left a rolling mass of woods was pierced by one long green avenue, at the summit of which stretched the grey front and towers of the Château de St. Étarpe. Wrayson looked long at the fertile and beautiful country, which seemed to fade so softly away in the horizon; but he looked longest at the chateâu amongst the woods.

"I wonder who lives there," he remarked. "I meant to have asked the waiter."

"I can tell you," the stranger said. "The château belongs to the Baroness de Sturm."

"A Frenchwoman?" Wrayson asked.

"Half French, half Belgian. She has estates in both countries, I believe," his companion answered. "As a matter of fact, I believe that this château is hers in her own right as a daughter of the Étarpes. She married a Belgian nobleman."

"You seem well acquainted with the neighbourhood," Wrayson remarked.

"I have been here before," was the somewhat short answer.

Wrayson produced his card-case.

"As we seem likely to see something of one another during the next few days, *nolens volens*," he remarked, "may I introduce myself? My name is Wrayson, Herbert Wrayson, and I come from London."

The stranger took the card a little doubtfully.

"I am much obliged," he said. "I do not carry a card-case, but my name is Duncan."

"An Englishman, of course?" Wrayson remarked smiling.

"I am English," Mr. Duncan answered, "but I have not been in England for many years."

There was something about his manner which forbade any further questioning on Wrayson's part. The two men sat together in silence, and Wrayson, although not of a curious turn of mind, began to feel more than an ordinary interest in his companion. One thing he noticed in particular. Although, as the sun sank lower, the beauties of the landscape below increased, Duncan's eyes scarcely for a moment rested upon them. He had turned his chair a little, and he sat directly facing the chateâu. The golden cornfields, the stained-glass windows of the grey church rising like a cathedral, as it were, in the midst of the daffodil-starred meadows, caught now with the flood of the dying sunlight mingled so harmoniously with their own time-mellowed richness, the increasing perfume of the flowers by which they were surrounded, - none of these things seemed for one moment to distract his attention. Steadily and fixedly he gazed up that deep green avenue, empty indeed of any moving object, and yet seemingly not empty to him. For he had the air of one who sees beyond the world of visible objects, of one who sees things dimmed to those of only natural powers. With what figures, Wrayson wondered, idly, was he peopling that empty avenue, what were the fancies which had crept out from his brain and held him spellbound? He had admitted a more or less intimate acquaintance with the place: was he, perhaps, a former lover of the Baroness, when she had been simply Amy de St. Étarpe? Wrayson forgot, for a while, his own affairs, in following out these mild speculations. The soft twilight stole down upon them; here and there little patches of grey mist came curling up the valley. A bat came flying about their heads, and Wrayson at last rose.

"I shall take a stroll." he remarked, "and turn in. Good night, if I don't see you again!"

The man named Duncan turned his head.

"Good night!" he said, mechanically.

Wrayson walked down the garden and passed through a wicket-gate into the broad white road. Setting his back to the village, he came, in a few minutes, to the great entrance gate of the château, hung from massive stone pillars of great age, and themselves fashioned of intricate and curiously wrought ironwork. The gates themselves were closed fast, and the smaller ones on either side, intended for pedestrians, were fastened with a padlock. Wrayson stood for a moment looking through the bars into the park. The drive ran for half a mile perfectly straight, and then, taking an abrupt bend, passed upwards into the woods, amongst which was the château.

"What do you want?" an abrupt voice demanded.

Wrayson looked round in surprise. A man in gamekeeper's clothes had issued from the lodge, carrying a gun.

"Good evening!" Wrayson said. "Is it permitted for the public to enter the park?"

"By no means," was the surly answer. "Cannot monsieur see that the gates are locked?"

"I understood from the landlord of the *Lion d'Or*" Wrayson said, "that the villagers were allowed the privilege of walking in the park."

The man looked at him suspiciously.

"You are not of the village," he said.

E. Phillips Oppenheim

"I am staying there," Wrayson answered.

"It makes nothing. For the present, villagers and every one are forbidden to enter. There are visitors at the château."

Wrayson turned away.

"Very well," he said. "Good night!"

The man did not answer him. Wrayson continued to climb the hill which skirted the park. He did not turn round, but he heard the gates open, and he was convinced that he was being watched, if he was not followed. He kept on, however, until he came to some more iron gates, from which stretched the grass avenue which led straight to the gardens of the château. Dimly, through the gathering dusk, he caught a view of it, which was little more than an impression; silver grey and quiet with the peace which the centuries can bring, it seemed to him, with its fantastic towers, and imperfectly visible outline, like a palace of dreams rather than a dwelling house, however magnificent, of material stone and brick. An owl flew out from the trees a few yards to the left of him, and drifted slowly over his head, with much flapping of wings, and a weird, soft call, faintly answered in the distance by his mate; from far away down in the valley came the slow ringing of a single evening bell. Save for these things, a silence almost wonderful reigned. Gradually Wrayson began to feel that sense of soothed nerves, of inexpressible relief, which Nature alone dispenses - her one unequalled drug! All the agitation and turmoil of the last few months seemed to fall away from him. He felt that he had been living in a world of false proportions; that the maze of doubts and fears through which he had wandered was, after all, no part of life itself, merely a tissue of irrelevant issues, to which his distorted imagination had affixed a purely fictitious importance. What concern of his was it how Morris Barnes had lived or died? And who was Bentham that his fate should ever disturb him? The secrets of other people were theirs to keep. His own secret was more wonderful by far. Alone, from amidst the tangle of his other emotions, he felt its survival - more than its survival, its absolute conquest of all other feelings and considerations. It was truth, he knew, that men sought after in the quiet places, and it was the truth which he had found. If he could but see her coming down the avenue, coming to him across the daisy-strewn grass, beneath the shadow of the stately poplars! The very thought set his heart beating like a boy's. He felt the blood singing in his veins, the love-music swelling in his heart. He shook the gates. They, too, were padlocked. Then he listened. There was no sound of any footfall in the road. He moved a few steps higher up, and, making use of the pillars of the gate, he climbed on to the wall. It was a six-foot drop, but he came down noiselessly into a bed of moss. Once more he paused to listen. There was no sound save the burring of some night insect over his head. Stealthily, and keeping in the shadow of the trees, he began to climb the grassy avenue towards the château.

E. Phillips Oppenheim

CHAPTER XXIII

A PASSIONATE PILGRIM

It seemed to Wrayson, as by and by he began to make bolder and more rapid progress, that it was an actual fairy world into which he was passing with beating heart and this strange new sense of delicious excitement. As he drew nearer, the round Norman towers and immense grey front of the château began to take to themselves more definite shape. The gardens began to spread themselves out; terraced lawns, from whose flower-beds, now a blurred chaos so far as colour was concerned, waves of perfume came stealing down to him; statuary appeared, white and ghostly in the half light, and here and there startlingly lifelike; there were trimmed shrubs, and a long wall of roses trailed down from the high stone balcony. But, as yet, there was no sound or sign of human life! That was to come.

Wrayson came to a pause at last. He had passed from the shelter of the woods into a laurel walk, but further than this he could not go without being plainly visible to any one in the château. So he waited and watched. There were lights, he could see now, behind many of the ground floor windows of the chateâu, and more than once he fancied that he could catch the sound of music. He tried to fancy in which room she was, to project his passionate will through the twilight, so that she should come to him. But the curtains remained undrawn, and the windows closed. Still Wrayson waited!

Then at last Providence intervened. Above the top of the woods, over on the other side of the château, came first a faint lightening in the sky, which gradually deepened into a glow. Slowly the rim of the moon crept up, and very soon the spectral twilight was at an end. The shadowy landscape became real and vivid. It was a new splendour creeping softly into the night. Wrayson moved a little further back into his shelter, and even as he did so one of the lower windows of the château was thrown open, and two women, followed by a man, stepped out. Their appearance was so sudden that Wrayson felt his breath almost taken away. He leaned a little forward and watched them eagerly.

The woman, who was foremost of the little group, was a stranger to him, although her features, and a somewhat peculiar headdress which she wore, seemed in a sense familiar. She was tall and dark, and she carried herself with the easy dignity of a woman of rank. Her face was thoughtful and her expression sweet; if she was not actually beautiful, she was at least a woman whom it was impossible to ignore. But Wrayson glanced at her only for a minute. It was Louise who stood by her side! - the music of her voice came floating down to him. Heavens! had he ever realized how beautiful she was? He devoured her with his eyes, he strained his nerves to hear what they were saying. He was ridiculously relieved to see that the man who stood by their side was grey-headed. He was beginning to realize what love was. Jealousy would be intolerable.

E. Phillips Oppenheim

They moved about the terrace. He scarcely knew whether he hoped or feared the more that they would descend and come nearer to him. After all, it was cruelly tantalizing. He dared not disobey the Baroness, or he would have stepped boldly from his hiding-place and gone up to them. But that, by the terms of his promise, was impossible. He was to make his presence known to Louise only if he could do so secretly. He was not to accost her in the presence of any other person. It might be days or weeks before the opportunity came - or it might - it might be minutes! For, almost without warning, she was alone. The others had left her, with farewells, if any, of the briefest. She came forward to the grey stone parapet, and, with her head resting upon her hand, looked out towards the woods.

His heart began to beat faster - his brain was confused. Was there any chance that she would descend into the gardens - dare he make a signal to her? Her head and shoulders were bare, and a slight breeze had sprung up during the last few minutes. Perhaps she would feel the cold and go in! Perhaps -

He watched her breathlessly. She had abandoned her thoughtful attitude and was standing upright, looking around her. She looked once at the window. She was apparently undecided whether to go in or not. Wrayson prayed then, if he had never prayed before. He didn't know to whom! He was simply conscious of an intense desire, which seemed somehow formulated into an appeal. Before he was fully conscious of it, she was coming down the steps. She stood on the edge of the lawn for a moment, as though considering; then, carefully raising her skirts in both hands, she picked her way amongst the flower-beds, coming almost directly towards him. Glancing round, he saw her objective - a rustic seat under a dark cedar tree, and he saw, too, that she must pass within a few feet of where he stood. She walked as one dreaming, or whose thoughts are far distant, her head thrown back, her eyes half closed. The awakening, when it came, was sudden enough.

"Louise," he called to her softly, "Louise!"

She dropped her skirts. For a moment he feared that she was going to cry out.

"Who is that?" she asked sharply.

"It is I, Herbert Wrayson," he answered. "Don't be afraid. Shall I come out to you, or will you come down the laurel path?"

"You!" she murmured. "You!"

He saw the light in her face, and his voice was hoarse with passion.

"Come," he cried, "or I must fetch you! Louise! Sweetheart!"

She came towards him a little timidly, her eyebrows arched, a divine smile playing about her lips. She stood at the entrance to the laurel grove and peered a little forward.

"Where are you?" she asked. "Is it really you? I think that I am a little afraid! Oh!"

He took her into his arms with a little laugh of

E. Phillips Oppenheim

happiness. Time and life itself stood still. Her feeble remonstrances were swept away in the tide of his passion. His lips hung burning against hers.

"My sweetheart!" he murmured. "Thank God you came!"...

She disengaged herself presently. A clock from the stables was striking. She counted the hours.

"Eleven o'clock!" she exclaimed. "Herbert, how long have I been here?"

"Don't ask me that," he answered. "Only tell me how long you are going to stay."

"Not another minute, really," she declared. "They will be sending out search parties for me directly. And - Herbert - how did you get here?" she demanded anxiously.

"I climbed over the wall," he answered cheerfully. "There didn't seem to be any other way."

She seemed almost incredulous.

"Didn't you see any watchmen?" she asked.

"There was one at the gates," he answered. "I fancied he followed me up the road, but I gave him the slip all right."

"Be careful how you go back," she begged. "This place is supposed to be closely watched."

"Watched! Why?" he asked. "Are you afraid of robbers?"

"How much did the Baroness tell you?" she asked.

"Nothing, except that I should find you here," he declared. "She made me promise that I would wait for an opportunity of seeing you alone."

"And why," she asked, "have you come?"

He took her into his arms again.

"I have learnt what love is," he murmured, "and I have forgotten the other things."

"That is all very well," she laughed, smoothing out her hair; "but the other things may be very important to me."

"A man named Stephen Heneage has taken up this Barnes affair," he answered. "He saw you leave the flats that night, and he is likely, if he thinks that it might lead to anything, to give the whole show away. He warned me to get away from England and - but you want the truth, don't you? All these are excuses! I came because I wanted you! - because I couldn't live without you, Louise! Couldn't we steal away somewhere and never go back? Why need we? We could go to Paris to-morrow, catch the Orient express the next day - I know a dozen hiding-places where we should be safe enough. We will make our own world and our own life - and forget!"

"Forget!" She drew a little away from him. Her tone chilled him.

E. Phillips Oppenheim

"Herbert," she said, "whatever happens, I must go now - this moment. Where are you stopping?"

"The *Lion d'Or*," he answered, "down in the village."

"I will send a note in the morning," she said eagerly. "Only you must go now, dear. Some one will be out to look for me, and I cannot think – I must have a little time to decide. Be very careful as you go back. If you are stopped, be sure and make them understand that you are an Englishman. Good night!"

He kissed her passionately. She yielded to his embrace, but almost immediately drew herself away. He clutched at her hand, but she eluded him. With swift footsteps she crossed the lawn. Just as she reached the terrace, the windows opened once more and some one called her name.

"I am coming in now," he heard her answer. "It has been such a wonderful night!"

CHAPTER XXIV

AN INVITATION TO DINNER

The landlord of the *Lion d'Or,* who had appeared for a moment to chat with his guests while they took their morning coffee, pointed downwards into the valley, where little clouds of mist hung over the lowlands.

"The *messieurs* will find themselves hot to-day," he remarked. "Here, only, there will be a breeze. Eleven hundred feet up, and only three miles from the sea! It is wonderful, eh?"

Wrayson pointed across towards the château, whose towers rose from the bosom of the cool green woods.

"There, also," he said, "it will be very pleasant. The château is as high as we are, is it not so?"

The landlord shrugged his shoulders.

"There is little difference," he admitted, "and in the woods there is always shade. But who may go there? Never was an estate kept so zealously private, and, does monsieur know? Since yesterday a new order has been issued. The villagers were forbidden even their ancient rights of walking across the park! The head forester has posted a notice in the village."

E. Phillips Oppenheim

"I have heard something of it," Wrayson admitted. "Has any reason been given. Are the family in residence there?"

The landlord shook his head.

"Madame la Baronne was never so exacting," he replied. "One hears that she has lent the château to friends. Two ladies are there, and one gentleman. It is all."

"Do you know who they are?" Wrayson asked.

The landlord assumed an air of mystery.

"One," he said, "is a young English lady. The other - well, they call her Madame de Melbain."

"What?"

The exclamation came like a pistol-shot from Wrayson's fellow-guest at the inn, who, up to now, had taken no part in the conversation. He had turned suddenly round, and was facing the startled landlord.

"Madame de Melbain," he repeated. "Monsieur, perhaps, knows the lady?"

There was a moment's silence. Then the man who had called himself Duncan looked away, frowning.

"No!" he said, "I do not know her. The name is familiar, but there is no lady of my acquaintance bearing it at present."

The landlord looked a little disappointed.

"Ah!" he remarked, "I had hoped that monsieur would have been able to give us a little information. There are many people in the village who would like to know who this Madame de Melbain is, for it is since her coming that all has been different. The park has been closed, the peasants and farmers have received orders forbidding them to accept boarders at present, and I myself am asked - for a consideration, I admit - to receive no further guests. Naturally, we ask ourselves, monsieur, what does it mean? One does not wish to gossip, but there is much here to wonder at!"

"What is she like, this Madame de Melbain?" Duncan asked.

"No one has seen her, monsieur," the landlord answered. "She arrived in a close carriage, since when she has not passed the lodge gates. She has her own servants who wait upon her. Without doubt she is a person of some importance! Possibly, though, she is eccentric. They say that every entrance to the château is guarded, and that a cordon of men are always watching."

Wrayson laughed.

"A little exaggeration, my friend, there, eh?"

The landlord shrugged his shoulders.

"One cannot tell," he declared. "This, at least, is singular," he continued, bending forward confidentially. "Since the arrival of these two ladies several strangers have been observed about the place, some of whom have endeavoured to procure lodgings. They spoke French, but they were not Frenchmen or

Englishmen. True, this may be a coincidence, but one can never tell. Monsieur has any further commands?"

Monsieur had none, and the landlord withdrew, smiling and bowing.

Duncan leaned across the table.

"My French," he said deliberately, "is rotten. I couldn't understand half of what that fellow said. Do you mind repeating it to me?"

Wrayson did so, and his companion listened moodily. When he had finished, Duncan was gazing steadfastly over towards the château, and knocking the ashes from his pipe.

"Sounds a little feudal, doesn't it?" he remarked, drawing his pouch from his pocket. "However, I don't suppose it is any concern of yours or of mine."

Wrayson made no direct answer. He was fully conscious that his companion was watching him closely, and he affected to be deeply interested in the selection of a cigarette.

"No!" he said at last; "it is no concern of ours, of course. And yet one cannot help feeling a little interested. I noticed myself that the lodge gates of the château were rather strictly guarded."

"Very likely," the other answered. "Women of fashion who suffer from nerves take strange fancies nowadays. This Madame de Melbain is probably one of these."

Wrayson nodded.

"Very likely," he admitted. "What are you going to do with yourself all day?"

"Loaf! I am going to lie down in the fields there amongst the wild flowers, in the shade of the woods," Duncan answered; "that is, if one may take so great a liberty with the woods of madame! This sort of country rather fascinates me," he added thoughtfully. "I have lived so long in a land where the vegetation is a jungle and the flowers are exotics. There is a species of exaggeration about it all. I find this restful."

"Africa?" Wrayson asked.

The other nodded silently. He did not seem inclined to continue the conversation.

"You are the second man I have met lately who has come home from Africa," Wrayson remarked, "and you represent the opposite poles of life."

"It is very possible," Duncan admitted. "We are a polyglot lot who come from there."

"You were in the war, of course?" Wrayson asked.

"I was in the war," Duncan answered, "almost to the finish. Afterwards I went into Rhodesia, and incidentally made money. That's all I have to say about Africa. I hate the country, and I don't want to talk about it. See you later, I suppose."

He rose from his chair and stretched himself. Across the lawn the landlord came hurrying, his face perturbed and uneasy. His bow to Wrayson was subtly different. Here was perhaps an aristocrat under an assumed name, a person to be, without doubt, conciliated.

"Monsieur," he announced, with a little flourish of the white serviette which, from habit, he was carrying, "there is outside a young lady from the château who is inquiring for you."

"Which way?" Wrayson demanded anxiously.

"Monsieur will be pleased to follow me," the landlord answered.

Louise was alone in a victoria, drawn up before the front door of the inn. Wrayson saw at once that something had happened to disturb her. Even under her white veil he knew that she was pale, and that there were rings under her eyes. She leaned towards him and held out her hand in conventional manner for the benefit of the landlord, who lingered upon the steps.

"Come round to the other side of the carriage, Herbert," she said. "I have something to say to you. The coachman does not understand English. I have tried him."

Wrayson crossed behind the carriage and stood by her side.

"Herbert," she asked, anxiously, "will you do some-thing for me, something I want you to do very much?"

"If I can," he answered simply.

"You can do this," she declared. "It is very easy. I want you to leave this place this morning, go away, any-where! You can go back to London, or you can travel.

Only start this morning."

"Willingly," he answered, "on one condition."

"What is it?" she asked quickly.

"That you go with me," he declared.

She shook her head impatiently.

"You know that is not what I mean," she said reproachfully. "I was mad last night. You took me by surprise and I forgot everything. I was awake all night. This morning I can see things clearly. Nothing - of that sort - is possible between you and me. So I want you to go away!"

He shook his head, gently but firmly.

"It isn't possible, Louise," he said. "You mustn't ask me to do anything of that sort after last night. It's too late you see, dear. You belong to me now. Nothing can alter that."

"It is not too late," she answered passionately. "Last night was just an hour of madness. I shall cut it out of my life. You must cut it out of yours."

He leaned over till his head nearly touched hers, and under the holland dust-sheet which covered her knees he gripped her hand.

"I will not," he answered. "I will not go away. You belong to me, and I will have you!"

She looked at him for a moment without speech.

E. Phillips Oppenheim

Wrayson's features, more distinguished in a general way by delicacy than strength, had assumed a curiously set and dogged appearance. His eyes met hers kindly but mercilessly. He looked like a man who has spoken his last word.

"Herbert," she murmured, "there are things which you do not know and which I cannot tell you, but they stand between us! They must stand between us forever!"

"Of that," he said, "I mean to be the judge. And until you tell me what they are, I shall treat them as though they did not exist."

"I came here," she said, "to ask you, to beg you to go away."

"Then I am afraid you must write your mission down a failure," he answered doggedly, "for I refuse to go!"

Her eyes flashed at him from underneath her veil. He felt the pressure of her fingers upon his hand. He heard a little sigh - could it have been of relief?

"If I failed - " she began.

"And you have failed," he said decidedly.

"I was to bring you," she continued, "an invitation to dine to-night at the château. It is only a verbal one, but perhaps you will forgive that."

The colour streamed into his cheeks. He could scarcely believe his ears.

"Louise!" he exclaimed, "you mean it?"

"Yes!" she answered softly. "It would be better for you, better, perhaps, for me, if you would do as I ask - if you would go away and forget! But if you will not do that, there is no reason why you should not come to the château. A carriage will arrive for you at seven o'clock."

"And you will come with me again into the gardens?" he whispered passionately.

"Perhaps," she murmured.

The horses, teased by the flies, tossed their heads, and the jingling of harness reminded Louise that half the village, from various vantage points, were watching the interview between the young lady from the château and the visitor at the inn.

"I must go at once," she said to Wrayson. "About to-night, do not be surprised at anything you see at the château. I have no time to say more. If you notice anything that seems to you at all unusual, accept it naturally. I will explain afterwards."

She spoke a word to the immovable man on the box, and waved her hand to Wrayson as the horses started forward. They were round the corner in a moment, and out of sight. Wrayson turned back to the inn, but before he had taken half a dozen paces he stopped short. He had happened to glance towards the upper windows of the small hotel, and he caught a sudden vision of a man's face - a familiar face, transformed, rigid, yet with staring eyes following the departing carriage. Wrayson himself was conscious of a quick shock of surprise, followed by a sense of apprehension. What could there possibly have been in the appearance of Louise to have brought a look like that into the face of his fellow-guest?

CHAPTER XXV

THE MAN IN THE YELLOW BOOTS

The two men did not meet again until luncheon-time, Anglicized into a one-o'clock meal for their benefit. Already seated at the table they found a short fair man, in the costume of a pedestrian tourist. He wore a tweed knickerbocker suit, and a knapsack lay upon the grass by his side. As Wrayson and his fellow-guest arrived almost at the same time, the newcomer rose and bowed.

"Good morning, gentlemen!" he said. "I trust you will permit me a seat at your table. It appears to be the only one."

Duncan contented himself with a nod. Wrayson felt compelled to be a little more civil. The man certainly seemed harmless enough.

"A very delightful spot, gentlemen," he continued, "and a fine, a very fine church that in the valley. I am spending my holiday taking photographs of churches of a certain period in this vicinity. I am looking forward to explore this one."

"I am afraid," Wrayson remarked, "that I do not know much of ecclesiastical architecture, but the aesthetic

E. Phillips Oppenheim

effect of this one, at least, is very fine."

The newcomer nodded.

"You are an artist perhaps, sir?" he asked innocently.

"I hope so - in some degree," Wrayson answered.

"Every one is fundamentally an artist, I suppose, who is capable of appreciating a work of beauty."

Duncan smiled slightly to himself. So far he had not spoken.

"It is all new country to me," the newcomer continued, "but from what I have seen of it, I should think it a grand place for painters. Not much for the ordinary tourist, eh?"

"That depends," Wrayson answered, "upon the ordinary tourist."

"Exactly! Quite so!" the little man agreed. "Of course, if one wanted a quiet time, what could be better than this? There must be others who think so besides yourselves."

"Who?" Wrayson asked.

"Your fellow-guests here."

"We have no fellow-guests," Wrayson answered, a little incautiously.

The newcomer leaned back in his chair with a disconcerted look.

"Then I wonder why," he exclaimed, "the landlord told me that he had not a single room."

Wrayson bit his lip.

"I fancy," he said, "that he is not in the habit of having people stay here."

"I am afraid," the little fair man said, "that it is not an hospitable village. I tried to get a room elsewhere, but, alas! with no success. They do not seem to want tourists at St. Étarpe."

Wrayson looked at the knapsack, at the camera, and at the little man himself. He spoke English easily, and without any trace of an accent. His clothes, too, had the look of having come from an English ready-made shop. Yet there was something about the man himself not altogether British.

"I fancy the people are busy getting ready for the harvest," Wrayson remarked at last. "You will find lots of places as pretty as this along the coast."

"Perhaps so," the visitor admitted, "and yet when one has taken a fancy to a place, it seems a pity to have to leave it so soon. You couldn't speak a word to the landlord for me, sir, I suppose - you or your friend. I don't fancy he understood my French very well."

Wrayson shook his head.

"I'm afraid it wouldn't be any use," he said. "As a matter of fact, I know that he does not intend to take any more visitors. He has not the staff to deal with them."

"It is a pity," the little man said dejectedly. "I think that I must try again in the village. By the by, sir, perhaps you can tell me to whom the château there belongs?"

"Madame la Baronne de Sturm," Wrayson answered. "At least, so our host told me yesterday."

"It is a very beautiful place - very beautiful," the tourist said reverently. "I dare say there is a chapel there, too! Can one gain admission there, do you know, sir?"

Wrayson laid down his knife and fork.

"Look here," he said good-humouredly, "I'm not a guide-book, you know, and I only arrived here yesterday myself. You've reached the limit of my information. You had better try the landlord. He will tell you all that you want to know."

Duncan pushed his chair back. He had eaten very little luncheon, but he was filling his pipe preparatory to leaving the table. As soon as it began to draw, he rose and turned to Wrayson. The little tourist he absolutely ignored, as he had done all the time during the meal.

"I should like a word with you before you go out," he said.

Wrayson nodded, and followed him in a few minutes to the summer-house at the end of the lawn. Duncan did not beat about the bush.

"That little brute over there," he said, inclining his head towards the table, "is neither an Englishman nor a tourist. I have seen him before, and I never forget a face."

"What is he then?" Wrayson asked.

"Heaven knows what he is now," Duncan answered. "I saw him last at Colenso, where he narrowly escaped being shot for a spy. He is either a Dutchman or a German, and whatever he may be up to here, I'll swear ecclesiastical architecture is not his game."

There was a moment's silence. Wrayson had turned involuntarily towards the château, and Duncan had followed suit. They both looked up the broad green avenue to where the windows of the great building flashed back the sunlight. At the same moment their mutual action was realized by both of them.

Wrayson first turned away and glanced round at the table which they had just quitted. The little man, who was still seated there, had lit a cigar and was talking to the waiter. He looked back again and moved his head thoughtfully in the direction of the château.

"He asked questions about the château," Wrayson remarked. "Do you suppose that there can be anything going on there to interest him?"

"You should know better than I," Duncan answered. "You received a visit this morning from one of the two ladies who are staying there."

Wrayson turned a little pale. He looked at Duncan steadily for a moment. A giant in height, his features, too, were of a large and resolute type. His eyes were clear and truthful; his expression, notwithstanding a certain gloom which scarcely accorded with his years and apparent health, was unmistakably honest. Wrayson felt instinctively that he was to be trusted.

E. Phillips Oppenheim

"Look here," he said, "I should like to tell you the truth - as much of it as is necessary. I happen to know that the young lady with whom you saw me talking this morning, and who is a friend of the Baroness de Sturm's, is suspected in certain quarters of being implicated in a - criminal affair which took place recently in London. I myself, in a lesser degree, am also under suspicion. I came over here to warn her."

Duncan was looking very grave indeed.

"In a criminal affair," he repeated. "That is a little vague."

"I am sorry," Wrayson answered, "but I cannot very well be more explicit. The matter is one in which a good many other people are concerned, and I might add that it is a hopeless mystery to me. All I know is that a crime was committed; that this young lady was present under suspicious circumstances; that I, in certain evidence I had to give, concealed the fact of her presence; and that now a third person turns up, who also knew of the young lady's presence, but who was not called upon to give evidence, who is working on his own account to clear up the whole affair. He happens to be a friend of mine, and he warned me frankly to clear out."

"I am beginning to follow you," Duncan said thoughtfully. "Now what about Madame de Melbain?"

"I know absolutely nothing of her," Wrayson answered. "I found out where the young lady was from the Baroness de Sturm, with whom she was living in London, and I came over to warn her."

"The young lady was living with the Baroness de Sturm?" Duncan repeated. "Is she, then, an orphan?"

"No!" Wrayson answered. "She is, for some reason - I do not know why - estranged from her family. Now the question arises, has this fellow here come over to track her down? Is he an English detective?"

Duncan turned deliberately round and stared at the person whom they were discussing.

"I should doubt it very much," he answered. "For my part, I don't believe for a moment that he is an Englishman at all."

"I am very glad to hear you say so," Wrayson declared. "But the question is, if he is not on this business, what the devil is he doing here?"

"Have you the *entrée* to the chateâu?" Duncan asked abruptly.

"I am invited to dine there this evening," Wrayson answered.

"Then, if I were you," Duncan said, "I should make a point of ascertaining, if you can, the personality of this Madame de Melbain."

Wrayson nodded.

"I shall see her, of course," he said, "and I will do so."

"My own idea," Duncan said deliberately, "is that it is in connection with her presence here that the landlord of the inn and the villagers have received these

E. Phillips Oppenheim

injunctions about strangers. Try and find out what you can about her, and in the meantime I will look after the gentleman over there. He wants to be friendly - I will make a companion of him. When you come back to-night we will have another talk."

"It's awfully good of you," Wrayson said. "And now - I've one thing more to say."

Duncan nodded.

"Go on," he said.

"I have taken you into my confidence so far as was possible," Wrayson said slowly. "I am going to ask you a question now."

"I cannot promise to answer it," Duncan declared, taking up his pipe and carefully refilling it.

"Naturally! But I am going to ask it," Wrayson said. "An hour or so ago I was talking to the young lady in front of the inn, and you were watching us. I saw your face at the window as she was driving off."

"Well?"

The monosyllable was hard and dry.

"You are neither an inquisitive nor an emotional person," Wrayson said. "I am sure of that. I want an explanation."

"Of what?"

"Of your suddenly becoming both!"

Duncan had lit his pipe now, and smoked for a few moments furiously.

"I will not bandy words with you," he said at last. "You want an explanation which I cannot give."

Wrayson looked as he felt, dissatisfied.

"Look here," he said, "I'm not asking for your confidence. I'm simply asking you to explain why the sight of that young lady should be a matter of emotion to you. You know who she is, I am convinced. What else?"

Duncan shook his head.

"I'm sorry," he said. "You may trust me or not, as you like. All I can say about myself is this. I've been up against it hard - very hard. So far as regards the ordinary affairs of life I simply don't count. I'm a negation - a purely subjective personage. I may be able to help you a little here - I shall certainly never be in your way. My interest in the place - there, I will tell you that - is purely of a sentimental nature. My interest in life itself is something of the same sort. Take my advice. Let it go at that."

"I will," Wrayson declared, with sudden heartiness.

Duncan nodded.

"I'll go and look after our little friend in the yellow boots," he said.

CHAPTER XXVI

MADAME DE MELBAIN

Punctually at half-past seven the carriage arrived to take Wrayson to the château. A few minutes' drive along a road fragrant with the perfume of hay, and with the pleasant sound of the reaping machines in his ears, and the carriage turned into the park through the great iron gates, which opened this time without demur. By the side of the road was a clear trout stream, a little further away a herd of deer stood watching the carriage pass. The park was uncultivated but picturesque, becoming more wooded as they climbed the hill leading to the chateâu. Wrayson smiled to himself as he remembered that this magnificent home and estate belonged to the woman who was his neighbour at Battersea, and whom he himself had been more than half inclined to put down as an adventuress.

A major-domo in quiet black clothes, who seemed to reflect in his tone and manner the subdued splendour of the place, received him at the door, passing him on at once to a footman in powdered hair and resplendent livery. Across a great hall, whose white stone floor, height, and stained-glass windows gave Wrayson the impression that he had found his way by mistake into the nave of a cathedral, he was ushered into a drawing-room, whose modernity and comparatively low ceiling were almost a relief. Here there were books and flowers and music, some exquisite water-colours upon the white walls, newspapers and magazines lying about, which gave the place a habitable air. A great semicircular window commanded a wonderful view of the park, but Wrayson had little time to admire it. A door was opened at the further end of the room, and he heard the soft rustling of a woman's gown upon the carpet. It was Louise who came towards him.

She was dressed in white muslin, unrelieved by ornament or any suggestion of colour. Her cheeks were unusually pale, and the shadows under her eyes seemed to speak of trouble. Yet Wrayson thought that he had never seen her look more beautiful. She gave him her hand with a faint smile of welcome, and permitted him to raise it to his lips.

"This is very, very foolish," she said softly, "and I know that I ought to be ashamed of myself."

"On the contrary," he answered, "I think that it is very natural. But, seriously, I feel a little overpowered. You won't want to live always in a castle, will you, Louise?"

She sighed, and smiled, and sighed again.

"I am afraid that our castle, Herbert," she murmured, "will exist only in the air! But listen. I must speak to you before the others come in."

"I am all attention," he assured her.

"It is about Madame de Melbain," she began, a little hesitatingly.

E. Phillips Oppenheim

He waited for her to continue. She seemed to be in some difficulty.

"I want you to watch and do just what we others do," she said, "and not to be surprised if some of our arrangements seem a little curious. For instance, although she is the elder, do not give her your arm for dinner. She will go in first alone, and you must take me."

"I can assure you," Wrayson said, smiling, "that I shall make no difficulty about that."

"And she doesn't like to be talked to very much," Louise continued.

"I will humour her in that also," Wrayson promised. "She is a good sort to let me come here at all."

"She is very kind and very considerate," Louise said, "and her life has been a very unhappy one."

Wrayson moved his chair a little nearer.

"Need we talk about her any more?" he asked. "There is so much I want to say to you about ourselves."

She looked at him for a moment, a little sadly, a little wistfully.

"Ah! don't," she murmured. "Don't talk about definite things at all. For to-night - to-night only, let us drift!"

He smiled at her reassuringly.

"Don't be afraid," he said. "I am not going to ask you

any questions. I am not going to ask for any explanations. I think that we have passed all that. It is of the future I wanted to speak."

"Don't," she begged softly. "Of the past I dare not think, nor of the future. It is only the present which belongs to us."

"The present and the future," he answered firmly.

She rose suddenly to her feet, and Wrayson instinctively followed her example. They were no longer alone. Two women, who had entered by a door at the further end of the apartment, were slowly approaching them. The foremost was tall and dark, a little slim, perhaps, but with an elegant figure, and a carriage of singular dignity. Her face was youthful, and her brown eyes were soft and clear as the eyes of a girl, but her dark hair was plentifully streaked with grey, and there was about her whole appearance an air of repressed sadness.

"This is Mr. Wrayson, is it not?" she asked, in a very sweet voice, but with a strong foreign accent. "We have so few visitors that one can scarcely make a mistake. You are very welcome."

She did not offer to shake hands, and Wrayson contented himself with a low bow.

"You are very kind," he murmured.

"Monsieur le Baron," she remarked, turning to an elderly gentleman who had just entered, "will doubtless find your coming pleasant. The entertainment of three ladies must have seemed at times a little trying.

E. Phillips Oppenheim

Let me make you gentlemen known to one another, Monsieur Wrayson, Monsieur le Baron de Courcelles. And Ida," she added, turning to her companion, who had moved a few steps apart, "permit that I present to you, also, Mr. Wrayson - Mademoiselle de Courcelles."

The conversation for a moment or two followed the obvious lines. Madame de Melbain and Louise had drawn a little apart; a few remarks as to the beauty of the chateâu and its situation passed between Wrayson and the Baron. The name of its owner was mentioned, and Wrayson indicated his acquaintance with her. At the sound of her name, Madame de Melbain turned somewhat abruptly round, and seemed to be listening; but at that moment the door was thrown open, and the major-domo of the household, who had received Wrayson, announced dinner. He directly addressed Madame de Melbain.

"Madame is served," he murmured respectfully.

The little procession arranged itself as Louise had intimated. Madame de Melbain led the way, ushered by the major-domo and followed immediately by the Baron and Mademoiselle de Courcelles. Wrayson, with Louise, brought up the rear. They crossed the white flagged hall and entered an apartment which Wrayson, although his capacity for wonder was diminishing, felt himself compelled to pause and admire. It was of great height, and again the curiously shaped windows were filled with stained glass. The oak-panelled walls, black with age, were hung with portraits, sombre and yet vivid, and upon a marble pedestal at the end of the room, lifelike, and untouched by the centuries, stood a wonderful presentation of Ralph de St. Étarpe, the founder of the house, clad in the armour of his days. The dinner table, with its brilliant and modern appurtenances of flowers and plate, standing in the middle of the floor, seemed like a minute and yet startling anachronism. The brilliant patches of scarlet geranium, the deep blue livery of the two footmen, the glitter of the Venetian glass upon the table, were like notes of alien colour amongst surroundings whose chief characteristic was a magnificent restraint, and yet such dignity as it was possible to impart into the everyday business of eating and drinking was certainly manifest in the meal, which presently took its leisurely course.

Wrayson, although no one could accuse him of a lack of *savoir faire*, found himself scarcely at his ease. Madame de Melbain; erect; dignified, and beautiful, sat at the head of the table, and although she addressed a remark to each of them occasionally, she remained always unapproachable. The Baron made only formal attempts at conversation, and Mademoiselle de Courcelles was absolutely silent. Wrayson was unable to divest himself of the feeling of representing an alien presence amongst a little community drawn closely together by some mysterious tie. Louise was his only link with them, and to Louise he decided to devote himself entirely, regardless of the apparent demands of custom. His position at the table enabled him to do this, and very soon he discovered that it was precisely what was expected of him. The conversation between the others, such as it was, lapsed into German, or some kindred tongue. Wrayson found himself able presently to talk confidentially with Louise.

"Remember," he said, after a slight pause, "that I have finished altogether with the role of investigator. I no

E. Phillips Oppenheim

longer have any curiosity about anything. Still, I think that there is something which I ought to tell you."

She smiled.

"You may tell me as much as you like," she said, "as long as you don't ask questions."

"Exactly! Well, there is another Englishman staying at the *Lion d'Or*. He appears to be a decent fellow, and a gentleman. I am not going to talk about him. I imagine that he is harmless."

"We have heard of him," Louise murmured. "It certainly appears as though he were only an ordinary tourist. Has any one else arrived?"

"Yes!" Wrayson answered, "some one else has arrived, and I want to tell you about him."

Louise was obviously disturbed. She refused a course a little impatiently, and turned towards Wrayson anxiously.

"But the landlord," she said in a low tone, "has orders to receive no more guests."

"This man arrived to luncheon to-day," Wrayson answered. "The landlord could not refuse him that. He wished for a room and was told that he could not be taken in."

"Well, who is he, what is he like?" she demanded.

"He is a miserable sort of bounder - an imitation cockney tourist, with ready-made English clothes, a knapsack, and a camera. I should have felt suspicious about him myself, but the other fellow whom I told you about, who is staying at the inn, recognized him. He had seen him abroad, and what he told me seems decisive. I am afraid that he is a spy."

Wrayson cursed himself for a moment that he had been so outspoken, for the girl by his side seemed almost on the point of collapse. Her eyes were full of fear, and she clutched at the tablecloth as though overcome with a spasm of terror.

"Don't be alarmed," Wrayson whispered in her ear. "I am sure, I am quite sure that he is not here for what you may fear. I don't believe he is an Englishman at all."

The girl recovered herself amazingly.

"I was not thinking of myself," she said quietly; and Wrayson noticed that her eyes were fixed upon the pale, distinguished face of the woman who sat with a certain air of isolation at the head of the table.

E. Phillips Oppenheim

CHAPTER XXVII

THE SPY

Wrayson found himself a few minutes later alone with the Baron, who, with some solemnity, rose and took the chair opposite to him. Conversation between them, however, languished, for the Baron spoke only in monosyllables, and his attitude gave Wrayson the idea that he viewed his presence at the chateâu with disfavour. With stiff punctiliousness, he begged Wrayson to try some wonderful Burgundy, and passed a box of cigarettes. He did not, however, open any topic of conversation, and Wrayson, embarrassed in his choice of subjects by the fact that any remark he could make might sound like an attempt at gratifying his curiosity, remained also silent. In a very few minutes the Baron rose.

"You will take another glass of wine, sir?" he asked.

Wrayson rose too with alacrity, and bowed his refusal. They recrossed the great hall and entered the drawing-room. Louise and Madame de Melbain were talking earnestly together in a corner, and from the look that the latter threw at him as they entered, Wrayson was convinced that in some way he was concerned with the subject of their conversation. It was a look deliberate and scrutinizing, in a sense doubtful, and yet not unkindly. Behind it all, Wrayson felt that there was something which he could not understand, there was something of the mystery in those dark sad eyes which seemed to pervade the whole atmosphere of the place and the lives of these people.

Louise rose as he approached and motioned him to take her vacated place.

"Madame de Melbain would like to talk to you for a few moments," she said quietly. "Afterwards will you come on to the terrace?"

She swept away through the open window, and was at once followed by the Baron. Mademoiselle de Courcelles was playing very softly on a grand piano in an unseen corner of the apartment. Wrayson and his hostess were alone.

She turned towards him with a faint smile. She spoke with great deliberation, but very clearly, and there was in her voice some hidden quality, indefinable in words, yet both musical and singularly attractive.

"I shall not keep you very long, Mr. Wrayson," she said. "Louise has been talking to me about you. She is happy, I think, to have found a friend so chivalrous and so discerning."

Wrayson smiled doubtfully as he answered.

"It is very little that I have been able to do for her," he said. "My complaint is that she will not give me the opportunity of doing more."

"You are too modest," Madame de Melbain said

E. Phillips Oppenheim

slowly. "Louise has told me a good deal. I think that you have been a very faithful friend."

Wrayson bowed but said nothing. If Madame de Melbain had anything to say to him, he preferred to afford her the opportunity of an attentive silence.

"Louise and I," Madame de Melbain continued, "were school friends. So you see that I have known her all my life. She has had her troubles, as I have! Only mine are a righteous judgment upon me, and hers she has done nothing to deserve. It is the burden of others which she fastens upon her back."

Wrayson felt instinctively that his continued silence was what she most desired. She was speaking to him, but her eyes had travelled far away. It was as though she had come into touch with other and greater things.

"Louise has not told me everything," she continued. "There is much that she will not confess. So it is necessary, Mr. Wrayson, that I ask you a question. Do you care for her?"

"I do!" Wrayson answered simply.

"You wish to marry her?"

"To-morrow, if she would!"

Madame de Melbain leaned a little forward. Her cheeks were still entirely colourless, but some spark of emotion glittered in her full dark eyes.

"You will be alone with her presently. Try and persuade her to marry you at once. There is nothing but an absurd scruple between you! Remember that always."

"It is a scruple which up till now has been too strong for me," Wrayson remarked quietly.

She measured him with her eyes, as though making a deliberate estimate of his powers.

"A man," she said, "should be able to do much with the woman whom he cares for - the woman who cares for him."

"If I could believe that," he murmured.

She shrugged her shoulders slightly. He understood the gesture.

"You are right," he declared, with more confidence. "I will do my best."

She moved her head slowly, a sign of assent, also of dismissal. He rose to his feet.

"Louise is on the terrace," she said. "Will you give me your arm? The Baron is there also. We will join them."

They stepped through the high French windows on to the carpeted terrace. It seemed to Wrayson that they had passed into a veritable land of enchantment. The service of dinner had been a somewhat leisurely affair, and the hour was already late. The moon was slowly rising behind the trees, but the landscape was at present wrapped in the soft doubtful obscurity of a late twilight. The flowers, with whose perfume the air was faintly fragrant, remained unseen, or visible only in blurred outline; the tall trees, whose tops were unstirred by even the slightest breeze, stood out like silent sentinels against the violet sky. Madame de Melbain stopped short upon the threshold of the terrace, with head slightly thrown back, and half-closed eyes.

"Suzanne was right," she murmured, "there is peace here - peace, if only it would last!"

The Baron came hastily forward. He seemed to be eyeing Wrayson a little doubtfully. Madame de Melbain pointed down the avenue.

"I think," she said, "that it would be pleasant to walk for a little way. Give me your arm, Baron. We will go first. Mr. Wrayson will follow with Louise."

They descended the steps, crossed the lawn, and through a gate into the broad grass-grown avenue, cut through the woods to the road. Wrayson at first was silent, and Louise seemed a little nervous. More than once she started at the sound of a rabbit scurrying through the undergrowth. There was something a little mysterious about the otherwise profound silence of the impenetrable woods. Even their footsteps fell noise-lessly upon the spongy turf.

Wrayson spoke at last. They had fallen sufficiently far behind the others to be out of earshot.

"Do you know what Madame de Melbain has been saying to me?" he asked.

Louise turned her head a little. There was the faintest flicker of a smile about her lips.

"I cannot imagine", she declared, looking once more straight ahead.

"She has been inciting me to bold deeds," Wrayson said. "How should you like to be carried off in mediaeval fashion - married, willing or unwilling?"

"Is that what Madame de Melbain has been recommending you to do?" she asked.

He nodded.

"Yes! And I am thinking of taking her advice," he said coolly.

She laughed quietly, yet his ears were quick, and he caught the note of sadness which a moment later crept into her eyes.

"It would solve so much that is troublesome, wouldn't it?" she remarked. "May I ask if that has been the sole topic of your conversation?"

"Absolutely! Louise! Dear!"

She turned a little towards him. His voice was compelling. The fingers of her hand closed readily enough upon his, and the soft touch thrilled him.

"You have some fancy in your brain," he said, in a low, passionate whisper. "It is nothing but a fancy, I am assured. You have heard what your own friend has advised. You don't doubt that I love you, Louise, that I want to make you happy."

She leaned a little towards him. A sudden wave of

abandonment seemed to have swept over her. He drew her face to his and kissed her with a sudden passion. Her lips met his soft and unresisting. Already he felt the song of triumph in his heart. She was his! She could never be anybody else's now. Very softly she disengaged herself. The other two were still in sight, and already the curve of the moon was creeping over the trees.

"Don't spoil it," she murmured. "Don't talk of to-morrow, or the future! We have to-night."...

There followed minutes of which he took no count, and then of a sudden her hand clutched his arm.

"Listen," she whispered hoarsely.

He came suddenly down to earth. They were walking in the shadow of the trees, close to the side of the wood, and their footsteps upon the soft turf were noiseless. Wrayson almost held his breath as he leaned towards the dark chaos of the thickly planted trees. Only a few yards away he could distinctly hear the dry snapping of twigs. Some one was keeping pace with them inside the wood, now he could see the stooping figure of a man creeping stealthily along. A little exclamation broke from Louise's lips.

"It is a spy after all," she muttered. "They said that every entrance to the place was guarded."

Wrayson had time to take only one quick step towards the wood, when a shrill cry rang out upon the still night. Then there was the trampling under foot of bushes and undergrowth, the sound of men's voices, one English and threatening, the other guttural and terrified. Madame de Melbain and her escort had paused and were looking back. Louise was moving towards them, and Wrayson was on the point of entering the wood. Into the little semicircle formed by these four people there suddenly strode Wrayson's friend from the inn, grasping by the collar a shrinking and protesting figure in a much dishevelled tweed suit.

"We were right, Mr. Wrayson," the former remarked quietly. "This fellow has been spying round all day. You had better ask your friends what they wish done with him."

E. Phillips Oppenheim

CHAPTER XXVIII

THE SCENE IN THE AVENUE

There followed a few minutes of somewhat curious silence. At the first sound of the voice of the man who had made so startling an appearance in their midst, a cry, only half suppressed, had broken from Madame de Melbain's lips. She had moved impulsively a little forward; the moon, visible now from over the tree tops, was shining faintly upon her absolutely colourless face and dilated eyes. For some reason she seemed terror-stricken, both she and Louise, who was clinging now to her arm. Neither of them seemed even to have glanced at the cowering figure of the man, who had relapsed now into a venomous silence. Both of them were gazing at his captor, and upon their faces was the strangest expression which Wrayson had ever seen on any human features. It was as though they stood upon the edge of the world and peered downwards, into the forbidden depths; as though they suddenly found themselves in the presence of a thing so wonderful that thought and speech alike were chained. Wrayson involuntarily followed the direction of their rapt gaze. The stranger certainly presented a somewhat formidable appearance. He was standing upon slightly higher ground, and the massive proportions of his tall, powerful figure stood out with almost startling distinctness against the empty background. His face was half in the shadow, yet it seemed to Wrayson that some touch of the mystery which was quivering in the drawn face of the two women was also reflected in his dimly seen features. Something indefinable was in the air, something so mysterious and wonderful, that voices seemed stricken dumb, and life itself suspended. An owl flew slowly out from the wood with ponderous flapping of wings, and sailed over their heads. Every one started: Madame de Melbain gave a half-stifled shriek. The strain was over. Louise and she were half sobbing now in one another's arms.

"I will leave this fellow to be dealt with as the owners of the chateâu may direct," the stranger said stiffly, turning to Wrayson. "You can tell them all that we know about him."

He turned on his heel, but the Baron laid his hand upon his shoulder and peered into his face inquisitively.

"*We* should like to know," he said, "whom we have to thank for the capture of this intruder!"

"I am a stranger here, and to all of you," was the quiet answer. "You owe me no thanks. I have seen something of this fellow before," he added, pointing to his captive, who was now standing sullenly in the centre of the group. "I felt sure that he was up to no good, and I watched him."

For the first time the fair-haired little tourist, who had been dragged so submissively into their midst, suffered a gleam of intelligence to appear in his face. He changed his position so that he could see his captor better.

E. Phillips Oppenheim

"Ah!" he muttered, "you have seen me before, eh? And I you, perhaps! Let me think! Was it -"

Wrayson's friend leaned a little forwards, and with the careless ease of one flicking away a fly, he struck the speaker with the back of his hand across the face. The blow was not a particularly severe one, but its victim collapsed upon the turf.

"Look here," his assailant said, standing for a moment over him, "you can go on and finish your sentence if you like. I only want to warn you, that if you do, I will break every bone in your body, one by one, the next time we meet. Go on, if you think it worth while."

The man on the ground was dumb, because he was afraid. But the same thought presented itself to all of them. The Baron, who was least of all affected, expressed it.

"Perhaps, sir," he said, "you will not object to telling me - the Baron de Courcelles - whom we have to thank for the discovery of this - intruder!"

Wrayson's friend edged a little away. There was no response in his manner to the courtesy with which the Baron had sought to introduce himself.

"You have nothing to thank me for," he said shortly. "My name would be quite unknown to you, and I am leaving this part of the world at once. Permit me to wish you good evening!"

He had already turned on his heel when Madame de Melbain's voice arrested him. Clear and peremptory, the first words which had passed her lips since the surprise had come to them, seemed somehow to introduce a new note into an atmosphere from which an element of tragedy had never been lacking.

"Please stop!"

He turned and faced her with obvious unwillingness. She stretched out her hand as though forbidding him to go, but addressed at the same time the two men, apparently gamekeepers, who had suddenly emerged from the wood.

"Monsieur Robert," she said, "we have caught this man trespassing in the woods here, notwithstanding the precautions which I understood you had taken. Take him away at once, if you please. I trust that you will be able to hand him over to the gendarmes."

Monsieur Robert, the steward of the estates, an elderly man, whose face was twitching with anxiety, stepped forward with a low bow.

"Madame," he said, "we had word of this intrusion. We were even now upon the track of this ruffian. There was another, also, who climbed the wall - ah! I see him! The Englishman there!"

"He is our friend," Madame de Melbain said. "You must not interfere with him."

"As Madame wills! Come, you rascal," he added, gripping his prisoner by the shoulder. "We will show you what it means to climb over walls and trespass on the estate of Madame la Baronne. Come then!"

The intruder accepted the situation with the most

philosophic calm. Only one remark he ventured to make as he was led off.

"It is not hospitable, this! I only wished to see the chateâu by moonlight!"

Wrayson's fellow guest at the *Lion d'Or* turned to follow them.

"The fellow might try to escape," he muttered; but again Madame de Melbain called to him.

"You must not go away," she said, "yet!"

Then she moved forward with smooth, deliberate footsteps, yet with something almost supernatural in her white face and set, dilated eyes. It was as though she were looking once more through the windows of the world, as though she could see the figures of dead men playing once more their part in the game of life. And she looked always at the Englishman.

"Listen," she said, "there is something about you, sir, which I do not understand. Who are you, and where do you come from?"

He made no answer. Only he held out his hand as though to keep her away, and drew a little further back.

"You shall not escape," she continued, the words leaving her lips with a sort of staccato incisiveness, crisp and emotional. "No! you are here, and you shall answer. Who are you who come here to mock us all; because it is a dead man who speaks with your voice, and looks with your eyes? You will not dare to say that you are Duncan Fitzmaurice!"

The figure in the shadows seemed to loom larger and larger. He was no longer shrinking away.

"I know nothing of the man of whom you speak!" he declared. "I am a wanderer. I have no name and no home."

Madame de Melbain reeled and would have fallen. Then for a moment events seemed to leap forward. White and fainting, she lay in the arms of the man who had sprung to her succour, yet through her half-opened eyes there flashed a strange and wonderful light - a light of passionate and amazing content. He held her, almost roughly, for several moments, yet his lips were pressed to hers with a tenderness almost indescribable. No one of the little group moved. Wrayson felt simply that events, impossible for him to understand, had marched too quickly for him. He stood like a man in a dream, whose limbs are rigid, whose brain alone is working. And the others, too, seemed to have become part of a silent and wonderful tableau. For years after Wrayson carried with him the memory of those few minutes, - the perfume from the woods, faint but penetrating; the shadowy light, the passionate faces of the man and the woman, the woman yielding to a beautiful dream, and the man to a moment of divine madness. Movement, when it came, came from the principal actors in that wonderful scene. Madame de Melbain was alone, supported in Louise's arms, the Englishman's heavy footsteps were already audible, crashing through the undergrowth. Louise pointed to the wood and called out to Wrayson:

"Follow him! Don't let him out of your sight! Quick!"

Wrayson turned and sped down the avenue. When he

E. Phillips Oppenheim

reached the wall, he stood there and waited. Presently Duncan came crashing through the wood and vaulted the wall. Wrayson met him in the middle of the hard white road.

"We will walk back to the *Lion d'Or* together," he said calmly, "I have a few things to say to you!"

CHAPTER XXIX

A SUBSTANTIAL GHOST

Monsieur Jules, of the *Lion d'Or,* was in a state of excitement bordering upon frenzy. Events were happening indeed with him, this placid August weather. First the occupancy of the château by the mysterious lady, and the subsequent edict of the steward against all strangers; then the coming of this tourist yesterday, who had gone for an evening stroll without paying his bill, and was now a prisoner of the law, Heaven only knew on what charge! Added to this - a matter of excitement enough surely - the giant Englishman, who had been his guest for nearly three weeks - a model guest too, - had departed at a minute's notice, though not, the saints be praised, without paying his bill. And now, though the hour was yet scarcely nine o'clock, a carriage with steaming horses was standing at his door, and the beautiful young English lady was herself inside his inn. He was indeed conducting her down the grey stone passage out on to the rose-bordered garden, which was the pride of his heart, and where monsieur, the remaining Englishman, was smoking his morning cigarette.

She barely waited until Monsieur Jules had bowed himself out of hearing distance. She looked at Wrayson, at the table laid for one only, and at the

E. Phillips Oppenheim

empty garden.

"Where is he - your friend?" she demanded breathlessly.

"Gone," Wrayson answered. "I am sorry, but I did my best. He went away at daylight. I saw him off, but I could not keep him."

"Where to?" she asked. "You know that, at least."

He pointed towards the distant coast line.

"In that direction! That is all I know."

"He told you nothing before he went?" she asked eagerly.

"Nothing at all," he answered. "He refused to discuss what had happened. Sit down, Louise," he added firmly. "I want to talk to you."

He placed a chair for her under the trees. She sank into it a little wearily.

"A certain measure of ignorance," he said, "I am willing to put up with, but when you exhibit such extraordinary interest in another man, I really feel that my limit has been reached. Who is he, Louise? You must tell me, please!"

"I wish I could tell you," she answered. "I wish I could say that I knew. Half the night the three of us have talked and wondered. I have heard plenty of theories as to a second life on some imaginary planet, but I never heard of the dead who lived again here, in this world!"

He looked puzzled.

"Do you mean," he asked, "that he was like some one whom you believed to be dead?"

She was silent for a moment. The sun was hot even where they sat, but he fancied that he saw her shiver. She looked into his face, and something of the terror of the night before was in her eyes.

"To us," she said slowly, "to Madame de Melbain and to me, he was a ghost, an actual apparition. He spoke to us with the voice of one whom we know to be dead. He came to us, in his form."

Wrayson looked across at her with a quiet smile.

"There was nothing of the ghost about Duncan!" he remarked. "I should consider him a remarkably substantial person. Don't you think that we were all a little overwrought last night? A strong likeness and a little imagination will often work wonders."

"If it was a likeness only," she said, "why did he leave us so abruptly, why has he left this place at a moment's notice to avoid us?"

Wrayson was silent for a few seconds.

"Look here," he said, "this is a matter of common sense after all. If you were *not* deceived by a likeness, it was the man himself! That goes without saying. What reasons had you for supposing that he was dead?"

"The newspapers, the War Office, even the return of

E. Phillips Oppenheim

his effects."

"From where?" Wrayson asked.

"From South Africa. He was shot through the lungs in Natal!"

"Men have turned up before, after having been reported dead," he remarked sententiously.

"But he was in the army," she replied. "Don't you see that if he was alive now, he would be a deserter. He has never rejoined. He was certified as having died in the hospital at Ladysmith!"

Wrayson looked steadily into her agitated face.

"Supposing," he said, "that he turned out to be the man whom you have in your mind, what is he to you?"

"My brother," she answered simply.

Wrayson's first impulse was of surprise. Then he drew a long breath of relief. He looked back upon his long hours of anxiety, and cursed himself for a fool.

"What an idiot I have been!" he declared. "Of course, I know that you lost a brother in South Africa. But - but what about Madame de Melbain?"

"Madame de Melbain and my brother were friends," she said quietly. "There were obstacles or they would have been more than friends."

Wrayson nodded.

"Now supposing," he said, "that, by some miracle, your brother still lived, that this was he, is there any reason why he should avoid you both?"

She thought for a moment.

"Yes!" she said slowly, "there is."

"I suppose," he continued tentatively, "you couldn't tell me all about it?"

"I couldn't," she answered. "It isn't my secret."

Wrayson looked for a moment away from her, across the valley with its flower-spangled meadows, parted by that sinuous poplar-fringed line of silver, the lazy, slow-flowing river stealing through the quiet land to the sea. The full summer heat was scarcely yet in the air, but already a faint blue haze was rising from the lowlands. Up on the plateau, where they were sitting, a slight breeze stirred amongst the trees; Monsieur Jules had indeed some ground for his pride in this tiny sylvan paradise.

"I think," he said, "that for one day we will forget all this tangle of secrets and unaccountable doings. What do you say, Louise?" he whispered, taking her unresisting hand into his. "May I tell Monsieur Jules to serve breakfast for two in the arbour there?"

She laughed softly into his face. There was the look in her eyes which he loved to see, half wistful, half content, almost happy.

"But you are never satisfied," she declared. "If I give

E. Phillips Oppenheim

you a day, a whole precious day out of my valuable life -"

"They belong to me, all of them," he declared, bending over her till his lips touched her cheek. "Some day I am very sure that I shall take them all into my charge."

She disengaged herself from his embrace with a sudden start. Wrayson turned his head. Within a yard or two of them, Madame de Melbain had paused in the centre of the little plot of grass. She was looking at them from underneath her lace parasol, with faintly uplifted eyebrows, and the dawn of a smile upon her beautiful lips. Louise sprang to her feet, and Wrayson followed her example. Madame de Melbain lowered her parasol as though to shut out the sight of the two.

"May I come on?" she asked. "I want to speak to Louise, althou gh I am afraid I am shockingly *de trop.*"

Wrayson had an idea, and acted upon it promptly.

"Madame de Melbain," he said, "I believe that you have some influence with Louise, I am sure that you are one of those who sympathize with the unfortunate. Can't I bespeak your good offices?"

She lowered her parasol to the ground, and leaned a little forward upon it. Her eyes were fixed steadily upon Wrayson.

"Go on," she said briefly.

"I love Louise," Wrayson said, "and I believe she cares for me.

Nevertheless, she refuses to marry me, and will give no intelligible reason. My first meeting with her was of an extraordinary nature. I assisted her to leave a house in which a murder had been committed, since which time I think we have both run a risk of trouble with the authorities. Louise lives always in the shadow of some mystery, and when I, who surely have the right to know her secrets, beg for her confidence, she refuses it."

"And what is it that you wish me to do?" Madame de Melbain asked softly.

"To use your influence with Louise," Wrayson pleaded. "Let her give me her confidence, and let her accept from me the shelter of my name."

Madame de Melbain was silent for several moments. She seemed to be thinking. Louise's face was expressionless. She had made one attempt to check Wrayson, but recognizing its futility she had at once abandoned it. From below in the valley came the faint whir of the reaping machines, from the rose garden a murmur of bees. But between the two women and the man there was silence - silence which lasted so long that Monsieur Jules, who was watching from a window, called softly upon all the saints of his acquaintance to explain to him of what nature was this mystery, which seemed to be developing, as it were, under his own surveillance.

At last Madame de Melbain appeared to come to a decision. She moved slowly forward, until she stood within a few feet of him. Then she raised her eyes to his and looked him long and earnestly in the face.

E. Phillips Oppenheim

"You look," she said, half under her breath, "like a man who might be trusted. I will trust you. I will be kinder to you than Louise, for I will tell you all that you want to know. But when I have told you, you will have in your keeping the honour of an unfortunate woman whose name alone is great."

Wrayson looked her for a moment in the eyes. Then he bowed low.

"Madame," he said, "that trust will be to me my most sacred possession."

She smiled at him faintly, nodding her head as though to keep pace with her thoughts.

"I believe you, Mr. Wrayson," she said. "Yes, I believe you! Let me tell you this, then. I count it amongst my misfortunes that my own troubles have become in so large a manner the troubles of my friends. You will appreciate that the more, perhaps, when I tell you that Madame de Melbain is not the name by which I am generally known. I am that unfortunate woman the Queen of Mexonia!"

CHAPTER XXX

THE QUEEN OF MEXONIA

Wrayson, who had been prepared for something surprising, was yet startled out of his composure. The affairs of the unhappy Royal House of Mexonia were the property of the world. He half rose to his feet, but Madame de Melbain instantly waved him back again.

"My friends," she said, "deem it advisable that my whereabouts should not be known. I certainly am very anxious that my incognita should be preserved."

She paused, and Wrayson, without hesitation, answered her unspoken question. Unconsciously, too, he found himself using the same manner of address as the others.

"Madame," he said, "whatever you choose to tell me will be sacred."

She bowed her head slightly.

"I am going to tell you a good deal," she said, glancing across at Louise.

Louise opened her lips as though about to intervene.

E. Phillips Oppenheim

Madame de Melbain continued, however, without a break.

"I am going to tell you more than may seem necessary," she said, "because I believe that I am one of those unfortunate persons whose evil lot it is to bring unhappiness upon their friends. So far as I can avoid this, Mr. Wrayson, I mean to. Further - it is possible that I may ask you - presently - to render me a service."

Wrayson bowed low. He felt that she was already well aware of his willingness.

"First, then, let me tell you," she continued, leaning back in her chair, and looking away across the valley with eyes whose light was wholly reminiscent, "that we three were schoolgirls together, Louise, Amy – whom you know better, perhaps, as the Baroness de Sturm - and myself. We were at a convent near Brussels. There were not many pupils, and we three were friends....

"We had a great deal of liberty - more liberty, perhaps, than our friends would have approved of. We worked, it is true, in the mornings, but in the afternoons we rode or played tennis in the Bois. It was there that I met Prince Frederick, who afterwards became my husband.

"I was only sixteen years old, and just as silly, I suppose, as a girl brought up as I had been brought up was certain to be. I was very much flattered by Prince Frederick's attentions, and quite ready to respond to them. My own family was noble, and the match was not considered a particularly unequal one, for though

Frederick was of the Royal House, he was a long way from the succession. Still, there was a good deal of trouble when a messenger from Frederick went to my father. He declared that I was altogether too young; my mother, on the other hand, was just as anxious to conclude the match. Eventually it was arranged that the betrothal should take place in six months - and Frederick went back to Mexonia."

Madame de Melbain paused for a moment. Wrayson felt, from her slightly altered attitude and a significant lowering of her voice, that she was reaching the part of her narrative which she found the most difficult.

"We girls," she continued, "went back to school, and just at that time Louise's brother came over to Brussels. I think that I have already told you that the supervision over us was far from strict. There was nothing to prevent Captain Fitzmaurice being a good deal with us. We had picnics, tennis parties, rides! Long before the six months were up I understood how foolish I had been. I wrote to Prince Frederick and begged him to release me from our uncompleted engagement. His answer was to appear in person. He made a scene. My mother and father were now wholly on his side. Within a few weeks he had lost both a cousin and a brother. His succession to the throne was almost a certainty. His own people were just as anxious to have him married. I did not know why then, but I found out later on. They had their way. I believe that things are different in an English home. In mine, I can assure you that I never had any chance. I entered upon my married life without the least possibility of happiness. Needless to say, I never realized any! For the last four years my husband has been trying for a divorce! Very soon it is possible that he will succeed."

E. Phillips Oppenheim

Wrayson leaned a little towards her.

"Is it permitted, Madame, to ask a question?"

"Why not?"

"You have fought against this divorce, you and your friends, so zealously. Yet your life has been unhappy. Release could scarcely have been anything but a relief to you!"

Madame de Melbain raised her head slightly. Her brows were a little contracted. From her eyes there flashed the silent fire of a queen's disdain.

"Release! Yes, I would welcome that! If it were death it would be very welcome! But divorce - he to divorce me, he, whose brutality and infidelities are the scandal of every Court in Europe! No! A divorce I never shall accept. Separation I have insisted upon."

Wrayson hesitated for a moment.

"May I be pardoned," he said, "if I repeat to you what I saw in print lately - in a famous English paper? They spoke of this divorce case which has lasted so long; they spoke of it as about to be finally decided. There was some fresh evidence about to be produced, a special court was to be held."

Madame de Melbain turned, if possible, a shade paler.

"Yes!" she said slowly, "I have heard of that. We have all heard of that. I want to tell you, Mr. Wrayson, what that fresh evidence consists of."

Wrayson bowed and waited. Somehow he felt that he was on the eve of a great discovery.

"Both before my marriage and afterwards," Madame de Melbain said quietly, "I wrote to - Captain Fitzmaurice. I was always impulsive - when I was younger, and my letters, especially one written on the eve of my marriage, would no doubt decide the case against me. Captain Fitzmaurice was killed - in Natal, but in a mysterious way news has reached me of the letters since his death."

"In what way?" Wrayson asked.

For the first time, Madame de Melbain glanced a little nervously about her. Against listeners, however, they seemed absolutely secure. There was no hiding-place, nor any one within sight. Upon the land was everywhere the silence of a great heat. Even in the shade where they sat the still air was hot and breathless. Down in the valley the cows stood knee deep in the stream, and a blue haze hung over the vineyards.

"Nearly eighteen months ago," Madame de Melbain continued, "I received a letter signed by the name of Morris Barnes. The writer said that he had just arrived from South Africa, and had picked up on one of the battlefields there a bundle of letters, which he had come to the conclusion must have been written by me. He did not mince matters in the least. He was a blackmailer pure and simple. He had given me the first chance of buying these letters! What was my offer?"

A sharp ejaculation broke from Wrayson's lips. Louise signed to him to be silent.

E. Phillips Oppenheim

"Amy was with me when the letters came," Madame de Melbain continued. "She left at once for England to see this man. The sum he demanded was impossible. All that she could do was to ask for time, and to arrange to pay him so much a month whilst we were considering how to raise the money. He accepted this, and promised to keep silence. He kept his word, but for a time only. He made inquiries, and he seems to have come to the conclusion that the money was on the other side. At any rate, he approached the advisers of my husband. He was in treaty with them for the letters - when he - when he met with his death!"

Wrayson had a feeling that the heat was becoming intolerable. He dared not look at Louise. His eyes were fixed upon the still expressionless face of the woman whose story was slowly unfolding its tragic course.

"A rumour of this," Madame de Melbain continued, "reached us in Mexonia! I telegraphed to Amy! She and Louise were at their wits' ends. Louise decided to go and see this man Barnes, to make her way, if she could, into his flat, to search for and, if she could find them, to steal these letters. She carried out her purpose or rather her attempted purpose. The rest you know, for it was you who saved her!"

"The man," Wrayson said hoarsely, "was murdered."

Madame de Melbain inclined her head.

"So I have understood," she remarked.

"He was murdered," Wrayson continued in a harsh, unnatural voice, "on that very night, the night when he was to have made over these letters to your - enemies!

The message was telephoned to me! He was to go to the Hotel Francis. He was warned that there was danger. And there was! He was murdered - while the cab waited - to take him there!"

Her eyes held his - she did not flinch.

"The man who telephoned to me - Bentham his name was, the agent of your enemies, - he, too, was murdered!"

"So I have heard," she said calmly.

"The letters!" he faltered. "Where are they?"

"No one knows," she answered. "That is why I live always on the brink of a volcano. Many people are searching for them. No one as yet has succeeded. But that may come at any moment."

"Madame," he said, "can you tell me who killed these men?"

She raised her eyebrows.

"I cannot," she answered coldly.

"Madame," he declared, "the man Barnes was a pitiful blackmailing little Jew! For all I know, he deserved death a dozen times over - ay, and Bentham too! But the law does not look upon it like that. Whoever killed these men will assuredly be hanged if they are caught. Don't you think that your friends are a little too zealous?"

She met his gaze unflinchingly.

E. Phillips Oppenheim

"If friends of mine have done these things," she said, "they are at least unknown to me!"

He drew a short choking breath of relief. Yet even now the mystery was deeper than ever! He began to think out loud.

"A friend of yours it must have been," he declared. "Barnes was murdered when in a few hours he would have parted with those letters to your enemies; Bentham was murdered when he was on the point of discovering them! There is some one working for you, guarding you, who desires to remain unknown. I wonder!"

He stopped short. A sudden illumining idea flashed through his mind. He looked at Madame de Melbain fixedly.

"This man Duncan who has disappeared so suddenly," he said thickly. "Whom did you say - who was it that he reminded you of?"

Madame de Melbain lost at last her composure. She was white to the lips, her eyes seemed suddenly lit with a horrible dread. She pushed out her hands as though to thrust it from her.

"He was killed!" she cried. "It was not he! He is dead! Don't dare to speak of anything so horrible!"

Then, before they could realize that he was actually amongst them, he was there. They heard only a crashing of boughs, the parting of the hedge. He was there on his knees, with his arms around the terrified woman who had sobbed out his name. Louise, too, swayed upon her feet, her fascinated eyes fixed upon the newcomer. Wrayson understood, then, that in some way this man had indeed come back from the dead.

E. Phillips Oppenheim

CHAPTER XXXI

RETURNED FROM THE TOMB

The intervention which a few seconds later abruptly terminated an emotional crisis was in itself a very commonplace one. Monsieur the proprietor deemed the moment advisable for solving a question which was beginning to distract his better half in the kitchen. He advanced towards them, all smiles and bows and gestures.

"Monsieur would pardon his inquiring - would Monsieur and the ladies be taking *dejeuner?* A fowl of excellence unusual was then being roasted, the salad - Monsieur could see it growing! And Madame had thought of an omelet! There was no cooler place in all France on a day of heat so extraordinary as the table under the trees yonder. And as for strawberries - well, Monsieur could see them grow for himself! Or if it was *fraises de Bois* that Madame preferred, the children had brought in baskets full only that morning, fresh and juicy, and of a wonderful size."

Wrayson interrupted him at last.

"Let luncheon be served as you suggest," he directed. "In the meantime -"

Monsieur Jules understood and withdrew with more bows and smiles. The significance of his brief appearance upon the lawn was a thing of which he had not the least idea. Yet after his departure, the strain to a certain extent had passed away. Only Madame de Melbain's eyes seemed scarcely to leave the face of the man who stood still by her chair.

"Alive!" she murmured, grasping his hand in hers. "You alive!"

Louise had taken his other hand. He was imprisoned between the two.

"Yes!" he said, "I made what they called a wonderful recovery. I suppose it was almost a miracle."

"But your death," Louise declared, "was never contradicted."

"A good deal of news went astray about that time," he remarked grimly. "I was left, and forgotten. When I found what had been done, I let it go. It seemed to me to be better. I went up to Rhodesia, and of course I had the devil's luck. I've come back to Europe simply because I couldn't stand it any longer. I was not coming to England, and I had no idea of seeing you, Emilie! I travelled here on a little pilgrimage."

"It was fate," she murmured.

"But since I am here," he continued, "and since we have met again, I must ask you this. Your husband is trying to divorce you?"

"Yes!" she murmured.

"And why?"

"Because he is a brute," she answered quietly. "We have been separated for more than a year. I think that he wants to marry again."

"And you permit this?" he asked.

"No!" she answered, "I contest it. Up to now, the courts have been in my favour."

"Up to now! They must always be in your favour!" he declared vehemently. "What can they say against a saint like you?"

She smiled up at him tenderly, a little wistfully.

"They would say a good deal," she whispered, "if they could see you here now."

He drew abruptly away.

"I am a thoughtless brute," he declared. "It was for that that I decided to remain dead. I will go away at once."

Her fingers closed over his. She drew him a little nearer with glad recklessness.

"You shall not," she murmured. "It is worth a little risk, this."

Wrayson touched Louise on the arm and they turned away. He found her a seat in a quiet corner of the fruit garden, where a tall row of hollyhocks shielded them from observation. She was very white, and in a semi-hysterical state.

"I can't believe," she said, "that that is really Duncan - Duncan himself. It is too wonderful!"

"There is no doubt about it being your brother," he answered. "What I don't quite understand is why he has kept away so long."

"It is because of her," she answered. "If they had been on the same continent, I believe that nothing could have kept them apart!"

"And now?" he asked.

"I cannot tell," she answered, "I, nor any one else! God made them for one another, I am very sure!"

He took her hand and held it tightly in his.

"And you for me, dearest," he whispered. "Shall I tell you why I am sure of it?"

She leaned back with half-closed eyes. Endurance has its limits, and the mesmeric influence of the drowsy summer day was in her veins.

"If you like," she murmured, simply....

And only a few yards away, the man from the dead and the woman who had loved him seemed to have drifted into a summer day-dream. The strangeness of this thing held them both - ordinary intercourse seemed impossible. What they spoke about they scarcely knew! There were days, golden days to be whispered about and lived again; treasured minutes to be recalled, looks and words remembered. Of the future, of the actual present, save of their two selves, they scarcely spoke. It was an hour snatched from Paradise for her! She would not let it go lightly. She would not suffer even a cloud to pass across it!

In time, Monsieur Jules found himself constrained to announce that *dejeuner* was served. He found it useless to try to attract the attention of either Madame de Melbain or Duncan, so he went in search of Wrayson.

"Monsieur is served," he announced, looking blandly upwards at a passing cloud. "There remains the wine only."

"Chablis of the best, and ice, and mineral water," Wrayson ordered. "Come, Louise."

She sighed a little as she rose and followed him along the narrow path, where the rose-bushes brushed against her skirt, and the air was fragrant with lavender. It had been an interlude only, after all, though the man whose hand she still held would never have admitted it. But - he did not know! She prayed to Heaven that he never might.

Luncheon, after all, with a waiter within hearing, and Monsieur Jules hovering round, banished in a great measure the curious sense of unreality from which none of them were wholly free. And when coffee came, Madame leaned a little towards Duncan, and with her hand upon his arm whispered a question.

"My letters, Duncan! What became of them?"

He sighed.

"I was a little rash, perhaps," he said, "but - they were

all I had left. They were with me at Colenso, in an envelope, sealed and addressed, to be burnt unopened. When I was hit, I got a Red Cross man to cut them out of my coat and destroy them."

Madame de Melbain looked at him for a moment, and her eyes were soft with unshed tears. Then she turned away, though her hand still rested upon his.

"Duncan," she said quietly, "don't think that I mind. You did all that you could, and indeed I would rather that you cared so much. But the letters were not destroyed."

For a moment he failed to realize the import of her words.

"Not destroyed?" he repeated, a little vaguely.

"No!" she answered. "They came into the hands of some one in London. Terrible things have happened in connexion with them. Duncan, if you will listen to me quietly, I will tell you about it. Sit down, dear."

She saw the gathering storm. The man's face was black with anger. He was still a little dazed however.

"You mean - that the man to whom I trusted them - "

"He kept them for his own purpose," she said softly.

"Don't look like that, Duncan. He has paid his debt. He is dead!"

"And the letters?"

"We do not know. My husband's advisers are trying to get possession of them. That is why the courts have not yet pronounced their judgment."

He had risen to his feet, but she drew him gently down again.

"Remember, Duncan, that the man is dead! Be calm, and I will tell you all about it."

He looked at her wonderingly.

"You are not angry with me?"

"Angry! Why should I be? I am only happy to know that you never forgot - that you could not bear to destroy the only link that was left between us. Do you know, I am almost sorry that I spoke to you about this! We seem to have snatched an hour or two out of Paradise, and it is I who have stirred up the dark waters. Let us forget it for a few more minutes!"

He drew her away with him towards their seat under the trees. Wrayson looked across at Louise with a smile.

"You, too," he said. "May we not forget a little longer?"

She smiled at him sadly, and shook her head.

"No!" she answered. "With them it is different. I can scarcely yet realize that I have a brother: think what it must be to Emilie to have the man whom she loved come back from the grave. Listen!"

Outside they heard the sound of galloping horses. A moment later the Baron de Courcelles issued from the inn and crossed the lawn towards Madame de Melbain.

"Madame," he said, "the man who was caught in the park last night is, without doubt, a spy from Mexonia! He can be charged with nothing more serious than trespass, and in a few minutes he will be free. Should he return, this" - he glanced towards Duncan - "would be the end. I have a carriage waiting for you."

Madame de Melbain rose at once. With a little gesture of excuse she drew Duncan on one side.

"Wait here," she begged, "until you hear from me. Baron de Courcelles is my one faithful friend at Court. I am going to consult with him."

"I shall see you again?" he asked.

She hesitated.

"Is it wise?" she murmured. "If my enemies knew that you were alive, that I had seen you here, what chance should I have, do you think, before the courts?"

He bent over her hands.

"I have brought enough trouble upon you," he said simply. "I will wait! Only I hope that there will be work for me to do!"

E. Phillips Oppenheim

CHAPTER XXXII

AT THE HÔTEL SPLENDIDE

"I asked you," the Baron remarked, helping himself to *hors d'oeuvres,* to dine with me here, because I fancy that the little inn at St. Étarpe is being closely watched. Always when one has private matters to discuss, I believe in a certain amount of publicity. Here we are in a quiet corner, it is true, but we are surrounded by several hundreds of other people. They are far too occupied with their own affairs to watch us. It is the last place, for instance, where our friend from Mexonia would dream of looking for us."

The three men were seated at a small round table in the great dining-room of the *Hôtel Splendide* of Dinant-on-Sea. The season was at its height, and the room was full. On every side they were surrounded by chattering groups of English tourists and French holiday makers. Outside on the promenade a band was playing, and a leisurely crowd was passing back and forth.

"The lady whom we will continue, if you please, to call Madame de Melbain," the Baron continued, "has desired me to take you two gentlemen into our entire confidence. You are both aware that for eighteen months the suit for divorce brought by that lady's husband has been before a special court."

"One understands," Wrayson remarked, "that the sympathies of all Europe are with - the lady."

The Baron bowed.

"Entirely. Her cause, too, is the popular one in Mexonia. It is the ministry and the aristocracy who are on the other side. These are anxious for an alliance which will safeguard Mexonia from certain dangers to which she is at present exposed. Madame de Melbain, as you are both aware, comes from one of the oldest families of Europe, but it is a family without any political significance. The betrothal was completed before Frederick stood so near to the throne. If his accession had seemed even a likely thing at the time, it would not have been sanctioned. I speak as the staunch friend of the lady whose cause is so dear to us, but I wish you to grasp the facts."

There was a brief pause whilst a fresh course was served by an apologetic and breathless waiter. The three men spoke together for a while on some chance subject. Then, when they were alone, the Baron continued.

"The court, although powerful influences were at work, found itself unable to pronounce the decree which those in authority so much desired. All that those who were behind the scenes could do was to keep the case open, hoping that while living apart from her husband some trifling indiscretion on the part of Madame would afford them a pretext for giving the desired verdict. I need not say that, up to the present, no such indiscretion has occurred. But all the time we have been on the brink of a volcano!"

E. Phillips Oppenheim

"The letters!" Duncan muttered.

The Baron nodded.

"About a year ago," he said, "Madame de Melbain received a terrifying letter from the miscreant into whose hands they had fallen. Madame very wisely made a confidant of me, and, with the Baroness de Sturm, I left at once for London, and saw this man. I very soon persuaded myself that he had the letters and that he knew their value. He asked a sum for them which it was utterly unable for us to pay."

"Did he explain," Duncan asked, "how they came into his hands?"

"He said that they were picked up on the battlefield of Colenso at first," the Baron declared. "Afterwards he was brutally frank. You see your death was gazetted, a fact of which he was no doubt aware. He admitted that they had been given to him to destroy."

Duncan leaned across the table.

"Baron," he said, "who killed that man? He cheated me of my task, but I should like to know who it was."

"So would a great many more of us," the Baron answered. "The fact is, we are in the curious position of having an unknown friend."

"An unknown friend?" Duncan repeated.

The Baron nodded.

"We paid that man two thousand a year," he said, "but

he was not satisfied. He communicated secretly with the other side, and they agreed to buy the letters for ten thousand pounds. We knew the very night when he had arranged to hand them over to a man named Bentham in London. But we were powerless. We could not have found the half of ten thousand pounds. One thing only was tried, and that very nearly ended in disaster. An attempt was made to steal the letters. Mr. Wrayson will tell you about that - presently."

A *maître d'hôtel* paused at their table to hope that messieurs were well served. In a season so busy it was not possible to give the attention to every one they would like! Was there anything he could do? Messieurs were drinking, he noticed, the best wine in the cellars! He trusted that they approved of it. The young lady there with the diamond collar and the wonderful eyes? He bent a little lower over the table. That was Mademoiselle Diane, of the Folies Bergères! And the gentleman? He had registered under another name, but he was well known as the Baron X -, a great capitalist in Paris!

The *maître d'hôtel* passed on, well satisfied that he had interested the three distinguished looking gentlemen who dined alone. Wrayson, as soon as he was out of hearing, leaned over the table.

"It is on that night," he said to Duncan, "that I come into touch with the affairs of which our friend has spoken. The man Barnes had a flat corresponding to mine on the floor above. I returned home about midnight and found a young lady, who was a complete stranger to me, engaged in searching my desk. I turned up the lights and demanded an explanation. She was apparently quite as much surprised to see me as I was to see her. It appeared that she had imagined herself in Barnes' flat. Whilst I was talking to her, the telephone bell rang. Some unknown person asked me to convey a message to Barnes. When I had finished she was gone. I sat down and tried to make head or tail of the affair. I couldn't. Barnes was a disreputable little bounder! This girl was a lady. What connexion could there be between the two? I fancied what might happen if she were surprised by Barnes, and I determined not to go to bed until I heard her come down. I fell asleep over my fire, and I woke with a start to find her once more upon the threshold of my room. She was fainting - almost on the point of collapse! I gave her some brandy and helped her downstairs. At the door of the flat was a cab, and in it was the man Barnes, dead - murdered!"

The breath came through Duncan's teeth with a little hiss. One could fancy that he was wishing that his had been the hand to strike the blow. The Baron glanced round casually. He called a waiter and complained of the slow service, sent for another bottle of wine, and lit a cigarette.

"I think," he said, "that we will pause for a moment or so. Mr. Wrayson's narrative is a little dramatic! Ah! Mademoiselle la danseuse goes! What a toilet!"

Mademoiselle favoured their table with her particular regard as she passed out, and accepted with a delightful smile the fan which she dropped in passing, and which the Baron as speedily restored. He resumed his seat, stroking his grey moustache.

"A very handsome young lady," he remarked. "I think that now we may continue."

"The girl?" Duncan asked quickly.

"Was your sister," Wrayson answered.

There was a moment's intense silence. Duncan was doing his best to look unconcerned, but the hand which played with his wineglass shook.

"How - was he murdered?"

"Strangled with a fine cord," Wrayson answered.

"In the cab?"

"There or inside the building! It is impossible to say."

"And no one was ever tried for the murder?" "No one," Wrayson answered.

Duncan swallowed a glassful of wine.

"But my sister," he said, "was in his rooms - she might have seen him!"

"Your sister's name was never mentioned in the matter," Wrayson said. "I was the only witness who knew anything about her - and - I said nothing."

Duncan drew a little breath.

"Why?" he asked.

"An impulse," Wrayson answered. "I felt that she could not have been concerned in such a deed, and I felt that if I told all that I knew, she would have been suspected. So I said nothing. I saved her a good deal of

E. Phillips Oppenheim

trouble and anxiety I dare say, and I do not believe that I interfered in any way with the course of justice."

Duncan looked across the table and raised his glass.

"I should like to shake hands with you, Mr. Wrayson," he said, "only the Baron would have fits. You acted like a brick. I only hope that Louise is as grateful as she ought to be."

"My silence," Wrayson said, "was really an impulse. There have been times since when I have wondered whether I was wise. There are people now at work in London trying to solve the mystery of this murder. I acted upon the supposition that no one had seen your sister leave the flat except myself. I found afterwards that I was mistaken!"

The Baron leaned forward.

"One moment, Mr. Wrayson," he interrupted. "You have said that there are people in London who are trying to solve the mystery of Barnes' death. Who are they?"

"One is the man's brother," Wrayson answered, "if possible, a more contemptible little cur than the man himself was. His only interest is to discover the source of his brother's income. He wants money! Nothing but money. The other is a much more dangerous person. His name is Heneage, and he is an acquaintance of my own, a barrister, and a man of education."

"Why does he interest himself in such an affair?" Duncan asked.

"Because the solution of such matters is a hobby of his," Wrayson answered. "It was he who saw your sister and I come out from the flat that morning. It was he who warned us both to leave England."

The Baron leaned forward in his chair.

"Forgive me, Mr. Wrayson," he said, "but there is a - lady at your right who seems anxious to attract your attention. We are none of us anxious to advertise our presence here. Is she, by any chance, a friend of yours?"

Wrayson looked quickly round. He understood at once the Baron's slight pause. The ladies of the French half-world are skilled enough, when necessary, in concealing their profession: their English sister, if she attempts it at all, attempts a hopeless task. Over-powdered, over-rouged, with hair at least two shades nearer copper coloured than last time he had seen her, badly but showily dressed, it was his friend from the Alhambra whose welcoming smile Wrayson received with a thrill of interest. She was seated at a small table with a slightly less repulsive edition of herself, and her smile changed at once into a gesture of invitation. Wrayson rose to his feet almost eagerly.

"This is a coincidence," he said under his breath. "She, too, holds a hand in the game!"

CHAPTER XXXIII

A HAND IN THE GAME

The diners at the *Hotel Splendide* were a little surprised to see the tall, distinguished-looking Englishman leave his seat and accost with quiet deference the elder of the two women, whose entrance a few minutes before had occasioned a good many not very flattering comments. The lady who called herself Blanche meant to make the most of her opportunity.

"Fancy meeting you here," she remarked. "Flo, this is a friend of mine. Mrs. Harrigod! Gentleman's name doesn't matter, does it?" she added, laughing.

Wrayson bowed, and murmured something inaudible. Blanche's friend regarded him with unconcealed and flattering approval.

"Over here for a little flutter, I suppose?" she remarked. "It is so hot in town we had to get away somewhere. Are you alone with your friends?"

"Quite alone," Wrayson answered. "We are only staying for a day or two."

The lady nodded.

"We shall stay for a week if we like it," she said. "If not, we shall go on to Dieppe. Did you get my letter?"

"Letter!" Wrayson repeated. "No! Have you written to me?"

She nodded.

"I wrote to you a week ago."

"I have been staying near here" Wrayson said, "and my letters have not been forwarded."

He bent a little lower over the table. The perfume of violet scent was almost unbearable, but he did not flinch.

"You had some news for me?" he asked eagerly.

"Yes!" she answered. "I'm not going to tell you now. We are going to sit outside after dinner. You must come to us there. No good having smart friends unless you make use of them," she added, with a shrill little laugh.

"I shall take some chairs and order coffee," Wrayson said. "In the meantime - ?"

"If you like to order us a bottle of champagne and tell the waiter to put it on your bill, we shan't be offended," Blanche declared. "We were just wondering whether we could run to it."

"You must do me the honour of being my guests for dinner also," Wrayson declared, calling a waiter. "It was very good of you to remember to write."

The friend murmured something about it being very kind of the gentleman. Blanche shrugged her shoulders.

"Oh! I remember right enough," she said. "It wasn't that. But there, wait until I've told you about it. It's an odd story, and sometimes I wish I'd never had anything to do with it. I get a cold shiver every time I think of that old man who took me to dine at Luigi's. Outside in three-quarters of an hour, then!"

"I will keep some chairs and order coffee," Wrayson said, turning away.

"And bring one of your friends," Blanche added. "It won't do him any harm. We shan't bite him!"

"I will bring them both," Wrayson promised.

He went back to his own table and people watched him curiously.

"I believe," he said quietly, as he sat down, "that if there is a person in the world who can put us on the track of those letters, it is the lady with whom I have just been talking."

The Baron looked across at the two women with new interest.

"What on earth have they got to do with it, Wrayson?" he asked.

"The fair one was a friend of Barnes'," Wrayson answered. "It was at her flat that he called the night he was murdered."

"You are sure," Duncan asked, "that the letters have not been found yet by the other side?"

"Quite sure," the Baron answered. "We have agents in Mexonia, even about the King's person, and we should hear in an hour if they had the letters."

"Presuming, then," Duncan said thoughtfully, "that Barnes was murdered for the sake of these letters - and as he was murdered on the very night he was going to hand them over to the other side, I don't see what else we can suppose, - the crime would appear to have been committed by some one on our side."

"It certainly does seem so," the Baron admitted.

"And this man Bentham! He was the agent for - the King's people. He too was murdered! Baron!"

"Well?"

"Who killed Barnes? He robbed me of my right, but I want to know."

The Baron shook his head.

"I have no idea," he said gravely. "We have agents in London, of course, but no one who would go to such lengths. I do not know who killed Barnes, nor do I know who killed Bentham."

There was a short silence. The Baron's words were impressively spoken. It was impossible to doubt their veracity. Yet both to Wrayson and to Duncan they had a serious import. The same thought was present in the mind of all three of them - and each avoided the others' eyes. Wrayson, however, was not disposed to let the matter go without one more effort. The corners of his mouth tightened, and he looked the Baron steadily in the face.

"Baron," he said, "I have told you that there is a man in London who has set himself to solve the mystery of Barnes' death. The two people whom he would naturally suspect are Miss Fitzmaurice and myself. There is strong presumptive evidence against us, owing to my silence at the inquest, and at any moment we might either of us have to face this charge. Knowing this, do I understand you to say that, if the necessity arose, you would be absolutely unable to throw any light upon the matter?"

"Absolutely!" the Baron declared. "Both those murders are as complete an enigma to me as to you."

"You have agents in London?"

"Agents, yes!" the Baron declared, "but they are in the nature of detectives only. They would not dream of going to such lengths, either with instructions or without them. Neither, I am sure, would any one who was employed to collect evidence upon the other side."

There was no more to be said. Wrayson rose to his feet a little abruptly.

"The air is stifling here," he said. "Let us go outside and take our coffee."

They found seats on the veranda, looking out upon the promenade. The Baron looked a little dubiously at the stream of people passing backwards and forwards.

"Are we not a little conspicuous?" he remarked.

"Does it really matter?" Wrayson asked. "It is only for this evening. I shall leave for London tomorrow, in any event. Besides, it is part of the bargain that we take coffee with these ladies. Here they are."

Wrayson introduced his friends with perfect gravity. Chairs were found, and coffee and liqueurs ordered. Wrayson contrived to sit on the outside, and next to his copper-haired friend.

"Now for our little talk," he said. "Will you have a cigarette? You'll find these all right."

She threw a sidelong glance at him and sighed. What an exceedingly earnest young man this was!

"Well," she said, "I know you'll give me no peace till I've told you. There may be nothing in it. That's for you to find out. I think myself there is. It was last Thursday night in the promenade at the Alhambra that I saw her!"

"Saw whom?" Wrayson interrupted.

"I'm coming to that," she declared. "Let me tell you my own way. I was talking to a friend, and I overheard all that she said. She was quietly dressed, and she looked frightened; a poor, pale-faced little thing she was anyway, and she was walking up and down like a stage-doll, peering round corners and looking everywhere, as though she'd lost somebody. Presently she went up to one of the attendants, and I heard her ask him if he knew a Mr. Augustus Howard who came there often. The man shook his head, and then she tried to describe him. It was a bit flattering, but an idea jumped into my head all of a sudden that it was Barnes she was looking for."

"By Jove!" Wrayson muttered, under his breath. "Did you speak to her?"

She nodded.

"I waited till she was alone, and then I made her sit down with me and describe him all over again. By the time she'd finished, I was jolly well sure that it was Barnes she was after."

"Did you tell her?" Wrayson asked.

"Not I!" she answered. "I didn't want a scene there, and besides, it's your little show, not mine. I told her that I felt sure I recognized him, and that if she would be in the same place at nine o'clock a week from that night, I could send some one whom I thought would be able to tell her about her friend. That was last Thursday. You want to be just outside the refreshment-room at nine o'clock to-morrow night, and you can't mistake her. She looks as though she'd blown in from an A B C shop."

Wrayson possessed himself of her hand for a moment in an impulse of apparent gallantry. Something which rustled pleasantly was instantly and safely transferred to the metal purse which hung from her waistband.

"You will allow me?" he murmured.

"Rather," she answered, with a little laugh. "What a stroke of luck it was meeting you here! Flo and I were both stony. We hadn't a sovereign between us when we'd paid for our tickets."

"Have you seen anything of Barnes' brother?" he asked.

"Once or twice at the Alhambra," she answered.

"He was wearing his brother's clothes, but he looked pretty dicky."

"You didn't mention this young woman to him, I suppose?" he asked.

She shook her head.

"Not I! You're the only person I've told. Hope it brings you luck."

Wrayson rose to his feet. The Baron and Duncan followed his example. They took leave of the ladies and turned towards the promenade.

"I'm going to London by the morning boat," Wrayson announced. "I believe I'm on the track of those letters."

They walked up and down for a few moments talking. As they passed the front of the hotel, they heard a shrill peal of laughter. Blanche and her friend were talking to a little group of men. The Baron smiled.

"We have broken the ice for them," he said, "but I am afraid that we are already forgotten."

CHAPTER XXXIV

AN ILL-ASSORTED COUPLE

Wrayson looked anxiously at his watch. It was already ten minutes past nine, and although he was standing on the precise spot indicated, there was no one about who in the least resembled the young woman of whom he was in search. The overture to the ballet was being played, a good many people were strolling about, or seated at the small round tables, but they were all of the usual class, the ladies ornate and obvious, and all having the air of *habitués*. In vain Wrayson scanned the faces of the passers-by, and even the occupants of the back seats. There was no sign of the young woman of whom he was in search.

Presently he began to stroll somewhat aimlessly about, still taking note of every one amongst the throng, and in a little while he caught sight of a familiar figure, sitting alone at one of the small round tables. He accosted him at once.

"How are you, Heneage?" he said quietly. "What are you doing in town at this time of the year?"

Heneage started when he was addressed, and his manner, when he recognized Wrayson, lacked altogether its usual composure.

"I'm all right," he answered. "Beastly hot in town, though, isn't it? I'm off in a day or two. Where have you been to?"

"North of France," Wrayson answered. "You look as though you wanted a change!"

"I'm going to Scotland directly I can get away."

The two men looked at one another for a moment. Heneage was certainly looking ill. There were dark lines under his eyes, and his face seemed thinner. Then, too, he was still in his morning clothes, his tie was ill arranged, and his linen not unexceptionable. Wrayson was puzzled. Something had gone wrong with the man.

"You see," he said quietly, "I have been forced to disregard your warning. I shall be in England for some little time at any rate. May I ask, am I in any particular danger?"

Heneage shook his head.

"Not from me, at any rate!"

Wrayson looked at him for a moment steadily.

"Do you mean that, Heneage?" he asked.

"Yes!"

"You are satisfied, then, that neither I nor the young lady had anything to do with the death of Morris Barnes?" Heneage moved in his chair uneasily.

"Yes!" he answered. "Don't talk to me about that damned business," he added, with a little burst of half-suppressed passion. "I've done with it. Come and have a drink."

Wrayson drew a sigh of relief. Perhaps, for the first time, he realized how great a weight this thing had been upon his spirits. He had feared Heneage! - not this man, but the cold, capable Stephen Heneage of his earlier acquaintance; feared him not only for his own sake, but hers. After all, his visit to the Alhambra had brought some good to him.

Heneage had risen to his feet.

"We'll go into the American bar," he said. "Not here. The women fuss round one so. I'm glad you've turned up, Wrayson. I've got the hump!"

The bar was crowded, but they found a quiet corner. Heneage ordered a
large brandy and soda, and drunk half of it at a gulp.

"How's every one?" Wrayson asked. "I haven't been in the club yet."

"All right, I believe. I haven't been in myself for a week," Heneage answered.

Wrayson looked at him in surprise.

"Haven't been in the club for a week?" he repeated. "That's rather unusual, isn't it?"

"Damn it all! I'm not obliged to go there, am I?" Heneage exclaimed testily.

Wrayson looked at him in amazement. Heneage, as a rule, was one of the most deliberate and even-tempered of men.

"Of course not," he answered. "You won't mind telling me how the Colonel is, though, will you?"

"I believe he is very well," Heneage answered, more calmly. "He doesn't come up to town so often this hot weather. Forgive me for being a bit impatient, old fellow. I've got a fit of nerves, I think."

"You want a change," Wrayson said earnestly. "There's no doubt about that."

"I am going away very soon," Heneage answered. "As soon as I can get off. I don't mind telling you, Wrayson, that I've had a shock, and it has upset me."

Wrayson nodded sympathetically.

"All right, old chap," he said. "I'm beastly sorry, but if you take my advice, you'll get out of London as soon as you can. Go to Trouville or Dinard, or some place where there's plenty of life. I shouldn't busy myself in the country, if I were you. By the bye," he added, "there is one more question I should like to ask you, if you don't mind."

Heneage called a waiter and ordered more drinks. Then he turned to Wrayson.

"Well," he said, "go on!"

"About that little brute, Barnes' brother. Is he about still?"

Heneage's face darkened. He clenched his fist, but recovered himself with a visible effort.

"Yes!" he answered shortly, "he is about. He is everywhere. The little brute haunts me! He dogs my footsteps, Wrayson. Sometimes I wonder that I don't sweep him off the face of the earth."

"But why?" Wrayson asked. "What does he want with you?"

"I will tell you," Heneage answered. "When he first turned up, I was interested in his story, as you know. We commenced working at the thing together. You understand, Wrayson?"

"Perfectly!"

"Well - after a while it suited me - to drop it. Perhaps I told him so a little abruptly. At any rate, he was disappointed. Now he has got an idea in his brain. He believes that I have discovered something which I will not tell him. He follows me about. He pesters me to death. He is a slave to that one idea - a hideous, almost unnatural craving to get his hands on the source of his brother's money. I think that he will very soon be mad. To tell you the truth, I came in here to-night because I thought I should be safe from him. I don't believe he has five shillings to get in the place."

Wrayson lit a cigarette and smoked for a moment in silence. Then he turned towards his companion.

"Heneage," he said, "I don't want to annoy you, but you must remember that this matter means a good deal to me. I am forced to ask you a question, and you must answer it. Have you really found anything out? You don't often give a thing up without a reason."

Heneage answered him with greater composure than he had expected, though perhaps to less satisfactory effect.

"Look here, Wrayson," he said, "you appreciate plain speaking, don't you?"

Wrayson nodded. Heneage continued:

"You can go to hell with your questions! You understand that? It's plain English."

"Admirably simple," Wrayson answered, "and perfectly satisfactory."

"What do you mean?"

"It answers my question," Wrayson declared quietly.

Heneage shrugged his shoulders.

"You can get what satisfaction you like out of it," he said doggedly.

"It isn't much," Wrayson admitted. "I wish I could induce you to treat me a little more generously."

Heneage looked at him with a curious gleam in his eyes.

"Look here," he said. "Take my advice. Drop the whole affair. You see what it's made of me. It'll do the same to you. I shan't tell you anything! You can swear to that. I've done with it, Wrayson, done with it! You understand that? Talk about something else, or leave me alone!"

Wrayson looked at the man whom he had once called his friend.

"You're in a queer sort of mood, Heneage," he said.

"Let it go at that," Heneage answered. "Every man has a right to his moods, hasn't he? No right to inflict them upon his friends, you'd say! Perhaps not, but you know I'm a reasonable person as a rule. Don't - don't - "

He broke off abruptly in his sentence. His eyes were fixed upon a distant corner of the room. Their expression was unfathomable, but Wrayson shuddered as he looked away and followed their direction. Then he, too, started. He recognized the miserable little figure whose presence a group just broken up left revealed. Heneage rose softly to his feet.

"Let us go before he sees us," he whispered hurriedly. "Look sharp!"

But they were too late. Already he was on his way towards them, shambling rather than walking down the room, an unwholesome, unattractive, even repulsive figure. He seemed to have shrunken in size since his arrival in England, and his brother's clothes, always too large, hung about him loose and ungraceful. His tie was grimy; his shirt frayed; his trousers turned up, but still falling over his heels; his hat, too large for him, came almost to his ears. In the increased pallor and thinness of his face, his dark eyes seemed to have come nearer together. He would have been a ludicrous object but for the intense earnestness of his expression. He came towards them with rapidly blinking eyes. He took no notice of Heneage, but he insisted upon shaking hands with Wrayson.

"Mr. Wrayson," he said, "I am glad to see you again, sir. You always treated me like a gentleman. Not like him," he added, motioning with his head towards Heneage. "He's a thief, he is!"

"Steady," Wrayson interrupted, "you mustn't call people names like that."

"Why not?" Barnes asked. "He is a thief. He knows it. He knows who robbed me of my money. And he won't tell. That's what I call being a thief."

Wrayson glanced towards Heneage and was amazed at his demeanour. He had shrunk back in his chair, and he was sitting with his hands in his pockets and his eyes fixed upon the table. Of the two, his miserable little accuser was the dominant figure.

"He's very likely spending it now - my money!" Barnes continued. "Here am I living on crusts and four-penny dinners, and begging my way in here, and some one else is spending my money. Never mind! It may be my turn yet! It may be only a matter of hours," he added, leaning over towards them and showing his yellow teeth, "and I may have the laugh on both of you."

Heneage looked up quickly. He was obviously discomposed.

"What do you mean?" he asked.

E. Phillips Oppenheim

Sydney Barnes indulged in the graceless but expressive proceeding of sticking his tongue in his cheek. After which he turned to Wrayson.

"Mr. Wrayson," he said, "lend me a quid. I've got the flat to sleep in for a few more weeks, but I haven't got money enough for a meal. I'll pay you back some day - perhaps before you expect it."

Wrayson produced a sovereign and handed it over silently.

"If I were you," he said, "I'd spend my time looking for a situation, instead of hunting about for this supposed fortune of your brother's."

Barnes took the sovereign with hot, trembling fingers, and deposited it carefully in his waistcoat pocket. Then he smiled in a somewhat mysterious manner.

"Mr. Wrayson," he said, "perhaps I'm not so far off, after all. Other people can find out what he knows," he added, pointing at Heneage. "He ain't the only one who can see through a brick wall. Say, Mr. Wrayson, you've always treated me fair and square," he added, leaning towards him and dropping his voice. "Can you tell me this? Did Morry ever go swaggering about calling himself by any other name - bit more tony, eh?"

Wrayson started. For a moment he did not reply. Thoughts were rushing through his brain. Was he forestalled in his search for this girl? Meanwhile, Barnes watched him with a cunning gleam in his deep-set eyes.

"Such as Augustus Howard, eh? Real tony name that

for Morry!"

Wrayson, with a sudden instinctive knowledge, brushed him on one side, and half standing up, gazed across the room at the corner from which his questioner had come. With her back against the wall, her cheap prettiness marred by her red eyes, her ill-arranged hair, and ugly hat, sat, beyond a doubt, the girl for whom he had waited in the promenade.

E. Phillips Oppenheim

CHAPTER XXXV

HIS WIFE

Wrayson drew a little breath and looked back at Sydney Barnes.

"You asked me a question," he said. "I believe I have heard of your brother calling himself by some such name."

Barnes grasped him by the arm.

"Look here," he said, "come and repeat that to the young lady over there. She's with me. It won't do you any harm."

Wrayson rose to his feet, but before he could move he felt Heneage's hand fall upon his arm.

"Where are you going, Wrayson?" he asked.

Barnes looked up at him anxiously. His pale face seemed twisted into a scowl.

"Don't you interfere!" he exclaimed. "You've done me enough harm, you have. You let Mr. Wrayson pass. He's coming with me."

Heneage took no more notice of him than he would of a yapping terrier. He looked over his head into Wrayson's eyes.

"Wrayson," he said, "don't have anything more to do with this business. Take my advice. I know more than you do about it. If you go on, I swear to you that there is nothing but misery at the end."

"I know more than you think I do," Wrayson answered quietly. "I know more indeed than you have any idea of. If the end were in hell I should not hold back."

Heneage hesitated for a moment. He stood there with darkening face, an obstinate, almost a threatening figure. Passers-by looked with a gleam of interest at the oddly assorted trio, whose conversation was obviously far removed from the ordinary chatter of the loungers about the place. One or two made an excuse to linger by - it seemed possible that there might be developments. Heneage, however, disappointed them. He turned suddenly upon his heel and left the room. Those who had the curiosity to follow along the corridor saw him, without glancing to the right or to the left, descend the stairs and walk out of the building. He had the air of a man who abandons finally a hopeless task.

The look of relief in Barnes' face as he saw him go was a ludicrous thing. He drew Wrayson at once towards the corner.

"Queer thing about this girl," he whispered in his ear. "She ain't like the others about here. She just comes to make inquiries about a friend who's given her the chuck, and whose name she says was Howard. I believe it's Morry she means. Just like him to take a toff's name!"

"Wait a moment before we speak to her," Wrayson said. "How did you find her out?"

"She spoke to me," Barnes answered. "Asked me if my name was Howard, said I was a bit like the man she was looking for. Then I palled up to her, and I'm pretty certain Morry was her man. I want her to go to the flat with me and see his clothes and picture, but she's scared. Mr. Wrayson, you might do me a good turn. She'll come if you'd go too!"

"Do you know why I am here to-night?" Wrayson asked.

"No! Why?"

"To meet that young woman of yours," Wrayson answered.

Barnes looked at him in amazement.

"What do you mean?" he asked quickly. "You don't know her, do you?"

His sallow cheeks were paler than ever. His narrow eyes, furtively raised to Wrayson's, were full of inquisitive fear.

"No! I don't know her," Wrayson answered, "but I rather fancy, all the same, that she is the young person whom I came here to meet to-night."

Barnes waited breathlessly for an explanation. He did

not say a word, but his whole attitude was an insistent interrogation point.

"You remember," Wrayson said, "that when you and I were pursuing these investigations together, I made some inquiries of the woman at whose flat your brother called on the night of his murder. I saw her again at Dinant yesterday, and she told me of this young person. She also evidently believed that the man for whom she was inquiring was your brother."

Barnes nodded.

"She told me that she was to have met a gentleman to-night," he said. "Here, we must go and speak to her now, or she'll think that something's up."

He performed something that was meant for an introduction.

"Friend of mine, Miss," he said, indicating Wrayson. "Knew my brother well, lived in the flat just below him, in fact. Perhaps you'd like to ask him a few questions."

"There is only one question I want answered," the girl replied, with straining eyes fixed upon Wrayson's face, and a little break in her tone. "Shall I see him again? If Augustus was really - his brother - where is he? What has happened to him?"

There was a moment's silence. Sydney Barnes had evidently said nothing as to his brother's tragic end. Wrayson could see, too, that the girl was on the brink of hysterics, and needed careful handling.

"We will tell you everything," he said presently. "But first of all we have to decide whether your Augustus Howard and Morris Barnes were the same person. I think that the best way for you to decide this would be to come home to my flat. Mr. Barnes' is just above, and I dare say you can recognize some of his brother's belongings, if he really was - your friend."

She rose at once. She was perfectly willing to go. They left the place together and entered a four-wheeler. During the drive she scarcely opened her lips. She sat in a corner looking absently out of the window, and nervously clasping and unclasping her hands. She answered a remark of Sydney Barnes' without turning her head.

"I always watch the people," she said. "Wherever I am, I always look out of the window. I have always hoped - that I might see Augustus again that way."

Wrayson, from his seat in the opposite corner of the cab, watched her with growing sympathy. In her very conformity to type, she represented so naturally a real and living unit of humanity. Her poor commonplace prettiness was already on the wane, stamped out by the fear and trouble of the last few months. Yet inane though her features, lacking altogether strength or distinction, there was stamped into them something of that dumb, dog-like fidelity to some object which redeemed them from utter insignificance. Wrayson, as he watched her, found himself thinking more kindly of the dead man himself. In his vulgar, selfish way, he had probably been kind to her: he must have done something to have kindled this flame of dogged, persevering affection. Already he scarcely doubted that Morris Barnes and Augustus Howard had been the same person. Within a very few minutes of her entering the flats there remained no doubt at all. With a low moan, like a dumb animal mortally hurt, she sank down upon the nearest chair, clasping the photograph which Sydney Barnes had passed her in her hands.

For a few moments there was silence. Then she looked up - at Wrayson. Her lips moved but no words came. She began again. This time he was able to catch the indistinct whisper.

"Where is he?"

Wrayson took a seat by her side upon the sofa.

"You do not read the newspapers?" he asked.

She shook her head.

"Not much. My eyes are not very good, and it tires me to read."

"I am afraid," he said gently, "that it will be bad news."

A little sob caught in her throat.

"Go on," she faltered.

"He is dead," Wrayson said simply.

She fainted quietly away.

Wrayson hurried downstairs to his own flat for some brandy. When he returned the girl was still unconscious. Her pocket was turned inside out and the front of her dress was disordered. Sydney Barnes was bending close over her. Wrayson pushed him roughly away.

"You can wait, at least, until she is well," he said contemptuously.

Sydney Barnes was wholly unabashed. He watched Wrayson pour brandy between the girl's lips, bathe her temples, and chafe her hands. All the time he stood doggedly waiting close by. No considerations of decency or humanity would weigh with him for one single second. The fever of his great desire still ran like fire through his veins. He did not think of the girl as a human creature at all. Simply there was a pair of lips there which might point out to him the way to his Paradise.

She opened her eyes at last. Sydney Barnes came a step nearer, but Wrayson pushed him once more roughly away.

"You are feeling better?" he asked kindly.

She nodded, and struggled up into a sitting posture.

"Tell me," she said, "how did he die? It must have been quite sudden. Was it an accident? - or - or -"

He saw the terror in her eyes, and he spoke quickly. All the time he found himself wondering how it was that she was guessing at the truth.

"We are afraid," he said "that he was murdered. It is surprising that you did not read about it in the papers."

She shook her head.

"I do not read much," she said, "and the name was different. Who was it - that killed him?"

"No one knows," he answered.

"When was it?" she asked.

He told her the date. She repeated it tearfully.

"He was down with me the day before," she said. "He was terribly excited all the time, and I know that he was a little afraid of something happening to him. He had been threatened!"

"Do you know by whom?" Wrayson asked.

She shook her head.

"He never told me," she answered. "He didn't tell me much. But he was very, very good to me. I was at the refreshment-room at London Bridge when I first met him. He used to come in and see me every day. Then he began to take me out, and at last he found me a little house down at Putney, and I was so happy. I had been so tired all my life," she added, with a little sigh, "and down there I did nothing but rest and rest and wait for him to come. It was too good to last, of course, but I didn't think it would end like this!"

Quietly but very persistently Sydney Barnes insisted on being heard.

"It's my turn now," he said, standing by Wrayson's side. "Look here, Miss, I'm his brother. You can see that, can't you?"

E. Phillips Oppenheim

"You are something like him," she admitted, "only he was much, much nicer to look at than you."

"Never mind that," he continued eagerly. "I'm his brother, his nearest relative. Everything he left behind belongs to me!"

"Not - quite everything," she protested.

"What do you mean?" he asked sharply.

"You may be his brother," she answered, "but I," holding out her left hand a little nervously, "I was his wife!"

CHAPTER XXXVI

THE MURDERED MAN'S EFFECTS

Both men had been totally unprepared for the girl's timid avowal. To Wrayson, however, after the first mild shock of surprise, it was of no special import. To Sydney Barnes, although he made a speedy effort to grapple with the situation, it came very much as a thunderclap.

"You have your certificate?" he asked sharply. "You were married properly in a church?"

She nodded. "We were married at Dulwich Parish Church," she answered. "It was nearly a year ago."

"Very well," Sydney Barnes said. "It is lucky that I am here to look after your interests. We divide everything, you know."

She seemed about to cry.

"I want Augustus," she murmured. "He was very good to me."

"Look here," he said, "Augustus always seemed to have plenty of oof, didn't he?"

She nodded.

"He was very generous with it, too," she declared. "He gave me lots and lots of beautiful things."

His eyes travelled over her hands and neck, destitute of ornaments.

"Where are they?" he asked sharply.

"I've had to sell them," she answered, "to get along at all, I hated to, but I couldn't starve."

The young man's face darkened.

"Come," he said. "We'd better have no secrets from one another. You know how to get at his money, I suppose?"

She shook her head.

"Indeed I don't know anything about it," she declared.

"You must know where it came from," he persisted.

"I don't," she repeated. "Indeed I don't. He never told me and I never asked him. I understood that he had made it in South Africa."

Sydney Barnes wiped the perspiration from his forehead.

"Look here," he said in a voice which, notwithstanding his efforts to control it, trembled a little, "this is a very serious matter for us. You don't want to go back to the refreshment bar again, do you?"

"I don't care what I do," she answered dully. "I hated that, but I shall hate everything now that he is gone."

"It's only for a day or two you'll feel like that," he declared. "We've got a right, you and I, to whatever Morry left behind, and whatever happens I mean to have my share. Look around you!"

It was not an inspiring spectacle. The room was dirty, and almost devoid of furniture.

"All that I've had out of it so far," he declared, "is free quarters here. The rent's paid up to the end of the year. I've had to sell the furniture bit by bit to keep alive. It was a cheap lot, cheap and showy, and it fetched jolly little. Morry always did like to have things that looked worth more than he gave for them. Even his jewellery was sham - every bally bit of it. There wasn't a real pearl or a real diamond amongst the lot. But there's no doubt about the money. I've had the bank-book. He was worth a cool two thousand a year was Morry - that's five hundred each quarter day, you understand, and somewhere or other there must be the bonds or securities from which this money came. He never kept them here. I'll swear to that. Therefore they must be somewhere that you ought to know about."

She nodded wearily.

"Very likely," she said. "I have a parcel he gave me to take care of."

The effect of her simple words on Barnes was almost magical. The dull colour streamed into his sallow cheeks, he shook all over with excitement. His voice, when he spoke, was almost hysterical. He had been so near to despair. This indeed had been almost his last hope.

"A parcel!" he gasped. "A parcel! What sort of a parcel? Did he say that it was important?"

"It's just a long envelope tied up with red tape and sealed," she answered. "Yes! he made a great fuss about leaving it with me."

"Tell us all about it," he demanded greedily. "Oh, Lord! Oh, Lord! Be quick!"

"It must have been almost the very day it happened," she said, with a little shudder. "He came down in the afternoon and he seemed a bit queer, as though he had something on his mind. He took out the envelope once or twice and looked at it. Once he said to me, 'Agnes,' he said, 'there are men in London who, if they knew that I carried this with me, would kill me for it. I was frightened, and I begged him to leave it somewhere. I think he said that he had to have it always with him, because he couldn't think of a safe hiding-place for it. Just as he was going, though, he came back and took it out of his pocket once more."

"He left it with you?" Barnes exclaimed. "You have it safe?"

She nodded.

"I was going to tell you. 'Look here, Agnes,' he said, 'I'm nervous to-night. I don't want to carry this about with me. I shall want it to-morrow and I'll come down for it. To-night's a dangerous night for me to be carrying it about.' Those were just about his last words.

He gave me the packet and I begged him to be careful. Then he kissed me and off he went, smoking a cigar, and as cheerful as though he were going to a wedding."

She began to cry again, but Barnes broke in upon her grief.

"Didn't he tell you anything more about it?" he demanded.

"He told me - if anything happened to him," she sobbed, "to open it."

"We must do so," he declared. "We must do so at once. There must be a quarter's dividends overdue. We can get the money to-morrow, and then - oh! my God!" he exclaimed, as though the very anticipation made him faint. "Where is the packet?"

"At the bottom of my tin trunk in my rooms," she answered. "I had to leave the house. I couldn't pay the rent any longer."

"Where are the rooms?" he demanded. "We'll go there now."

"In Labrador Street," she answered. "It's a poor part, but I've only a few shillings in the world."

"We'll have a cab," he declared, rising. "Mr. Wrayson will lend us the money, perhaps?"

"I will come with you," Wrayson said quietly.

"We needn't bother you to do that," Sydney Barnes declared, with a suspicious glance.

The young woman looked towards him appealingly. He nodded reassuringly.

"I think," he said, "that it will be better for me to come. I am concerned in this business after all, you know."

"I don't see how," Barnes declared sullenly. "*If* this young lady is my sister-in-law, surely she and I can settle up our own affairs."

Wrayson stood with his back to the door, facing them.

"I hope," he said, "that you will not, either of you, be disappointed in what you find in that packet. But I think it is only right to warn you. I have reason to believe that you will not find any securities or bonds there at all! I believe that you will find that packet to consist of merely a bundle of old letters and a photograph!"

Barnes spat upon the floor. He was shaking with fright and anger.

"I don't believe it," he declared. "What can you know about it?"

Wrayson shrugged his shoulders.

"Look here," he said, "the matter is easily settled. We will put this young lady in a cab and she shall bring the packet to my flat below. You and she shall open it, and if you find securities there I have no more to say, except to wish you both luck. If, on the other hand, you find the letters, it will be a different matter."

The girl had risen to her feet.

"I would rather go alone," she said. "If you will pay my cab, I will bring the packet straight back."

Wrayson and Barnes waited in the former's flat. Barnes drank two brandy and sodas, and walked restlessly up and down the room. Wrayson was busy at the telephone, and carried on a conversation for some moments in French. Directly he had finished, Barnes turned upon him.

"Whom were you talking to?" he demanded.

"A friend of yours," he answered. "I have asked her to come round for a few minutes."

"A friend of mine?"

"The Baroness!"

The colour burned once more in his cheeks. He looked down at his attire with dissatisfaction.

"I didn't want to see her again just yet," he muttered. Wrayson smiled.

"She won't look at your clothes," he remarked, "and I rather want her here."

Barnes was suddenly suspicious.

"What for?" he demanded. "What has she got to do with the affair? I won't have strangers present."

"My young friend," Wrayson said, "I may just as well warn you that I think you are going to be disappointed. I am almost certain that I know the contents of that packet. You will find that it consists, as I told you before, not of securities at all, but simply a few old letters."

Barnes' eyes narrowed.

"Whatever they are," he said, "they meant a couple of thousand a year to Morry, and they were worth his life to somebody! How do you account for that, eh?"

"You want the truth?" Wrayson asked.

"Yes!"

"Your brother was a blackmailer!"

The breath came through Barnes' teeth with a little hiss. He realized his position almost at once. He was trapped.

He walked up to Wrayson's side. His voice shook, but he was in deadly earnest.

"Look here," he said, "the contents of that packet, whatever they may be, are mine - mine and hers! You have nothing to do with the matter at all. I will not have you in the room when they are opened."

Wrayson shrugged his shoulders.

"The packet will be opened here," he said, "and I shall certainly be present."

Barnes ground his teeth.

"If you touch one of those papers or letters or whatever

they may be, you shall be prosecuted for theft," he declared. "I swear it!"

Wrayson smiled.

"I will run the risk," he declared. "Ah! Baroness, this is kind of you," he added, throwing open the door and ushering her in. "There is a young friend of yours here who is dying to renew his acquaintance with you."

She smiled delightfully at Sydney Barnes, and threw back her cloak. She had just come in from the opera, and diamonds were flashing from her neck and bosom. Her gown was exquisite, the touch of her fingers an enchantment. It was impossible for him to resist the spell of her presence.

"You have been very unkind," she declared. "You have not been to see me for a very long time. I do not think that I shall forgive you. What do you say, Mr. Wrayson? Do you think that he deserves it?"

Wrayson smiled as he threw open the door once more. He felt that the next few minutes might prove interesting.

E. Phillips Oppenheim

CHAPTER XXXVII

THE WIDOW'S ULTIMATUM

Sydney Barnes stepped quickly forward. If Wrayson had permitted it, he would have snatched the packet from the girl's fingers. Wrayson, however, saw his intent and intervened. He stepped forward and led her to his writing table.

"I want you to sit down here quietly and open the envelope," he said, switching on the electric lamp. "That is what he told you to do, isn't it? There may be a message for you inside."

She looked round a little fearfully. The presence of the Baroness evidently discomposed her.

"I thought," she said, "that we were going to be alone, that there would have been no one here but him and you."

"The lady is a friend of mine," Wrayson said, "and it is very likely that she may be interested in the contents of this envelope."

She untied the string with trembling fingers. Wrayson handed her a paper-knife and she cut open the top of the envelope. Then she looked up at him appealingly.

"I - I don't want to look inside," she half sobbed.

Wrayson took up the envelope and shook out its contents before her. There was a letter addressed simply to Agnes, and a small packet wrapped in brown oilcloth and secured with dark-green ribbon. Sydney Barnes' hand stole out, but Wrayson was too quick for him. He changed his position, so as to interpose his person between the packet and any one in the room.

"Read the letter," he told the girl. "It is addressed to you."

She handed it to him. Her eyes were blinded with tears.

"Read it for me, please," she said.

He tore open the envelope and read the few lines scrawled upon a half sheet of notepaper. He read them very softly into her ear, but the words were audible enough to all of them.

"MY DEAR AGNES, - I have just discovered that there are some people on my track who mean mischief. I have a secret they want to rob me of. I seem to be followed about everywhere I go. What they want is the little packet in this envelope. I'm leaving it with you because I daren't carry it about with me. I've had two narrow escapes already.

"Now you'll never read this letter unless anything happens to me. I've made up my mind to sell this packet for what I can get for it, and take you with me out of the country. It'll be a matter of ten thousand quid, and I only wish I had my fingers on it now and was well out of the country. But this is where the rub comes in. If anything happens to me before I can bring this off, I'm hanged if I know what to tell you to do with the packet. It's worth its weight in banknotes to more persons than one, but there's a beastly risk in having anything to do with it. I think you'd better burn it! There's money in it, but I don't see how you could handle it. Burn it, Agnes. It's too risky a business for you! I only hope that in a week or so I shall burn this letter myself, and you and I will be on our way to America.

"So long, Nessie,

"from your loving husband.

"P.S. - By the bye, my real name is Morris Barnes!"

There was an instant's pause as Wrayson finished reading. Then there came a long-drawn-out whisper from Sydney Barnes. He was close to the girl, and his eyes were riveted upon the little packet.

"Ten - thousand - pounds! Ah! Five thousand each! Give me the packet, sister-in-law!"

She stretched out her hand as though to obey. Wrayson checked her.

"Remember," he said, "what your husband told you. You were to burn that packet. He was right. Your husband was a blackmailer, Mrs. Barnes, and he paid the penalty of his infamous career with his life. I shall not allow either you or your brother-in-law to follow in his footsteps!"

She flashed an indignant glance upon him.

"Who are you calling names?" she demanded. "He was my husband and he was good to me!"

"I beg your pardon and his," Wrayson said. "I was wrong to use such a word. But I want you to understand that to attempt to make money by the contents of that packet is a crime! Your husband paid the penalty. He knew what he was doing when he commanded you to burn it."

She looked towards Sydney Barnes.

"What do you say?" she asked.

The words leaped from his mouth. He was half beside himself.

"I say let us open the packet and look it through ourselves before we decide. What the devil business is it of anybody else's. He was my brother and your husband. These people weren't even his friends. They've no right to poke their noses into our affairs. You tell them so; sister-in-law. Give me the packet. Come away with me somewhere where we can look it through quietly. I'm fair and straight. It shall be halves, I swear. I say, sister-in-law Agnes, you don't want to go back to the refreshment bar, do you?"

"No!" she moaned. "No! no!"

"Nor do I want to go back to the gutter," he declared fiercely. "But money isn't to be had for the picking up. Ten thousand pounds Morris expected to get for that packet. It's hard if we can't make half of that."

She looked up at Wrayson as though for advice.

"Mrs. Barnes," he said gravely, "I can tell you what is in that packet. You can see for yourself, then, whether it is anything by means of which you can make money. It consists of the letters of a very famous woman to the man whom she loved. They were stolen from him on the battlefield. I do not wish to pain you, but the thief was Morris Barnes. The friends of the lady who wrote them paid your brother two thousand pounds a year. Her enemies offered him - ten thousand pounds down. There is the secret of Morris Barnes' wealth."

Sydney Barnes leaned over the back of her chair. His hot whisper seemed to burn her cheek.

"Keep the packet, sister-in-law. Don't part!"

"Your brother-in-law," Wrayson remarked, "is evidently disposed to continue your husband's operations. Remember you are not at liberty to do as he asks. Your husband's words are plain. He orders you to burn the packet."

"How do I know that you are telling me the truth?" she asked abruptly.

"Undo the packet," he suggested. "A glance inside should show you."

For some reason or other she seemed dissatisfied. She pointed towards the Baroness.

"What is she doing here?" she asked.

"She is a friend of the woman who wrote those letters,"

Wrayson answered. "I want her to see them destroyed."

There was silence for several moments. The girl's fingers closed upon the packet. She turned round and faced them all. She faced them all, but she addressed more particularly Wrayson.

"You are wondering why I hesitate," she said slowly. "Augustus said destroy the packet, and I suppose I ought to do it."

"By God, you shan't!" Sydney Barnes broke in fiercely. "Morry didn't know that I should be here to look after things."

She waited until he had finished, but she seemed to take very little, if any, notice of his intervention.

"It isn't," she continued, "that I'm afraid to go back to the bar. I'll have to go to work some where, I suppose, but it isn't that. I want to know," she leaned a little forward, - "I want to know who it is that has robbed me of my husband. I don't care what he was to other people! He was very good to me, and I loved him. I should like to see the person who killed him hanged!"

Wrayson, for a moment, was discomposed.

"But that," he said, "has nothing to do with obeying your husband's directions about that packet."

She looked at him with tired eyes and changeless expression.

"Hasn't it?" she asked. "I am not so sure. You have explained about these letters. It is quite certain that my

E. Phillips Oppenheim

husband was killed by either the friends or the enemies of the woman who wrote these letters. I think that if I take this packet to the police it will help them to find the murderer!"

Her new attitude was a perplexing one. Wrayson glanced at the Baroness as though for counsel. She stepped forward and laid her hand upon the girl's shoulder.

"There is one thing which you must not forget, Mrs. Barnes," she said quietly. "Your husband knew that he was running a great risk in keeping these letters and making a living out of them. His letter to you shows that he was perfectly aware of it. Of course, it is a very terrible, a very inexcusable thing that he should have been killed. But he knew perfectly well that he was in danger. Can't you sympathize a little with the poor woman whose life he made so miserable? Let her have her letters back. You will not find her ungrateful!"

The girl turned slowly round and faced the Baroness. They might indeed have represented the opposite poles in femininity. From the tips of her perfectly manicured fingers to the crown of her admirably coiffured hair, the Baroness stood for all that was elegant and refined in the innermost circles of her sex. Agnes would have looked more in place behind the refreshment bar from which Morris Barnes had brought her. Her dress of cheap shiny silk was ill fitting and hopeless, her hat with its faded flowers and crushed shape an atrocity, boots and gloves, and brooch of artificial gems - all were shocking. Little was left of her pale-faced prettiness. The tragedy which had stolen into her life had changed all that. Yet she faced the Baroness without flinching. She seemed sustained by the suppressed emotion of the moment.

"He was my man," she said fiercely, "and no one had any right to take him away from me. He was my husband, and he was brutally murdered. You tell me that I must give up the letters for the sake of the woman who wrote them! What do I care about her! Is she as unhappy as I am, I wonder? I will not give up the letters," she added, clasping them in her hand, "except - on one condition."

"If it is a reasonable one," the Baroness said, smiling, "there will be no difficulty."

Agnes faced her a little defiantly.

"It depends upon what you call reasonable," she said. "Find out for me who it was that killed my husband, you or any one of you, and you shall have the letters."

Sydney Barnes smiled, and left off nervously tugging at his moustache. If this was not exactly according to his own ideas, it was, at any rate, a step in the right direction. Wrayson was evidently perplexed. The Baroness adopted a persuasive attitude.

"My dear girl," she said, "we don't any of us know who killed your husband. After all, what does it matter? It is terribly sad, of course, but he can't be brought back to life again. You have yourself to think of, and how you are to live in the future. Give me that packet, I will destroy it before your eyes, and I promise you that you shall have no more anxiety about your future."

The girl rose to her feet. The packet was already transferred to the bosom of her dress.

E. Phillips Oppenheim

"I have told you my terms," she said. "Some of you know all about it, I dare say! Tell me the truth and you shall have the packet, any one of you."

Wrayson leaned forward.

"The truth is simple," he said earnestly. "We do not know. I can answer for myself. I think that I can answer for the others."

"Then the packet shall help me to find out," she declared.

The Baroness shook her head.

"It will not do, my dear girl," she said quietly. "The packet is not yours."

The girl faced her defiantly.

"Who says that it is not mine?" she demanded.

"I do," the Baroness replied.

"And I!" Wrayson echoed.

"And I say that it is hers - hers and mine," Sydney Barnes declared. "She shall do what she likes with it. She shall not be made to give it up."

"Mrs. Barnes," the Baroness declared briskly, "you must try to be reasonable. We will buy the packet from you."

Sydney Barnes nodded his head approvingly.

"That," he said, "is what I call talking common sense."

"We will give you a thousand pounds for it," the Baroness continued.

"It's not enough, not near enough," Barnes called out hastily. "Don't you listen to them, Agnes."

"I shall not," she answered. "Ten thousand pounds would not buy it. I have said my last word. I am going now. In three days' time I shall return. I will give up the letters then in exchange for the name of my husband's murderer. If I do not get that, I shall go to the police!"

She rose and walked out of the room. They all followed her. The Baroness whispered in Wrayson's ear, but he shook his head.

"It is impossible," he said firmly. "We cannot take them from her by force."

The Baroness shrugged her shoulders. She caught the girl up upon the stairs and they descended together. Wrayson and Sydney Barnes followed, the latter biting his nails nervously and maintaining a gloomy silence. At the entrance, Wrayson whistled for a cab and handed Agnes in. Sydney Barnes attempted to follow her.

"I will see my sister-in-law home," he declared; but Wrayson's hand fell upon his arm.

"No!" he said. "Mrs. Barnes can take care of herself. She is not to be interfered with."

E. Phillips Oppenheim

She nodded back at him from the cab.

"I don't want him," she said. "I don't want any one. In three days' time I will return."

"And until then you will not part with the letters?" Wrayson said.

"Until then," she answered, "I promise."

The cab drove off. Sydney Barnes turned upon Wrayson, white and venomous.

"Where do I come in here?" he demanded fiercely.

"I sincerely trust," Wrayson answered suavely, "that you are not coming in at all. But you, too, can return in three days."

CHAPTER XXXVIII

INEFFECTUAL WOOING

"At last!" Wrayson said to himself, almost under his breath. "Shall we
have a hansom, Louise, or do you care for a walk?"

"A walk, by all means," she answered hurriedly.

"It is not far, is it?"

"A mile - a little more perhaps," he answered.

"You are sure that you are not tired?"

"Tired only of sitting still," she answered. "We had a delightful crossing. This way, isn't it?"

They left the Grosvenor Hotel, where Louise, with Madame de Melbain, had arrived about an hour ago, and turned towards Battersea. Louise began to talk, nervously, and with a very obvious desire to keep the conversation to indifferent subjects. Wrayson humoured her for some time. They spoke of the journey, suddenly determined upon by Madame de Melbain on receipt of his telegram, of the beauty of St. Étarpe, of the wonderful reappearance of her brother.

E. Phillips Oppenheim

"I can scarcely realize even now," she said, "that he is really alive. He is so altered. He seems a different person altogether."

"He has gone through a good deal," Wrayson remarked.

She sighed.

"Poor Duncan!" she murmured.

"He is very much to be pitied," Wrayson said seriously. "I, at any rate, can feel for him."

He turned towards her as he spoke, and his words were charged with meaning. She began quickly to speak of something else, but he interrupted her.

"Louise," he said, "is London so far from St. Étarpe?"

"What do you mean?" she asked.

"I think that you know very well," he answered. "I am sure that you do. At St. Étarpe you were content to accept what, believe me, is quite inevitable. Here - well, you have been doing all you can to avoid me, haven't you?"

"Perhaps," she admitted. "St. Étarpe was an interlude. I told you so. You ought to have understood that."

They entered the Park, and Wrayson was silent for a few minutes. He led the way towards an empty seat.

"Let us sit down," he said, "and talk this out."

She hesitated.

"I think - " she began, but he interrupted her ruthlessly.

"If you prefer it, I will come to the Baroness with you," he declared.

She shrugged her shoulders and sat down.

"Very well," she said, "but I warn you that I am in a bad temper. I am hot and tired and dusty. We shall probably quarrel."

He looked at her critically. She was a little pale, perhaps, but there was nothing else to indicate that she had just arrived from a journey. Her dress of dull black glace silk was cool and spotless, her hat and veil were immaculate. Always she had the air of having just come from the hands of an experienced maid. From the tips of her patent shoes to the fall of her veil, she was orderly and correct.

"It takes two," he said, "to quarrel. I shall not quarrel with you. All that I ask from you is a realization of the fact that we are engaged to be married."

She withdrew the hand which he had calmly possessed himself of.

"We are nothing of the sort," she declared.

He looked puzzled.

"Perhaps," he remarked, "I forgot to mention the matter last time I saw you, but I quite thought that you would take it for granted. In case I was forgetful, please let me impress the fact upon you now. We are going to be married, and very shortly. In fact, the sooner the better."

Of her own free will she laid her hand upon his. He fancied that behind her veil the tears had gathered in her eyes.

"Dear friend," she said softly, "I cannot marry you! I shall never marry any one. Will you please believe that? It will make it so much easier for me."

He was a little taken aback. She had changed her methods suddenly, and he had had no time to adapt himself to them.

"Don't hate me, please," she murmured. "Indeed, it would make me very happy if we could be friends."

He laughed a little unnaturally, and turned in his seat until he was facing her.

"Would you mind lifting your veil for a moment, Louise?" he asked her.

She obeyed him with fingers which trembled a little. He saw then that the tears had indeed been in her eyes. Her lips quivered. She looked at him sadly, but very wistfully.

"Thank you!" he said. "Now would you mind asking yourself whether friendship between us is possible! Remember St. Étarpe, and ask yourself that! Remember our seat amongst the roses - remember what you will of that long golden day."

She covered her face with her hands.

"Ah, no!" he went on. "You know yourself that only one thing is possible. I cannot force you into my arms, Louise. If you care to take up my life and break it in two, you can do it. But think what it means! I am not rich, but I am rich enough to take you where you will, to live with you in any country you desire. I don't know what your scruples are - I shall never ask you again. But, dear, you must not! You must not send me away."

She was silent. She had dropped her veil and her head had sunk a little.

"If I believed that there was anybody else," he continued, "I would go away and leave you alone. If I doubted for a single moment that I could make you happy, I would not trouble you any more. But you belong to me, Louise! You have taken up your place in my life, in my heart! I cannot live without you! I do not think that you can live without me! You mustn't try, dear! You mustn't!"

He held her unresisting hand, but her face was hidden from him.

"What it is that you fancy comes between us I cannot tell," he continued, more gravely. "Only let me tell you this. We are no longer in any danger from Stephen Heneage. He has abandoned his quest altogether. He has told me so with his own lips."

"You are sure of that?" she asked softly.

"Absolutely," he answered.

E. Phillips Oppenheim

She hesitated for a moment. He remained purposely silent. He was anxious to try and comprehend the drift of her thoughts.

"Do you know why?" she asked. "Did he find the task too difficult, or did he relinquish it from any other motive?"

"I am not sure," Wrayson answered. "I met him the night before last. He was very much altered. He had the appearance of a man altogether unnerved. Perhaps it was my fancy, but I got the idea - "

"Well?" she demanded eagerly.

"That he had come across something in the course of his investigations which had given him a shock," he said. "He seemed all broken up. Of course, it may have been something else altogether. At any rate, I have his word for it. He has ceased his investigations altogether, and broken with Sydney Barnes."

The afternoon was warm, but she shivered as she rose a little abruptly to her feet. He laid his hand upon her arm.

"Not without my answer," he begged.

She shook her head sadly.

"My very dear friend," she said sadly, "you must always be. That is all!"

He took his place by her side.

"Your very dear friend," he repeated. "Well, it is a

relationship I don't know much about. I haven't had many friendships amongst your sex. Tell me exactly what my privileges would be."

"You will learn that," she said, "in time."

He shook his head.

"I think not," he declared. "Friendship, to be frank with you, would not satisfy me in the least."

"Then I must lose you altogether," she murmured, in a low tone.

"I don't think so," he affirmed coolly. "I consider that you belong to me already. You are only postponing the time when I shall claim you."

She made no remark, and behind her veil her face told him little. A moment later they issued from the Park and stood on the pavement before the Baroness' flat. She held out her hand without a word.

"I think," he said, "that I should like to come in and see the Baroness."

"Not now," she begged. "We shall meet again at dinner-time."

"Where?" he asked eagerly.

"Madame desired me to ask you to join us at the Grosvenor," she answered, "at half-past eight."

"I shall be delighted," he answered, promptly. "You nearly forgot to tell me."

She shook her head.

"No! I didn't," she said. "I should not have let you go away without giving you her message."

"And you will let me bring you home afterwards?"

"We shall be delighted," she answered. "I shall be with Amy, of course."

He smiled as he raised his hat and let her pass in.

"The Baroness," he said, "is always kind."

He stood for a moment on the pavement. Then he glanced at his watch and hailed a cab.

"The Sheridan Club," he told the man. He had decided to appeal to the Colonel.

CHAPTER XXXIX

THE COLONEL'S MISSION

Wrayson was greeted enthusiastically, as he entered the club billiard-room, by a little circle of friends, unbroken except for the absence of Stephen Heneage. The Colonel came across and laid his hand affectionately on his arm.

"How goes it, Herbert?" he asked. "The seabreezes haven't tanned you much."

"I'm all right," Wrayson declared. "Had a capital time."

"You'll dine here to-night, Herbert?"

Wrayson shook his head.

"I meant to," he declared, "but another engagement's turned up. No! I don't want to play pool, Mason. Can't stop. Colonel, do me a favour."

The Colonel, who was always ready to do any one a favour, signified his willingness promptly enough. But even then Wrayson hesitated.

"I want to talk to you for a few minutes," he said, "without all these fellows round. Should you mind coming down into the smoking-room?"

The Colonel rose promptly from his seat.

"Not a bit in the world," he declared. "We'll go into the smoking-room. Scarcely a soul there. Much cooler, too. Bring your drink. See you boys later."

They found two easy-chairs in the smoking-room, of which they were the sole occupants. The Colonel cut off the end of his cigar and made himself comfortable.

"Now, my young friend," he said, "proceed."

Wrayson did not beat about the bush.

"It's about your daughter Louise, Colonel," he said. "She won't marry me!"

The Colonel pinched his cigar reflectively.

"She always was a most peculiar girl," he affirmed. "Does she give any reasons?"

"That's just what she won't do," Wrayson explained. "That's just why I've come to you. I - I - Colonel, I'm fond of her. I never expected to feel like it about any woman."

The Colonel nodded sympathetically.

"And although it may sound conceited to say so," Wrayson continued, "I believe - no! I'm sure that she's fond of me. She's admitted it. There!"

The Colonel smiled understandingly.

"Well." he said, "then where's the trouble? You don't want my consent. You know that."

"Louise won't marry me," Wrayson repeated. "That's the trouble. She won't explain her attitude. She simply declares that marriage for her is an impossibility."

The Colonel sighed.

"I'm afraid," he murmured, regretfully, "that my daughter is a fool."

"She is anything but that," Wrayson declared. "She has some scruple. What it is I can't imagine. Of course, at first I thought it was because we were, both of us, involved in that Morris Barnes affair. But I know now that it isn't that. Heneage, who threatened me, and indirectly her, has chucked the whole business. Such danger as there was is over. I - "

"Interrupting you for one moment," the Colonel said quietly, "what has become of Heneage?"

"He's in a very queer way," Wrayson answered. "You know he started on hot to solve this Morris Barnes business. He warned us both to get out of the country. Well, I saw him last night, and he was a perfect wreck. He looked like a man just recovering from a bout of dissipation, or something of the sort."

"Did you speak to him?" the Colonel asked.

"I was with him some time," Wrayson answered. "His manner was just as changed as his appearance."

The Colonel was looking, for him, quite grave. His

cigar had gone out, and he forgot to relight it.

"Dear me," he said, "I am sorry to hear this. Did he allude to the Morris Barnes affair at all?"

"He did," Wrayson answered. "He gave me to understand, in fact, that he had discovered a little more than he wanted to."

The Colonel stretched out his hand for a match, and relit his cigar.

"You believe, then," he said, "that Heneage has succeeded in solving the mystery of Barnes' murder, and is keeping the knowledge to himself?"

"That was the conclusion I came to," Wrayson admitted.

The Colonel smoked for a moment or two in thoughtful silence.

"Well," he said, "it isn't like Heneage. I always looked upon him as a man without nerves, a man who would carry through any purpose he set himself to, without going to pieces about it. Shows how difficult it is to understand the most obvious of us."

Wrayson nodded.

"But after all," he said, "it wasn't to talk about Heneage that I brought you down here. What I want to know, Colonel, is if you can help me at all with Louise."

The Colonel's forehead was furrowed with perplexity.

"My dear Herbert," he declared, "there is no man in the world I would sooner have for a son-in-law. But what can I do? Louise wouldn't listen to me in any case. I haven't any authority or any influence over her. I say it to my sorrow, but it's the truth. If it were my little girl down at home, now, it would be a different matter. But Louise has taken her life into her own hands. She has not spoken to me for years. She certainly would not listen to my advice."

"Then if you cannot help me directly, Colonel," Wrayson continued, "can you help me indirectly? I have asked you a question something like this before, but I want to repeat it. I have told you that Louise refuses to marry me. She has something on her mind, some scruple, some fear. Can you form any idea as to what it may be?"

The Colonel was silent for an unusually long time. He was leaning back in his chair, looking up through the cloud of blue tobacco smoke to the ceiling. In reflection his features seemed to have assumed a graver and somewhat weary expression.

"Yes!" he said at last, "I think that I can."

Wrayson felt his heart jump. His eyes were brighter. An influx of new life seemed to have come to him. He leaned forward eagerly.

"You will tell me what it is, Colonel?" he begged.

The Colonel looked at him with a queer little smile.

"I am not sure that I can do that, Herbert," he said. "I am not sure that it would help you if I did. And you are asking me rather more than you know."

Wrayson felt a little chill of discouragement.

"Colonel," he said, "I am in your hands. But I love your daughter, and I swear that I would make her happy."

The Colonel looked at his watch.

"Do you know where Louise is?" he asked quietly.

"Number 17, Frederic Mansions, Battersea," Wrayson answered.

The Colonel rose to his feet.

"I will go down and see her," he said simply. "You had better wait here for me. I will come straight back."

"Colonel, you're a brick," Wrayson declared, walking with him towards the door.

"I'll do my best, Herbert," he answered quietly, "but I can't promise. I can't promise anything."

Wrayson watched him leave the club and step into a hansom. He walked a little more slowly than usual, his head was a little bent, and he passed a club acquaintance in the hall without his customary greeting. Wrayson retraced his steps and ascended towards the billiard-room, with his first enthusiasm a little damped. Was his errand, he wondered, so grievously distasteful to his old friend, or was the Colonel losing at last the magnificent elasticity and vigour which had kept him so long independent of the years?

There were others besides Wrayson who noticed a certain alteration in the Colonel when he re-entered the billiard-room an hour or so later. His usual greeting was unspoken, he sank a little heavily into a chair, and he called for a drink without waiting for some one to share it with him. They gathered round him sympathetically.

"Feeling the heat a bit, Colonel?"

"Anything wrong downstairs?"

The Colonel recovered himself promptly. He beamed upon them all affectionately, and set down an empty tumbler with a little sigh of satisfaction.

"I'm all right, boys," he declared. "I couldn't find a cab - had to walk further than I meant, and I wanted a drink badly. Wrayson, come over here. I want to talk to you."

Wrayson sat down by his side.

"I've done the best I could," the Colonel said. "Things may not come all right for you quite at once, but within a week I fancy it'll be all squared up. I've found out why she refused to marry you, and you can take my word for it that within a week the cause will be removed."

"You're a brick, Colonel," Wrayson declared heartily. "There's only one thing more I'd love to have you to tell me."

"I'm afraid -" the Colonel began.

"That you and Louise were reconciled," Wrayson declared. "Colonel, there can't be anything between you two, of all the people in the world, there can't be anything sufficient to keep you and her, father and daughter, completely apart."

"You are quite right, Wrayson," the Colonel assented, a little more cheerfully. "Well, you may find that all will come right very soon now. By the by, I've been talking to the Baroness. I want you to let me be at your rooms to-morrow night."

Wrayson hesitated for a moment.

"You know how we stand?" he asked.

"Exactly," the Colonel answered. "I only wish that I had known before. You will have no objection to my coming, I suppose?"

"None at all," Wrayson declared. "But, Colonel! there is one more question that I must ask you. Did Louise speak to you about her brother?"

The Colonel nodded.

"She blamed me, of course," he said slowly, "because I had never told her. It was his own desire, and I think that he was right. I have telegraphed for him to come over. He will be here to-night or to-morrow."

Wrayson left the club, feeling almost light-hearted. It was the old story over again - the Colonel to the rescue!

CHAPTER XL

BLACKMAIL

Sydney Barnes staggered into his apartment with a little exclamation of relief which was almost a groan. He slammed the door and sank into an easy-chair. With both his hands he was grasping it so that his fingers were hot and wet with perspiration. At last he had obtained his soul's desire!

He sat there for several minutes without moving. The blinds were close drawn and the room was in darkness. Gradually he began to be afraid. He rose, and with trembling fingers struck a match. On the corner of the table - fortunately he knew exactly where to find it - was a candle. He lit it, and holding it over his head, peered fearfully around. Convinced at last that he was alone, he set it down again, wiped the perspiration from his forehead, and opening a cupboard in the chiffonnier, produced a bottle and a glass.

He poured out some spirits and drank it. Then, after rummaging for several moments in his coat pocket, he produced several crumpled cigarettes of a cheap variety. One of these he proceeded to smoke, whilst, with trembling fingers, he undid the packet which he had been carrying, and began a painstaking study of its contents. A delicate perfume stole out into the room

E. Phillips Oppenheim

from those closely pressed sheets, so eagerly clutched in his yellow-stained fingers. A little bunch of crushed violets slipped to the floor unheeded. Ghoul-like he bent over the pages of delicate writing, the intimate, passionate cry of a soul seeking for its mate. They were no ordinary love-letters. Mostly they were beyond the comprehension of the creature who spelt them out word for word, seeking all the time to appraise their exact monetary value to himself. But for what he had heard he would have found them disappointing. As it was, he gloated over them. Two thousand pounds a year his clever brother had earned by merely possessing them! He looked at them almost reverently. Then he suddenly remembered what else his brother had earned by their possession, and he shivered. A moment later the electric bell outside pealed, and there came a soft knocking at the door.

A little cry - half stifled - broke from his lips. With numbed and trembling fingers he began tying up the letters. The perspiration had broken out upon his forehead. Some one to see him! Who could it be? He was quite determined not to go to the door. He would let no one in. Again the bell! Soon they would get tired of ringing and go away. He was quite safe so long as he remained quiet. Quite safe, he told himself feverishly. Then his pulses seemed to stop beating. There was a rush of blood to his head. He clutched at the sides of his chair, but to rise was a sheer impossibility.

The thing which was terrifying him was a small thing in itself – the turning of a latch-key in the door. Before him on the table was his own - he knew of no other. Yet some one was opening, had opened his front door! He sprang to his feet at last with something which was almost a shriek. The door of the room in which he was, was slowly being pushed open. By the dim candlelight he could distinguish the figure of his visitor standing upon the threshold and peering into the room.

His impulse was, without doubt, one of relief. The figure was the figure of a complete stranger. Nor was there anything the least threatening about his appearance. He saw a tall, white-haired gentleman, carefully dressed with military exactitude, regarding him with a benevolent and apologetic smile.

"I really must apologize," he said, "for such an unceremonious entrance. I felt sure that you were in, but I am a trifle deaf, and I could not be sure whether or not the bell was ringing. So I ventured to use my own latch-key, with, as you are doubtless observing, complete success."

"Who are you, and what do you want?" Barnes asked, finding his voice at last.

"My name is Colonel Fitzmaurice," was the courteous reply. "You will allow me to sit down? I have the pleasure of conversing, I believe, with Mr. Sydney Barnes?"

"That's my name," Barnes answered. "What do you want with me?"

Despite his visitor's urbanity, he was still a little nervous. The Colonel had a somewhat purposeful air, and he had seated himself directly in front of the door.

"I want," the Colonel said calmly, "that packet which you have just stolen from Mrs. Morris Barnes, and which you have in your pocket there!"

Barnes rose at once, trembling, to his feet. His bead-like eyes were bright and venomous. He was terrified, but he had the courage of despair.

"I have stolen nothing," he declared, "I don't know what you're talking about. I won't listen to you. You have no right to force your way into my flat. Colonel or no colonel, I won't have it. I'll send for the police."

The Colonel smiled.

"No,'" he said, "don't do that. Besides, I know what I'm talking about. I mean the packet which I think I can see sticking out of your coat pocket. You have just stolen that from Mrs. Barnes' tin trunk, you know."

"I have stolen nothing," the young man declared, "nothing at all. I am not a thief. I am not afraid of the police."

The Colonel smiled tolerantly.

"That is good," he said. "I hate cowards. But I am going to make you very much afraid of me - unless you are wise and give me that packet."

Barnes breathed thickly for a moment. Coward he knew that he was to the marrow of his bones, but other of the evil passions were stirring in him then. His narrow eyes were alight with greed. He had the animal courage of vermin hard pressed.

"The packet is mine," he said fiercely. "It's nothing to do with you. Get out of my room."

He rose to his feet. The Colonel awaited him with equable countenance. He made, however, no advance.

"Young man," the Colonel said quietly, "do you know what happened to your brother?"

Sydney Barnes stood still and shivered. He could say nothing. His tongue seemed to cleave to the roof of his mouth.

"Your brother was another of your breed," the Colonel continued. "A blackmailer! A low-living, evil-minded brute. Do you know how he came by those letters?"

"I don't know and I don't care," Barnes answered with a weak attempt at bluster. "They're mine now, and I'm going to stick to them."

The Colonel shook his head.

"He broke his trust to a dying man," he said softly, - "to a man who lay on the veldt at Colenso with three great wounds in his body, and his life's blood staining the ground. He had carried those letters into action with him, because they were precious to him. His last thought was that they should be destroyed. Your brother swore to do this. He broke his word. He turned blackmailer."

"You're very fond of that word," Barnes muttered. "How do you know so much?"

"The soldier was my son," the Colonel answered, "and he did not die. You see I have a right to those letters. Will you give them to me?"

E. Phillips Oppenheim

Give them up! Give up all his hopes of affluence, his dreams of an easy life, of the cheap luxuries and riches which formed the Heaven of his desire! No! He was not coward enough for that. He did not believe that this mild-looking old gentleman would use force. Besides, he could not be very strong. He ought to be able to push him over and escape!

"No!" he answered bluntly, "I won't!"

The Colonel looked thoughtful.

"It is a pity," he said quietly. "I am sorry to hear you say that. Your brother, when I asked him, made the same reply."

Barnes felt himself suddenly grow hot and then cold. The perspiration stood out upon his forehead.

"I called upon your brother a few days before his death," the Colonel continued calmly. "I explained my claim to the letters and I asked him for them. He too refused! Do you remember, by the by, what happened to your brother?"

Sydney Barnes did not answer, but his cheeks were like chalk. His mouth was a little open, disclosing his yellow teeth. He stared at the Colonel with frightened, fascinated eyes.

"I can see," the Colonel continued, "that you remember. Young man," he added, with a curious alteration in his tone, "be wiser than your brother! Give me the packet."

"You killed him," the young man gasped. "It was you

who killed Morris."

The Colonel nodded gravely.

"He had his chance," he said, "even as you have it."

There was a dead silence. The Colonel was waiting. Sydney Barnes was breathing hard. He was alone, then, with a murderer. He tried to speak, but found a difficulty in using his voice. It was a situation which might have abashed a bolder ruffian.

The Colonel rose to his feet.

"I am sorry to hurry you," he said, "but we are already late for our appointment with Wrayson and his friends."

Sydney Barnes snatched up the packet and retreated behind the table. The Colonel leaned forward and blew out the candle.

"I can see better in the dark," he remarked calmly. "You are a very foolish young man!"

E. Phillips Oppenheim

CHAPTER XLI

THE COLONEL SPEAKS

Wrayson glanced at the clock for the twentieth time.

"I am afraid," he said gravely, "that Mr. Sydney Barnes has been one too many for us."

"Do you think," Louise asked, "that he has persuaded the girl to give him the packet?"

"It looks like it," Wrayson confessed.

Louise frowned.

"Of course," she said, "I think that you were mad to let her go before. She had the letters here in the room. You would have been perfectly justified in taking them from her."

"I suppose so," Wrayson assented, doubtfully. "Somehow she seemed to get the upper hand of us towards the end. I think she suspected that some of us knew more than we cared to tell her about - her husband's death."

Louise shivered a little and remained silent. Wrayson walked to the window and back.

"To tell you the truth," he said, "I expected some one else here to-night who has failed to turn up."

"Who is that?" the Baroness asked.

Wrayson hesitated for a moment and glanced towards Louise.

"Colonel Fitzmaurice," he said.

Louise seemed to turn suddenly rigid. She looked at him steadfastly for a moment without speaking.

"My father," she murmured at last.

Wrayson nodded.

"Yes!" he said.

"But - what has he to do with this?" Louise asked, with her eyes fixed anxiously, almost fearfully, upon his.

"I went to him for advice," Wrayson said quietly. "He has been always very kind, and I thought it possible that he might be able to help us. He promised to be here at the same hour as the others. Listen! There is the bell at last."

The Colonel entered the room. Louise half rose to her feet. Wrayson hastened to meet him.

"Herbert," he said, with an affectionate smile, "forgive me for being a little late. Baroness, I am delighted to see you - and Louise."

The Baroness held out both her hands, which the

Colonel raised gallantly to his lips. Louise he greeted with a fatherly and unembarrassed smile.

"I must apologize to all of you," he said, "but perhaps this will be my best excuse."

He took the packet from his breast pocket and handed it over to the Baroness. The room seemed filled with exclamations. The Colonel beamed upon them all.

"Quite simple," he declared. "I have just taken them from Mr. Sydney Barnes upstairs. He, in his turn, took them from -"

The door was suddenly opened. Mrs. Morris Barnes rushed into the room and gazed wildly around.

"Where is he?" she exclaimed. "He has robbed me. The little beast! He got into my rooms while I was out."

The Colonel led her gallantly to a chair.

"Calm yourself, my dear young lady," he said.

"Where is he?" she cried. "Has he been here?"

The Colonel shook his head.

"He is in his room upstairs, but," he said, "I should not advise you to go to him."

"He has my packet - Augustus' packet," she cried, springing up.

The Colonel laid his hand upon her arm.

"No!" he said, "that packet has been restored to its rightful owner."

She rose to her feet, trembling with anger. The Colonel motioned her to resume her seat.

"Come," he said, "so far as you are concerned, you have nothing to complain of. You offered, I believe, to give it up yourself on one condition."

She looked at him with sudden eagerness.

"Well?" she cried, impatiently.

"That condition," he said, "shall be complied with."

She looked into his face with strange intentness.

"You mean," she said slowly, "that I shall know who it was that killed my husband?"

"Yes!" the Colonel answered.

A sudden cry rang through the room. Louise was on her feet. She came staggering towards them, her hands outstretched.

"No!" she screamed, "no! Father, you are mad! Send the woman away!"

He smiled at her deprecatingly.

"My dear Louise!" he exclaimed, "our word has been passed to this young woman. Besides," he added, "circumstances which have occurred within the last hour with our young friend upstairs would probably

E. Phillips Oppenheim

render an explanation imperative! I am sorry for your sake, my dear young lady," he continued, turning to Mrs. Barnes, "to have to tell you this, but if you insist upon knowing, it was I who killed your husband."

Louise fell back into her chair and covered her face with her hands. The Baroness looked shocked but not surprised. Wrayson, dumb and unnerved, had staggered back, and was leaning against the table. Mrs. Barnes had already taken a step towards the door. She was very pale, but her eyes were ablaze. Incredulity struggled with her passionate desire for vengeance.

"You!" she exclaimed. "What should you want to kill him for?"

The Colonel sighed regretfully.

"My dear young lady," he said, "it is very painful for me to have to be so explicit, but the situation demands it. I killed him because he was unfit to live - because he was a blackmailer of women, an unclean liver, a foul thing upon the face of the earth."

"It's a damned lie!" the girl hissed. "He was good to me, and you shall swing for it!"

The Colonel looked genuinely distressed.

"I am afraid," he said, "that you are prejudiced. If he was, as you say, kind to you, it was for his own pleasure. Believe me, I made a careful study of his character before I decided that he must go."

She looked at him with fierce curiosity.

"Are you a god," she demanded, "that you should have power of life or death? Who are you to set yourself up as a judge?"

"Pray do not believe," he begged, "that I arrogate to myself any such position. Only, unfortunately, as regards your late husband's character there could be no mistake, and concerning such men as he I have very strong convictions."

Wrayson, who had recovered himself a little, laid his hand upon the Colonel's shoulder.

"Colonel," he said hoarsely, "you're not serious! You can't be! Be careful. This woman means mischief. She will take you at your word."

"How else should she take me?" the Colonel asked calmly. "I suppose her prejudice in favour of this man was natural, but all I can say is that, under similar circumstances, I should act to-day precisely as I did on the night when I found him about to sell a woman's honour, for money to minister to the degraded pleasures of his life."

The woman leaned towards him, venomous and passionate.

"You're a nice one to preach, you are," she cried hysterically, "you, with a man's blood upon your hands! You, a murderer! Degraded indeed! What were his poor sins compared with yours?"

The Colonel shook his head sadly.

"I am afraid, my dear young lady," he said, "that I

should never be able to convert you to my point of view. You are naturally prejudiced, and when I consider that I have failed to convince my own daughter" - he glanced towards Louise - "of the soundness of my views, it goes without saying that I should find you also unsympathetic. You are anxious, I see, to leave us. Permit me!"

He held open the door for her with grave courtesy, but Wrayson pushed him aside. He had recovered himself to some extent, but he still felt as though he were moving in some horrible dream.

"Colonel!" he exclaimed hoarsely, "you know what this means! You know where she will go!"

"If he don't, let me tell him," she interrupted. "To the nearest police station! That's where I'm off."

Wrayson glanced quickly at the Colonel, who seemed in no way discomposed.

"Naturally," he assented. "No one, my dear young lady, will interfere with you in your desire to carry out your painfully imperfect sense of justice. Pray pass out!"

She hesitated for a moment. Her poor little brain was struggling, perhaps, for the last time, to adapt itself to his point of view - to understand why, at a moment so critical, he should treat her with the easy composure and tolerant good-nature of one who gives to a spoilt child its own way. Then she saw signs of further interference on Wrayson's part, and she delayed no longer.

The Colonel closed the door after her, and stood for a moment with his back against it, for Wrayson had shown signs of a desire to follow the woman whose egress he had just permitted. He looked into their faces, white with horror - full of dread of what was to come, and he smiled reassuringly.

"Amy," he said, turning to the Baroness, "surely you and Wrayson here are possessed of some grains of common sense. Louise, I know, is too easily swayed by sentiment. But you, Wrayson! Surely I can rely on you!"

"For anything," Wrayson answered, with trembling lips. "But what can I do? What is there to be done?"

The Colonel smiled gently.

"Simply to listen intelligently - sympathetically if you can," he declared. "I want to make my position clear to you if I can. You heard what that poor young woman called me? Probably you would have used the same word yourself. A murderer!"

"Yes!" Wrayson muttered. "I heard!"

"When I came back from the Soudan twelve years ago, I had been instrumental in killing some thousands of brave men, I dare say I had killed a score or so with my own hand. Was I a murderer then?"

"No!" Wrayson answered. "It was a different thing."

"Then killing is not necessarily murder," the Colonel remarked. "Good! Now take the case of a man like Morris Barnes. He belonged to the class of humanity

E. Phillips Oppenheim

which you can call by no other name than that of vermin. Whatever he touched he defiled. He was without a single good instinct, a single passable quality. Wherever he lived, he bred contamination. Whoever touched him was the worse for it. His influence upon the world was an unchanging one for evil. Put aside sentiment for one moment, false sentiment I should say, and ask yourself what possible sin can there be in taking the life of such a one. If he had gone on four legs instead of two, his breed would have been exterminated centuries ago."

"We are not the judges," Wrayson began, weakly enough.

"We are, sir," the Colonel thundered. "For what else have we been given brains, the moral sense, the knowledge of good or evil? There are those amongst us who become decadents, whose presence amongst us breeds corruption, whose dirty little lives are like the trail of a foul insect across the page of life. I hold it a just and moral thing to rid the world of such a creature. The sanctity of human life is the canting cry of the falsely sentimental. Human life is sacred or not, according to its achievements. Such a one as Morris Barnes I would brush away like a poisonous fly."

"Bentham!" Wrayson faltered.

"I killed him, sir!" the Colonel answered, "and others of his kidney before him. Louise knew it. I argued with her as I am doing with you, but it was useless. Nevertheless, I have lived as seemed good to me."

"There is the law," Wrayson said, with a horrified glance towards Louise. He understood now.

The Colonel bowed his head.

"I am prepared," the Colonel answered, "to pay the penalty of all reformers."

There was a ring at the bell. Wrayson threw open the door. A small boy stood there. He held a piece of paper in his hand.

"The lidy said," he declared, "that the white-headed gentleman would give me 'arf a crown for this 'ere!"

Wrayson gave him the money, and stepped back into the room. He gave the paper to the Colonel, who read it calmly, first to himself and then aloud.

*　*　*　*　*

"I leave you to your conshens. He may have been bad, but he was good to me!

"AGNES B."

*　*　*　*　*

The Colonel's eyes grew very soft.

"Poor little woman," he said to himself. "Wrayson, you'll look after her. You'll see she doesn't come to grief!"

There was the sound of a heavy fall in the room above. The Colonel's face assumed an air of intense irritation.

"It's that infernal window pole," he declared. "I had doubts about it all the time."

Wrayson looked at him in horror.

"What do you mean?" he demanded.

"Perhaps you had better go up and see," the Colonel answered, taking up his hat. "A very commonplace tragedy after all! I don't quite see what else he could have done. He was penniless, half mad with disappointment; he'd been smoking too many cigarettes and drinking too much cheap liquor, and he was in danger of arrest for selling the landlord's furniture. No other end for him, I am afraid."

Wrayson threw open the door.

"Don't hurry," the Colonel declared. "You'll probably find that he has hanged himself, but he must have been dead for some time."

Wrayson tore up the stairs. The Colonel watched him for a moment. Then, with a little sigh, he began to descend.

"False sentiment," he murmured to himself sadly. "The world's full of it."

CHAPTER XLII

LOVE REMAINS

Wrayson rode slowly up the great avenue, and paused at the bend to see for the first time at close quarters the house, which from the valley below had seemed little more than a speck of white set in a deep bower of green. Seen at close quarters its size amazed him. With its cluster of outbuildings, it occupied nearly the whole of the plateau, which was like a jutting tableland out from the side of the mountain. It was of two stories only, and encircled with a great veranda supported by embowered pillars. Free at last from the densely growing trees, Wrayson, for the first time during his long climb, caught an uninterrupted view of the magnificent panorama below. A land of hills, of black forests and shining rivers; a land uncultivated but rich in promise, magnificent in its primitivism. It was a wonderful dwelling this, of which the owner, springing down from the veranda, was now on his way to meet his guest.

The two men shook hands with unaffected heartiness. Duncan Fitzmaurice, in his white linen riding clothes, seemed taller than ever, a little gaunt and thin, too, from a recent attack of fever. There was no doubt about the pleasure with which he received his guest.

E. Phillips Oppenheim

"Where is Louise?" he asked, looking behind down the valley.

"Coming up in the wagons," Wrayson answered. "She has been riding all day and was tired."

A Kaffir boy came out with a tray and glasses. Wrayson helped himself to a whisky and soda, and lit a cigar.

"I'll get my pony and ride back with you to meet them," Duncan said.

Wrayson detained him.

"One moment," he said, "I have something to say to you first."

Duncan glanced at him a little anxiously. Wrayson answered the look.

"Nothing - disturbing," he said. "You learnt the end of everything from my letters?"

"I think so," Duncan answered.

"The verdict on your father's death was absolutely unanimous," Wrayson said. "He was seen to stagger on the platform just as the train came in, and he seemed to make every effort to save himself. He was killed quite instantaneously. I do not think that any one had a suspicion that it was not entirely accidental."

Duncan nodded.

"And the other affair?"

"You mean the death of Sydney Barnes? No one has ever doubted that he committed suicide. Everything seemed to point to it. There is only one man who knew about Morris Barnes and probably guesses the rest. His name was Heneage, and he was your father's friend. He did not speak when he was alive, so he is not likely to now. There is the young woman, of course, Mrs. Morris Barnes. She has married again and gone to Canada. Louise looked after her."

Duncan took up his riding-whip from the table.

"Now tell me," he said, "what it is that you have to say to me."

"Do you read the papers?" Wrayson asked abruptly.

"Only so far as they treat of matters connected with this country," Duncan answered.

"You have not read, then, of the Mexonian divorce?"

The man's eyes were lit with fire. The handle of the riding-whip snapped in his hands.

"They have never granted it!" he cried.

"Not in its first form," Wrayson answered hastily. "The whole suit fell to the ground for want of evidence."

"It is abandoned, then?" Duncan demanded.

"On the contrary, the courts have granted the decree," Wrayson answered, "but on political grounds only. Every material charge against the Queen was withdrawn, and the divorce became a matter of

E. Phillips Oppenheim

of arrangement."

"She is free from that brute, then," Duncan said quietly. "I am glad."

Wrayson glanced down towards the valley. A couple of wagons and several Kaffir boys with led horses were just entering the valley.

"Yes!" he said, "she is free!"

Something in his intonation, some change in his face, gripped hold of Duncan. He caught his visitor by the shoulder roughly.

"What the devil do you mean?" he demanded, "What difference does it make? She would never dare - to - "

"You can never tell," Wrayson said, with a little sigh, "what a woman will dare to do. Tell me the truth, Duncan. You care for her still?"

"God knows it!" he answered fiercely. "There has never been another woman. There never could be."

"Jump on your pony, then, and ride down and meet them. Gently, man! Don't break your neck." ...

Later on they sat out upon the veranda. The swift darkness was falling already upon the land, the colour was fading fast from the gorgeous fragments of piled-up clouds in the western sky. Almost as they watched, the outline faded away from the distant mountains, the rolling woods lost their shape.

"It's a wonderful country, yours, Duncan," Wrayson said.

"It is God's own country," Duncan answered quietly. "What we shall make of it, He only knows! It is the country of eternal mysteries."

He pointed northwards.

"Think," he said, "beneath those forests are the ruins of cities, magnificent in civilization and art before a stone of Babylon was built, when Nineveh was unknown. What a heritage! What a splendid heritage, if only we can prove ourselves worthy of it!"

"Why not?" Wrayson asked quietly. "Our day of decline is not yet. Even the historians admit that."

"It is the money-grabbers of the world who belittle empire," Duncan answered. "It is from the money-grabbers of the Transvaal that we have most to fear. Only those can know what Africa is, what it might mean to us, who shake the dust of civilization from their feet, and creep a little way into its heart. It is here in the quiet places that one begins to understand. One has the sense of coming into a virgin country, strong, fresh, and wonderful. Think of the race who might be bred here! They would rejuvenate the world!"

"And yet," the woman at his side murmured, the woman who had been a queen, "it is not a virgin country after all. A little further northwards and the forests have in their keeping the secrets of ages. Shall we ever possess them, I wonder!"

In the darkness she felt his arms about her. Louise and

her husband had wandered away.

"One thing at least remains, changeless and eternal as history itself," he murmured, as their lips met. "Thank God for it!"